AN UNCERTAIN PEACE

by James Craig Tucker

To request permission, visit
www.wanderinginthewordspress.com.

Cover photo by George Barnard, a contract photographer for the Federal Army who arrived after Atlanta fell on Sept. 2, 1864.

PUBLISHED BY WANDERING IN THE WORDS PRESS

WANDERING
IN THE WORDS
PRESS

ISBN
Print: 979-8-9923121-1-9
Digital: 979-8-9923121-2-6
First Edition

To Noreen, who taught me that books and reading are important.
To Jan, who read all the early drafts, no matter how sketchy.
And most of all, to Deb, who never lost faith from that first day in
Mobile, Alabama.

. . . it is a fast place in every sense of the word and our friends in Atlanta are a fast people.
They live fast and die fast. They make money fast and they spend it fast.
To a stranger the whole city seems to be running on wheels.

—Milledgeville Federal Union (1867)

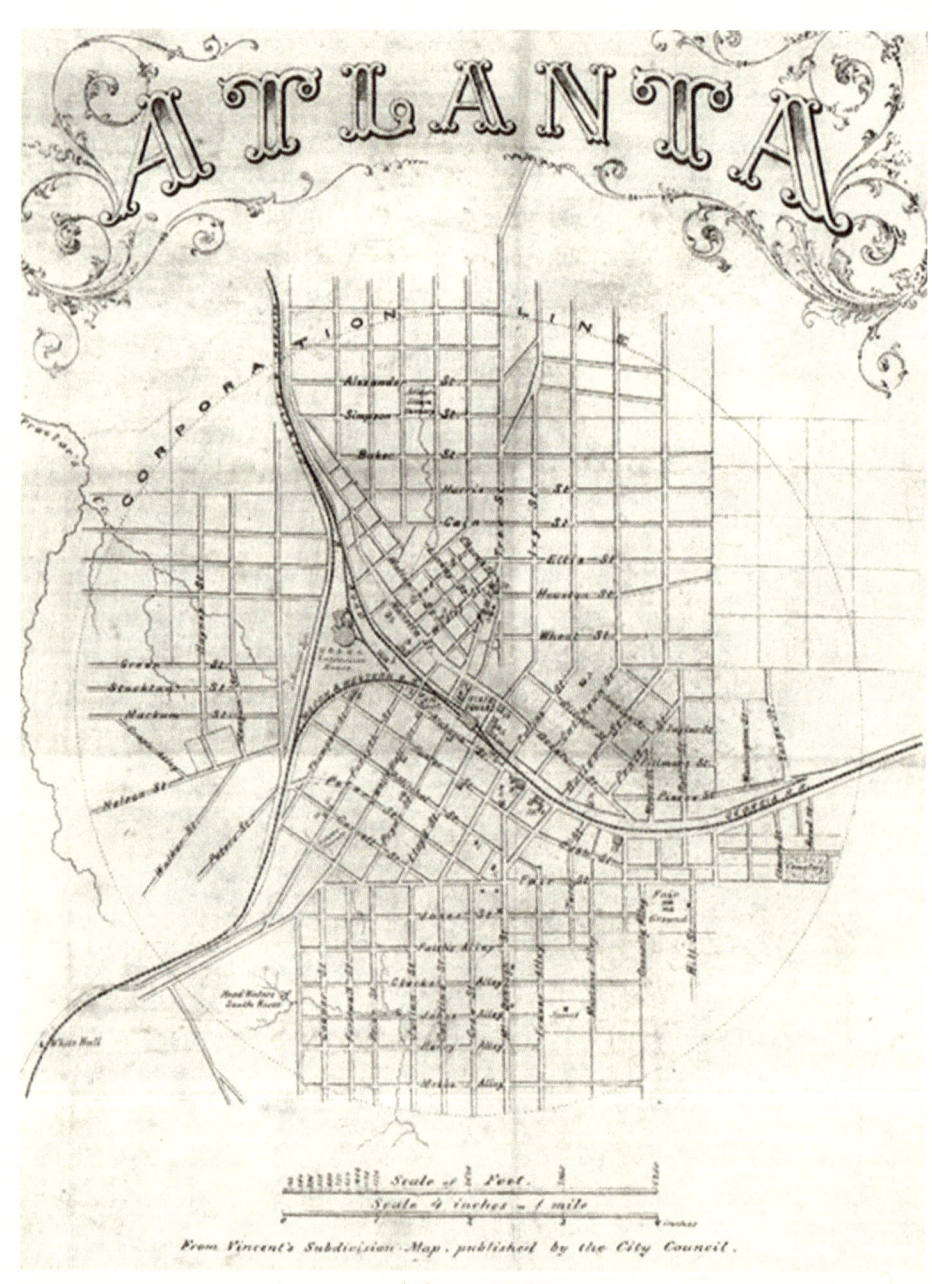

Atlanta 1864

Prologue

He lay in the tall grass watching the erratic flight of a dragonfly. The song of a wren floated above the metallic rhythm of grasshoppers. It carried him into a trance, his mind drifting, considering fact and illusion.

His world had changed. The hands that once held him so firmly were slack. He was, in a practical sense, free like the wild creatures Moses had taught him about. He had envied this freedom—and now longed for the changes to come. Moses feared for what was to be, but then Moses was old. The others were euphoric, their future unconsidered as they rushed toward the unknown. Were they fools?

Our eyes can deceive us, he thought. The rising heat waves transmuted the trees across the field into a gossamer shimmer. A growing drumbeat of horses' hooves in the distance made the stillness tangible and fragile.

He shook off his reverie and turned to look. Unhurried troopers slowly came into view—a wagon and mounted escort of six. Confederate.

Unseen in the tall grass, he watched them pass by.

He was poised on the brink of manhood, muscular and powerful. He might have fetched a good price not long before. Looking at him, poking his flesh, inspecting his teeth, they would have wanted him for a field hand. They would have approved of what they saw, but they considered only his physical strength. They would not have looked inside him as the Missus had. They could not know of his quick and clever ways. If they knew, they would have feared him, they would have broken him, they would have crushed him. She had seen but she did not fear. She taught him to read and talked to him of ideas. He'd worried she was lying, fooling him for cruel amusement. In time he came to believe her, and slowly, ever so slowly, his world grew into a place of magic and possibility.

A crack of gunfire shattered the silence. The driver of the wagon rolled forward and fell. Now the other horsemen were falling. One rider desperately spurred his horse, trying to flee. Soon he lay dead.

Then all was still.

Blue figures emerged from the wood. How long had they been there? The Yankees gathered up their grim harvest, throwing the bodies into the wagon or over the riderless horses. They fetched their mounts from the woods, and with the wagon and Confederate dead in tow, rode down the lane toward the Big House.

Fear cut deep into his chest—a primal fear that tells, far better than the mind, when danger is near. The fear grabbed him and spurred him on. He ran madly in the desire to raise the alarm. His legs weak, his lungs on fire, he started up the hill that overlooked the Big House.

A shot rang out. He fell as if shot himself, knocked down by exhaustion and fear.

He was too late. But too late to do what? He had been too far away; they had been too close. Another crack of a gunfire killed his purpose as others began to kill his world.

Alone and helpless, he crawled to the crest of the hill.

1866

I

The upper windows of the ramshackle storefront glowed from the fire within. Flames, masked by the outer walls, licked gently from under the eaves. A grayish-white cloud rising furiously into the night sky gave proof of the cancer raging within. The battered door, stained by the touch of many hands, stood ajar, revealing a strange calm in the untouched front room. Above the door, a sun-faded sign read MILLER'S TAVERN, beckoning the public to enter. None would, not now, not ever again.

Yet, in a city, even the meanest structure does not die alone. Around the flaming building, men worked feverishly. Fire Company Number One pulled a hand-pumper, the only usable firefighting apparatus in Atlanta, into position. The orderly bobbing of men working its handles formed a counterpoint to the frantic efforts of people slinging buckets of water. The stream from the pumper's hose broke the upper windows and sprayed into the flames with scant effect. All knew the building was lost, and few cared for its salvation. The saloon was disreputable. Even those fighting the blaze were happy to be rid of it.

A crowd gathered. Their upturned faces, lit golden by the fire, showed modest interest in the proceedings. Fires were not a novelty in the shanties and war-damaged structures that made up much of the city. Yet a fire is a fire. The crowd grew. Some were glad of an evening's amusement. More feared the fire might spread.

The crowd parted for an old woman who puffed her way to the front calling, "Tom! Tom! Be careful, Tom!" If Tom heard, he did not call back. Several wags in the crowd caught up the woman's words and called with mock concern for the unknown Tom.

The roar of the flames grew louder, as if to silence the cries of those who would drown them. The sky flashed bright with lightning. A roll of thunder answered moments later. Worried faces turned westward. If the rain arrived quickly, it would douse the burning building; if the winds came but the rain missed the city, the result would be disaster. A rising storm is a dubious friend.

Lightning flashed again, and as if in reply, part of the roof collapsed, sending up a shower of sparks. A man ran to the firemen and gestured desperately at the neighboring roofs to the right. The firefighters directed the spray onto those buildings.

Across the street, Allan Ramsey leaned against a doorjamb. He watched the proceedings and scribbled in a shabby leather notebook. As his material grew, he made fewer entries. Soon he stopped entirely and lingered only to see if the fire would spread.

A fair question. To the left of the burning building sat a pile of rubble that was in the process of being cleared out. That space formed a firebreak. If the wind came from the west—as it often did in Atlanta—the fire would spread to the east, away from the firebreak, and race across a block of buildings huddled like cattle in a slaughterhouse pen.

A man joined Ramsey in the doorway.

"Evening, Ed," Ramsey said. He did not look away from the burning building.

Deputy Marshal Edward Langley Sprague grunted and spit tobacco juice into the street.

"Looks like you got you a story, Ramsey. Might get a bigger one if this wind kicks up some more. Fire might run loose, burn down the *Intelligencer*."

"If that happens, it'll be in my story. I'll write it, and Steele will find a way to print it."

Ramsey shifted to look at the lawman. "You have anything you want to say to our readers?"

"Shit," Sprague muttered.

"Can't use that."

The two men watched the fire.

"This isn't an accident," Ramsey said.

Sprague spit again, a great shot arcing fifteen feet out into the street.

Ed Sprague had run a pack of bloodhounds before the war. Most said he was a bounty hunter. Some retold dark rumors that he went after fugitive slaves. No one really knew, and Sprague was a taciturn man. With his sleepy eyes, large bulbous nose, and sagging jowls, he even looked like an old bloodhound. Stocky, with a belly that lapped his belt, Sprague's appearance should have been comical, but somehow the deputy didn't inspire a desire to laugh.

The wind picked up, whipping the flames into a maelstrom of destruction. Lighted cinders fell onto the adjacent buildings. The men manning the pumper tried desperately to snuff them.

A spatter. Then another. The rain began.

Against the noise of the storm, Sprague finally spoke. "It's arson. Some damn fool threw lit bottles of kerosene through the back windows. I been talkin' to some folks who was inside at the time. 'Course most of 'em was drunk, but they all said the same thing."

"Who wanted to burn Miller out?"

"Hell, just about anybody but drunks, card sharks, and whores."

The remaining roof collapsed. A shower of embers flew up as if to spite the rain. "But the son of a bitch what done it," Sprague continued, "was most likely Rafe Jenkins."

"Is Jenkins stupid enough to burn out his competition?"

The rain was coming down in gusting sheets now, driving the crowd for shelter and ending the threat of the fire's spread.

"Rafe done it, all right," said Sprague, spitting again, this time a rifle shot into a growing puddle. "'Course he paid someone else to do it. Rafe ain't gonna be trottin' down an alley with flamin' kerosene bottles in his hands." The deputy chuckled at the thought. He stared at figures in the street, intently watching someone for a moment before going on. "Rafe done it 'cause he wants whores an' the gambling around here for himself."

Out in the street, the firemen coiled their hose in the rain. Ramsey scrawled a line in his notebook about the incongruous sight.

"I'll find the fool that done the burning," Sprague said wearily, "and he'll lead me to Rafe."

"Okay if I say it was arson? Everybody in town knows it anyway."

"I suppose, but you keep Rafe Jenkins to yourself."

The storm was blowing itself out. The air, normally freshened by a thunderstorm, was acrid with smoke. Across the street, John Norman, the president of Company No. 1, and some of his volunteer firemen watched the dwindling flames.

"I got another piece of news," said Sprague. "A while ago they found Otis Timmons. He was roughed up pretty bad. Ben Williford sent me word."

"Timmons, the Freedmen's Agent?"

"Yup. Weren't far from that smallpox hospital the city had Jim Dunning set up for the darkies. Timmons was beat damn good. Just don't make sense to whup a man that bad—he don't feel it after a while." Sprague shook his head at the folly. "I was on my way back from checking it out when Rafe turned firebug. If it ain't one damn thing, it's another."

"Any idea who might have done it?"

"Hell, that bastard Timmons damn near pissed off everybody in Atlanta. If word got out he was gonna get a lickin', folks'd wait in line for a chance to slug him. Ain't no telling who done it. Timmons ain't conscious, but he ain't gonna die, so I might hear more about it by morning."

"If you find anything out, Ed, you tell me, okay?"

The rain had stopped. Sprague stepped into the street and brushed spent cinders from his hat.

"Yeah, I'll let ya know," he called, crossing the street to join the men surveying the charred building.

Ramsey walked down Marietta Street, unsure whether to go to the newspaper office, to his boarding house, or for a drink. The drink was winning. The story could hold until morning. Maybe there would be an arrest during the night.

The street was muddy from the storm, but the weather had been dry of late, and footing was still fairly firm. He picked up his pace, his stride growing longer. A war-damaged leg gave him a rolling gait, but despite the pain, he liked to walk. He believed that someday, somehow, the exercise would heal him. Each day, he urged himself onward and searched for signs his body was repairing itself.

He breathed deeply as he drew away from the fire and smoke. At least for the present, the air was washed clean of the smell of horses and dust. The moon, visible between the scudding clouds, cast a pale light intermittently over the city. Ramsey walked on until his leg begged him to slacken his pace. He stopped to consider the evening and struck a match to light his pipe. A glance at his pocket watch told him it was 9:20 p.m.

A few months earlier, The Atlanta Gas Light Company had announced the city would soon have streetlights. The promise had not become fact. Darkness shrouded any place not lit by the glow of a nearby window or graced by the light of a privately owned lamp. It made little difference to Ramsey. Darkness did not bother him. Only the foolish or the easily frightened feared the dark. He ambled a few paces farther into the shadows. Back at the site of the fire, figures moved and men worked the pumper again.

John Norman had better watch himself, Ramsey thought, or he'll drain the cistern at Five Points and there'll be no water for the next fire.

And there would be a next fire. Burnings, accidental and intentional, were a plague on the city. Little could be done. The fire companies were crippled by a lack of equipment. City Hall had assured the citizens that this would be remedied—a steam pumper was on order and more cisterns were planned—but promises had once again outstripped actions. The only tools on hand were Company No. 1's worn hand-pumper and a legion of buckets.

Atlanta had no end of trouble. Camps of displaced people, both black and white, ringed the city. Smallpox raged among the malnourished and dispossessed of all races. Lawlessness bred of desperation was endemic. No one could be blamed. The city treasury was empty and the population's needs immense. Yankee troops and the civil authorities kept a rough peace—just.

And yet, ravaged and struggling as Atlanta might be, shops reopened and the railroads operated more dependably each month. The lifeblood of commerce was returning, and the debris of war was being cleared. Cocksure of itself and its future, Atlanta was a brash upstart of a city unloved by its neighbors, but each day brought more change than more sensible places saw in a month.

Ramsey unlocked the door to his room, lit a lamp, and removed his hat and coat. The flame rising on the wick sent the shadows into retreat. Movement on the other side of the room caught his attention, and his head snapped around.

"Hello, Allan," a voice said. A woman leaned against the wall, her arms crossed.

"Sam?"

"Sorry about the surprise," she said, "but you really have no reason to be cross. I was caught in the rain and needed a chance to dry off, so I let myself in." She moved out of the shadow and poured herself a glass of his whiskey. "And Allan, that lock"—she made a dismissive wave of her hand—"would only keep out the compulsively honest."

"The last I heard, you were being wined and dined in Memphis."

"That was rather pleasant, I must say. Unfortunately, Mr. James Daly's family had some pedestrian ideas about money and marriage. Despite my being a respectable war widow, their feelings for me had cooled by the time some of Mother Sally's jewelry went missing. Of course, I was horrified such a thing could happen, but the police insisted on asking me more questions than I was comfortable answering, so it seemed like a good time to leave."

Samantha Frazier had not lost her looks. Her black hair framed a superbly proportioned face.

"James Daly must greatly regret your decision," Ramsey said.

"Perhaps he does, though the rest of the family feels otherwise. They've sent James off to work with one of his cousins in Texas. All in all, I suppose it was for the best." She surveyed the room.

"Sam, why are you here? Or, more to the point, what do you want?"

"We made a good team back in the war, didn't we?" Sam said. "You, me, Vera, and Freddie Ross. How is Freddie? I haven't heard much from him. He's no better a correspondent than you are. Is he still working the clergyman bit? He married us more than once," she said with a laugh.

Ramsey poured himself a glass of whiskey. "You haven't answered my question."

"Well, Allan, if you must know, I'm on my way to New Orleans. I need a place to stay for a few days."

"Did you try the American Hotel? I'm sure they have a room for a respectable war widow."

"Hotels are fine things, but they are so very public. I was rather thinking of somewhere more private."

"So the police are looking for you."

"Well, they're not exactly looking for me, but there is some interest along those lines. After I left Memphis, I went to Nashville. It seems a Mr. Horace Somersby is angry about railroad bonds that Mrs. Dilys Lambert, a respectable war widow, found necessary to sell him. The dreadful man bargained the price down far below par value. I knew a man like that would check the serial numbers on the bonds with the issuing railroad, but he managed it more quickly than I anticipated. Do you remember the time we climbed down the trellis from a second-story hotel window in Port Gibson? Well, with the police pounding on the door, things went pretty much like that. I had to leave my entire wardrobe behind." She shook her head and finished her whiskey. "Damned telegraph. How can a girl make a living these days?"

"I see your problem."

"Wonderful! I can stay here very discretely. It will just be the two of us for a few days. I'll replenish my wardrobe and take the train south when the police return to chasing real criminals. It will be fun, just like the old days."

"You can't stay here, Sam. There would be too many questions."

She stood close to him. "It's just a few days."

"You can't stay here, but I suppose I can find a safe place where you can wait things out."

She poured herself another whiskey. "You always were the knight in shining armor."

A shadow of concern passed over her face. "I only found out you'd disappeared when I returned from Savannah in the fall of '64. Suddenly, Williams was running things, and no one would talk about you. Forgetting you'd ever existed was almost a standing order. It wasn't until later I heard about the ambush."

"I made a mistake."

"L. J. told me you went off on your own a lot after Vera disappeared and Burke and Rhodis were killed. You were looking for her, weren't you? That's how they caught you."

"Bringing Vera into the conversation is a poor move, Sam."

"Oh, Allan, I knew you loved her. I never cared. You and I were all about animal spirits and good times. What happened?"

"I don't know."

"Maybe you need to find out."

"Maybe it's none of your business, Sam. Leave it."

"Perhaps not, but you used to smile, and now you limp. You live in a shabby boarding house and work for a two-bit newspaper."

She surveyed the room with a frown. "Where's that carbine you used to carry when you went out into the field? You called it your guardian angel. I don't see it around here either. I don't see much of anything around here."

"The war is over. A man doesn't need a gun like that anymore. I'm doing just fine. I'm making a living and minding my own business."

Sam shook her head dismissively. "Leave the lying to me, Allan. I'm better at it than you." She clinked her glass against his and ruefully shook her head. "Oh, dear boy, what's become of you?"

"Ramsey!" Steele's voice boomed across the office.

Ramsey hung up his coat and joined his editor.

"What do you make of this?" John Steele thrust out a sheet of paper. "Man came in last night and gave it to Duncan after everyone left. Paid double the normal rate. He wants it to run in the personals three times. He rather frightened Duncan."

"Many things frighten Duncan," Ramsey muttered and glanced down at the paper.

CGNMZHESNVHCM.QKVOGWFMWNJ.A
CHUS.VA.NMKSRF.
BB.CHOMAZBCA.KBOMELXFPQZQF.VH
GFKPGM.YWGT.WUBB.
LQI.NWMBTVIGTL.

"Could that nonsense actually mean anything?" Steele asked.

"Have you run it?"

"No, but it's set."

Steele was a solid man of above-average height. His thatch of unkempt hair perched over deep blue eyes of remarkable vitality. He gave the impression of a man trying to look straight through the things around him.

"Well," Ramsey said, "it's most likely a code of some sort. It might be simple letter substitution, but I don't think so. The letters in the code seem too random. Perhaps the Vigenère Tableau was used. You Rebs called it the 'Vicksburg Code.'" He thought for a moment and shrugged his shoulders. "I don't really have any idea. There were many codes and ciphers around during the war."

Ramsey held the note up and examined it. "Cheap paper. The writing is that of a vigorous man with some education."

Steele frowned. "That doesn't help."

"What did the man look like?"

"A big fellow who wore glasses. Duncan didn't like his suit."

"What?"

"Some of Duncan's foolishness," Steele said. He took the note back from Ramsey. "It seems strange we were asked to run the ad three times."

"Perhaps the man who placed it wants to be certain an intended party sees it, but he isn't certain when that party will arrive in Atlanta. Maybe the repetitions themselves have some significance. I don't know. No doubt the lavish prepayment was intended to place you in your present dilemma."

"If it's a code, can you break it?" Steele's blue eyes flashed at the thought.

"Well, ethical questions aside, I doubt it. If I am right, a code like this is only decipherable by those who know a keyword. That word, along with an alphabetic tableau, establishes the meaning of the letters. The tableau is not unique. The keyword is the crucial part."

"So what do we do? If the message is sinister, I don't want trouble."

Ramsey understood. Atlanta had many conflicting
loyalties, and the Federal authorities were suspicious of
Southern intentions.

"Look, John, why not go ahead and run it. After all, people
put all sorts of idiotic things in personal ads. If there are any
questions later, we'll say we assumed it was given to us in good
faith."

Steele hesitated. "Okay, but we have to be careful. You go
see Havermeyer this afternoon and show it to him. That way
we keep our noses clean no matter what happens."

General Stevenson was in command of the city, but dealing
with the military meant dealing with the Provost's Office. And
dealing with the Provost's Office meant dealing with the
arrogant, efficient Major Wilhelm Havermeyer. At Army
headquarters, all knowledge of the city's problems flowed
upward through him, and just as surely, all commands and
edicts passed back down through him. Havermeyer was a man
wrestling chaos with little but a sense of order and iron will.
No doubt one day he would go mad.

Steele changed the subject. "Finished editing *Bingley's
Washington Letter*?"

"It's ready."

Ramsey took a manuscript from his desk drawer. Bingley
was a hack long past his prime. His "research" consisted of
spending days at the bar in Washington's Willard Hotel,
soaking up whiskey and rumor in prodigious quantities.
Bingley gave regional newspapers like the *Intelligencer* the
appearance of a presence on the national scene. His copy was
unreliable but cheap. Ramsey used his own contacts to wrestle
Bingley's verbiage into a modest conformity with reality.

Steele took the manuscript without comment. "When you
go to Army headquarters," he said, "take young Duncan. Show
him around. It will do him good." With that burden tossed on
Ramsey's shoulders, the editor disappeared into his office.

Rabun Perdido stared down at the chessboard, oblivious to the calls from his patrons at the bar. His large hand hovered over the queen bishop as he sought a move that would crack a defense he found impenetrable. Allan Ramsey leaned forward in concentration. Rabun's hand made a semicircular flight, hovering briefly over a knight before fluttering back to the queen bishop. He shook his head. The hand was withdrawn and planted on his hip.

"*Un moment, mon ami, un moment.*" Rabun walked away to help Mr. Winks, his barman, satisfy the thirst of the crowd filling the saloon.

"Allan, you play like an old lady," said Chatsworth White, a small man in a soiled beige linen suit. "Rabun's got you all backed up. If you had taken my earlier suggestion, that wouldn't be the case."

Ramsey reached for his glass of whiskey without reply. Chatsworth and the man standing next to him, Harold Streep, explained to each other the move Ramsey had missed. They could not agree what it was. Chatsworth's lumbering half-brother, Joe Frank, slapped at a fly that kept landing near a puddle of spilled beer.

Rabun—a tall, powerfully built man with an olive complexion and black hair that fell past his collar—appeared in Atlanta in the spring of 1865. At a time when some had fled and others had succumbed to despair, he pronounced Atlanta a fine city with a glorious future. He found a place for his business and soon had it fit for customers. Above the front door, a sign—painted with wild colors, depicting strange vegetation and bizarre animals—appeared. It announced to the world the name of the establishment: THE ISLE OF CAPRI.

Rabun labored over this creation for days and hung it with pride. Capri was, he explained, his favorite place in the whole world. Though dark forces kept him away at present, he would someday return. Perhaps that was true, but the odd sign suggested he had never set foot on the island.

His saloon occupied a room narrower than it was deep. Its whitewashed plaster walls rose from a well-worn planked floor. Unmatched wooden chairs surrounded unmatched tables. Along the wall an ancient potbelly stove provided comfort on cold nights. In stark contrast to the plainness of the room, an ornate and highly polished bar stood across from the stove and formed an elongated "L." It began just inside the door and ran the length of the room. Rabun had placed stools along the bar where his patrons could sit—an innovation other tavern owners scoffed at.

As the noise level grew, Ramsey's concentration remained on the game. Chatsworth was right: He had given up an alarming amount of space to his opponent. However, Chatsworth failed to see that Ramsey's pieces formed an interlocking defensive web. And contrary to White's thinking, Ramsey did have a place to go. When the time came, he would go straight through Rabun's marauding horde of attackers. He waited only for Rabun to move the queen bishop, a move that was obvious, logical—and fatal.

Ed Sprague joined the group. The deputy marshal glanced at Ramsey, then at the game, and then back at Ramsey. His jaw worked with bovine rhythm on a wad of tobacco.

"Have you made an arrest in the Miller Saloon fire?" Ramsey asked.

"They been complications," Sprague said, "but we sortin' 'em out."

"What about Otis Timmons? Any word on who jumped him last night?"

"No. An' besides, ain't my concern. Willis Lanier's on it now."

Harold Streep stepped forward. "You ain't heard nothing about them that attacked Timmons and you won't. The man had it coming! Those that beat him did their duty. This is a white man's town—you should know that. White man's town and white man's law!" He raised his voice in a flood of self-importance. "We don't need Yankee scum like Otis Timmons coming here to tell us how to treat our coloreds!"

Whatever impact these words had on the patrons was lost on the deputy.

"You know anything 'bout them that beat Timmons?"

"Deputy, I'm telling you—"

"Answer me, Streep!"

The two men stood face to face in the now silent saloon. Streep appeared to physically shrink as he glared at Sprague. A poor man, he had never owned a slave in his life. It didn't matter. Where once the freedmen had a specific owner, now white society was the master.

"Well!" Sprague spit, missing the spittoon. More silence. "If you ain't got nothin' to say to me, Streep, then you tell your damn friends I'm comin'. I'll find 'em!" Sprague's angry voice carried to every ear in the saloon. "I didn't like that son of a bitch neither, but the law's the law. You fools don't run this town." He poked a stubby finger into Streep's chest, knocking the smaller man back a step. "Go tell 'em that!"

"No call to yell at me!" Streep glanced around for support. None was offered. He turned back to face Sprague but avoided his eyes. "I just said what everybody knows."

Around the room, the bar patrons' faces were hard to read. No one was anxious to take on Sprague. Streep took a step toward the door. "If you throw in with them Yankees, you'd better watch yourself. You ain't no better than Timmons!" he said and rushed from the bar.

The room watched his retreat, then the hum of conversation resumed.

It occurred to Ramsey that Ed Sprague's low opinion of the human race resulted in a kind of primitive fairness with respect to law enforcement. It wasn't that he thought well of the freedmen—he didn't; Sprague didn't think much of anyone. His code was simple. Those who threatened the peace of the city were his enemies; those who didn't, he tolerated without affection.

"You said something about Timmons?" Sprague asked as if nothing had happened.

"You don't think Harold Streep had anything to do with the attack—do you?"

"Hell no. That little piece a shit would piss on himself if he thought he'd have to fight. But he's got a big mouth an' he's probably runnin' up the street right now telling anybody who'll listen what I said. Them's that did it are gonna know I ain't happy."

"Can I see Timmons tomorrow?"

"Yeah, I guess that would be okay with the doc. It's a waste a time, though. Timmons didn't see nothin'. They threw a blanket over his head before they commenced to beat him. Course that ain't stopped him from accusing half the damn city. Fact is, though, he don't know who did what. That worm Streep is right. We ain't gonna get nothin' on nobody."

Ramsey looked back at the board. Rabun returned, and the queen bishop was moved. Chatsworth White nodded his approval. Ramsey thrust forward his king bishop pawn and the counterattack was under way.

Ramsey left The Isle of Capri around midnight. The night air was clear and crisp. He stood on the wooden sidewalk in front of the saloon and looked up at the stars. Voices came from the darkness. A black man with a lantern led the way along the dark street for several white men who followed.

These ephemeral figures rounded a corner and disappeared. A dog barked and other dogs answered from different points nearby. Ramsey pulled up the collar of his coat against the spring air. He slowly raised his damaged leg and tried to touch the heel of his boot to the back of his thigh. No luck. His eyes were now used to the night. He strode off the sidewalk and into the darkness.

Ramsey set his pen down on the desk. The evening light grew dim in the window, and he lit the lamp on his desk. Blue-gray smoke from the spent match curled upward against its yellow glow. In the evening sky outside, the sun had slipped behind budding trees. Their limbs scratched a pattern of infinite complexity against the russet glow. A wagon rumbled past. In the distance a mother called her children home.

He had approached people he trusted about a place where Samantha Frazier could stay out of sight. Chatsworth White suggested his sister's farm. It was south of the city and near enough to the railroad so she could catch a train to New Orleans when she was ready and wouldn't have to board the train in Atlanta. Terms were agreed easily; Ramsey was more than generous with Sam's money, and having a paying guest meant desperately needed cash for Whitey's sister's family.

Ramsey squared his shoulders to continue and raised his pen. The blank sheet of paper stared him down. His pipe went out. He tried to balance his pen on his forefinger, but it soon clattered to his desk.

A banging on the door broke the silence.

"It's open," he called.

Duncan Moore bounded into the room.

"Ramsey, there's a dead man!"

"What?"

"A dead man!"

Duncan threw himself into a chair. "Down on the tracks at Butler Street!"

"What happened? How—"

"Run over by a train! Oh God, can you imagine?"

"Did they send you to get me? Weren't Henderson or Isaacs around?"

"No! Jared and I were alone in the office. Ed Sprague, damn him, stuck his head in the door and told us about it. He wanted to know where you were. Jared sent me to get you." Duncan imitated Jared Whitaker, the publisher of the *Intelligencer*, with savage accuracy. "'Duncan, my boy, this is a great opportunity! Run get Ramsey, but mind, you file your own story. Run on!'"

"It's a reporter's job, Duncan. Any man who falls under a train becomes news for readers who haven't."

"You think a mangled body is funny?"

"Calm down." Ramsey returned from the sideboard with a glass of water. "Drink this and get a hold on yourself."

Duncan took a sip, then ran a trembling hand through his hair. He struggled for control as he set down the glass. Duncan, Jared Whitaker's nephew, was a young man in search of a career. His family had sent him into his uncle's employ to learn the newspaper trade. Despite the Whitakers' assurances, progress was questionable.

Ramsey pulled on his coat. "Well, let's go. We've got a bit of a walk over to Butler Street."

Duncan's thin fingers gripped his knees tightly. Only fifteen years old, with a slight build and strands of wispy blond hair falling across his forehead, he resembled an exotic plant more than a newspaperman. Without looking up he mumbled, "I thought you could go without me. I mean, you've seen that sort of thing in the war, and . . . well . . . if you shared your notes, maybe I could write something and—"

"And you'd trick Whitaker. My answer is no."

"Oh for God's sake Ramsey, please! It wouldn't be a lie. I'd write the story. I would! Besides, you're the only one who gets on with Sprague. You know how he treats me."

"Duncan, we'll both go. We can have a look around and ask a few questions. By now Sprague can probably tell us everything we need to know. Most likely some drunk tried to wrestle a locomotive and lost. I'll handle Sprague. When we're done, you write your story."

"But—"

"On your feet, Duncan. They won't wait all night for us."

Duncan rose slowly from the chair, and without looking at Ramsey, made his way out the door.

Ramsey picked his way carefully along the dark tracks. Duncan followed at a distance.

"What we got, Ed?" Ramsey called out.

In a circle of lamplight, Sprague stood talking with George Monahan, the yard superintendent for the Western and Atlantic Railroad.

"Guess Duncan told you we got us a dead un." Sprague pointed in the direction of the corpse. "What's left is over there. Ain't pretty."

Sprague was right. It wasn't pretty. In the light from a constable's lantern, Ramsey saw the corpse. The body of a muscular man lay crumpled between the tracks. His cheap greenish suit was stained with dried blood. His right arm from the elbow down was missing, as was his right foot. Gold-rimmed spectacles still clung at an angle to his loutish face. A strong odor of whiskey hung in the air above him.

"Mind if I touch him, Ed?"

"Oh God," Duncan moaned in the darkness.

"Go ahead," Sprague said. "Done it myself a while ago." The deputy finished with Monahan and walked over. "Found him just like you see. Moved him just a little so's I could get at his wallet. Name's Jacob Brackman. From Chicago."

The two men looked down at the remains. Behind them, Duncan wretched.

"Was there money in his wallet?" Ramsey asked.

"Yup. A little over a hundred. Man's a fool to carry that kinda money in this town at night." He nodded at the corpse. "Whadaya think of our friend?"

"Well, he was dead when he went under the train, otherwise there'd be blood everywhere. And"—Ramsey turned the head with the tip of his boot—"he was shot. The bullet exited just behind the left ear. Wound looks like it was maybe a rifle or big handgun." He looked up from the body. "There's something else, Ed. His name isn't Brackman, it's Tully. Bill Tully."

"Thanks for introducin' us. How the hell ya know the likes of him?"

"Army. He was cavalry. I don't remember much about him except that he was trouble. He'd steal anything that wasn't nailed down and kill anyone that crossed him. I think toward the end of the war he was sent to prison. I don't really know much about it. There was a lot going on for me then."

"Maybe he was a badun, but he musta met someone worse. By the way, there's more of him around here. Foot and arm are twenty feet back that way." Sprague jerked his head in the direction of the body parts. "Betcha he weren't drunk, neither. Smell's too strong. Someone done poured it on him."

The deputy scratched the back of his neck. "So if it weren't robbery, then Mr. Brackman, or Tully, musta been killed by someone who took a personal interest in him. Huh? Ain't nobody heard a shot 'round here this evening. Least that's what George says. So that *somebody* took the trouble to drag the body down here. Why do ya think they done that?"

"I suppose they had a personal interest, like you said." Ramsey lifted the coat away from the body.

"If you lookin' for a label, the coat come from Chicago. What's more, he'd been to Georgiana's. Found a couple of her poker chips in the pocket. Maybe he was causing her trouble. Maybe she had him killed."

"Georgiana doesn't shoot a man who gets out of hand. She has Big Jake whack 'em on the head."

"Suppose so." Sprague nodded at the body. "God knows we get our share a drunks havin' at each other. A robbery goes bad an' some unlucky son of a bitch gets himself killed." The deputy frowned. "Kinda looks like somebody put some thought into this one, don't it?"

"It does."

"So whatcha gonna say about our friend here?" Sprague asked.

"I suppose you want me to write the story as an accident so I don't spook the killer. You want a quote?"

"Nah, just make sure ya talk accident. I wanna chance to collar the wolf right quick if I can."

"Ed, Doc Pierce is here to get the body," Al Bates shouted from the darkness, "and Ramsey, that colored boy of yours is looking for you."

"Tell Doc to come over here," Sprague called back. "The body sure as hell ain't comin' to him."

"Good night, Ed," Ramsey said.

"'Night, Ramsey. Don't write nothin' that's gonna piss me off, ya hear?"

The night was darker than ever outside the circle of light. When Ramsey reached the edge of the train yard, a voice said, "Your youngun don't look too good, Mr. Allan."

"What brings you out tonight, Mr. Henry?"

"Jist saw all the commotion. Mind if I come along?" The question was rhetorical. Mr. Henry came and went in Ramsey's life as he pleased.

Nearby, Duncan was seated on the ground cross-legged. Mr. Henry, his face barely visible in the darkness, stood over him.

"Let's go, Duncan," Ramsey said. "There's a story to write."

Duncan shuffled to his feet. They hadn't walked far when Duncan said in a trembling voice, "I looked at the body, Ramsey. I really did. It was awful. He . . . his . . . the arm—"

"I know, Duncan. Let's just get away from here."

"You don't understand. I looked at him! I looked at his face, Ramsey. I—"

"It's all right, Duncan. Things like that aren't easy."

"I know who that man is. It's . . . he's the one who placed the personal ad. The one with all the jumbled letters. He's the one."

Light from a nearby shanty fell on the boy through a swirl of shadow. Vomit spattered his shirt. Some still clung to his chin. His wild eyes echoed his unruly hair. He sniffed and wiped his nose on the back of his hand, then brushed the front of his shirt in a meaningless attempt to restore his appearance.

"Are you sure?" asked Ramsey. "You didn't get much of a look at—"

"I know what I saw!"

"Okay, okay. Why don't you go home and get some rest."

"The story! Whitaker wants my story!" It wasn't a call to action. It was a cry against the sole obstacle to flight.

"Well, I don't know about you, but I'm tired. We can do our stories in the morning. I've made some notes, and we can work from those. Besides, in the morning we can talk with Sprague. There might be some developments by then."

"Really?"

"Really."

Duncan looked back at the trainyard and trembled. "Thanks," he said and walked listlessly into the darkness.

"Mind if I come with you, young man?" Mr. Henry called to the retreating Duncan. "Dark night to be walkin' alone. Yes suh, a dark night."

Ramsey took his whiskey from the bar and retreated to a table in the corner. The Isle of Capri was quiet this evening. Rabun Perdido was away on business, and the chessboard rested somewhere under the bar. Across the room, a group of men, all regulars, discussed the news of the day. One of them had a folded newspaper to which he pointed with vehemence. At a table farther along, Jasper Dunlap dealt cards to a couple of young farm boys. He marveled at how well they played poker. Most likely they were in town for supplies and hoped for a bit of fun before they headed home. Jasper looked at his cards and smiled like a doting grandfather. The boys would leave poorer, but perhaps wiser in the ways of the world.

Bill Tully was dead. His death had occurred the evening after he'd run a strange message in the *Intelligencer*. It was a message that Tully had paid to run multiple times. What did the message say? Was he gathering others for some scheme, or was he trying to lure someone into a trap? Did the trap backfire? Was the message some sort of warning?

Ramsey sipped his whiskey. What about the murderer? A man like Tully would have many who wished him dead, but surely they'd shoot him and be done with it. Why risk moving the body? No one would care about a man like Tully. Maybe there was something meaningful in the place he died. At least Ramsey was certain Georgiana had nothing to do with it. That wasn't how she operated.

He turned the glass slowly in his fingers, the light dancing on the last of the amber liquid. Sprague wanted him along on the investigation. The deputy wouldn't have called at the *Intelligencer* if he didn't. Together they would search for the truth, teasing fact from conjecture. Was a man like Tully worth that? Any man's murder deserved concern, but Atlanta had more pressing problems. One thug's demise meant little in the scheme of things. Still, something would need to be done, if just for appearances. No doubt the whole thing would blow over in a day or two.

"Help me!"

The voice calls again. This time it's weaker. A woman? A boy?

Not even the horse moves in the stillness left by the voice.

Leaning forward in the saddle, ears straining, mind racing.

"Help me!"

Dismount. Running toward the house now to get to the voice.

In the shed doorway, a boy stands frozen, a hand on his shoulder. A man's hand.

Gunfire! Body slams to the ground.

Pain from a leg wet with blood.

A woodpile shimmers in the sun. A refuge?

Crawling. Bullets thud all around.

The world grows gray in the noonday glare.

Ramsey bolted upright, his bed a twisted shambles.
The dream again.

He hated the damn dream. He hated the day that spawned it.

In younger days, he thought death came only for the old or unlucky. It was his soldier's shield—a myth held against the horror of war. With death all around him, he had not personalized it, clinging to a belief that *he* would not die.

But he was wrong. He should be dead. Shot, gasping, bleeding, he lay insensible in the dust only to awaken to an old black woman who declared he would live. His mortality now lay on him like a cloak. He could only ask a god he did not believe in to keep him from dying too soon or at the wrong time.

He sat on the edge of his bed and stretched his leg. The glow of dawn lit two large windows across from him to reveal the room and its sparse furnishings. Between the windows sat a rolltop desk. Its pigeonholes were stuffed, but the writing surface was orderly, the inkwell full. Along the opposite wall, two ladder-back chairs flanked a table. The carpet beneath was worn. Several sketches and a watercolor were pinned without care above the desk. Toward the center of the room, two stuffed chairs faced each other, one in decent condition; the smaller companion, worn and shabby like a poor relation. A wardrobe and an ornate sideboard stood side by side. The latter held a wash basin and pitcher, the cheap crockery graced with an image of a nymph pouring water while an enraptured shepherd looked on.

Ramsey's second-story room offered two doors: one from the hallway, the other from an outside landing. A sturdy wooden staircase led up from the alley beside the house. This outside door caused Ramsey to take the room. A man who keeps odd hours and deals with questionable characters finds such a thing useful.

The brother of his landlady built the staircase and cut in the door. He had invented a new way of fitting corrective lenses for the shortsighted. Lacking financial resources, he prevailed on his sister for space in which to set up his business. She offered an upper-story room. Since those with poor vision are as robust as the eagle-eyed, a climb up stairs would harm neither them nor his business. Three months later, a farmer, angry and whipping his horses to a foolish speed, ran him down.

Ramsey sponged off at the basin, shivering against the cold water. He washed his face, his chest, his arms, but could not scrub away the dream. His simple toilet completed, he carried a glass of water across the room to the table.

Below him he heard a door quietly open and close. Mrs. Carraway, his landlady, made her way to the kitchen. He knew the sound well; it was his first human contact each morning. The footsteps ended. Another door quietly closed. The silence was healed, but she lingered in his mind. A plump woman whose efficient movements about the kitchen formed a domestic ballet. She carried in her dance the memory of a dead husband and a son swallowed by the war.

Other boarders stirred. Coughing from the next room announced the rising of the fair-haired man from Biloxi. His mechanical skills had saved him from the fighting, and now he was at work repairing the railroads. He was a man of energy and would be first at the breakfast table. No doubt he would go far in the world.

Ramsey dressed. His wardrobe did not confuse him with choices. Two shirts hung on pegs, one clean and the other passable. He chose passable and reached for the pants that lay across a chairback. They were new and dark gray. He finished with a vest. Mrs. Carraway had given it to him. "A man ain't complete without a vest," she said when she presented it to him the day he and Mr. Henry finished the repairs to the roof. Ramsey accepted the vest and wore it, though he knew his landlady had given the gift to herself, not him. The sight of it, like a conjurer's incantation, summoned her dead husband's presence.

Her husband was dead; she accepted that, but not the loss of her son. After the battle of Chickamauga, he was among the missing. The world considered the boy dead, but the letter from his colonel said only that her son was missing. The missing might be found. She kept her son's belongings locked away, enshrined for the day of his return.

If Allan Ramsey were asked why he returned to Atlanta after the war, he would struggle to answer. Certainly, better opportunities were elsewhere. The *New York Tribune* had offered a good job. The *Hartford Courant* wanted him back. General Grant made him a fine offer at the War Office. Despite it all, he'd chosen to stay here, drawn to a place where his past and future might one day intersect.

His current employment had come about by chance. In the early days after the war ended, he helped Judge Jared I. Whitaker, the publisher of the *Daily Intelligencer*, with a small matter. The judge was a practical man with an eye to the future. He thought Ramsey and his contacts among the new Union overlords would be useful. Whitaker offered Ramsey a job. The pay was meager and the duties ambiguous. Ramsey accepted.

The bargain proved fair for both sides. Ramsey looked into things for the judge and the powerful men aligned with him, helping them to anticipate trouble and walk a political tightrope. The arrangement gave him, a one-time Union officer, a degree of protection. Though as a former enemy, he was suspect in Southern eyes. To the Army, the arrangement gave him a taint of disloyalty. Both sides had their uses for him. Neither side quite trusted him.

Ramsey descended the stairs to breakfast. The meal rarely varied from bacon, biscuits, and coffee. This morning was no exception. Even so, as he finished sipping his coffee, he felt the day was starting well. He had avoided the man from Biloxi.

"Cassius!" Mrs. Carraway's maid, Katie, bellowed out the backdoor. "Cassius!"

"Katie," Ramsey called out, "Cassius will be back in a while. I sent him—"

"Sent him off?"

"He's carrying a message to Mr. Steele at the newspaper. He said he didn't have anything to do this morning. So—"

"Nothing to do! That boy's taken to lyin'. Cap'n Ramsey, you gonna be the ruin of that youngun. You give him a nickel, didn't you!"

"Well, yes."

"It's gettin' where he won't hardly do a thing without him bein' paid."

"A nickel is hardly—"

"It's a heap o' money to a lazy runaway scamp like Cassius." Katie placed her hands on her hips. "Next time, you ask me or the missus if he done his chores. He's got no business runnin' off with your notes and nickels."

"Sorry, Katie."

The whipping Katie intended for Cassius would never happen. Neither lazy nor a scamp, the boy was clever enough to evade that fate when he returned. He always did.

The message Cassius carried to Steele gave a brief description of the night's events and a promise that copy would follow. Returning to his desk, Ramsey found the story didn't take long to write. A few obvious facts, a fabricated quote from Sprague, and some comments about the dangers of the rail yard at night were enough. If Sprague made a quick arrest, perhaps tomorrow's story would reveal that the man had been murdered and the murderer caught.

Ramsey strolled down Ivy Street on his way to the newspaper. The warm clear day vibrated with energy. Staccato sounds of hammers clattered into and out of rhythm with each other. Ahead, the Methodist Church rose majestically, its steeple stabbing the blue spring sky. Farther along, a crowd gathered on Alabama Street.

He was fifty yards from the corner when he heard a female voice boom. Hattie, the street preacher, was beginning her day, a day in which she would amuse some and enrage others.

Nearby, Mr. Henry talked with three black men. The conversation ended when Mr. Henry noticed Ramsey. The old man strolled over.

Compact and muscular, Mr. Henry walked with catlike grace. His skin was so dark it had an iridescent quality, and he wore a battered hat to protect his bald head from the sun. From what people said, Mr. Henry had to be well past seventy, though he looked years younger. He spoke with a slightly clenched jaw, making his voice unmistakable.

"You get Duncan home all right?" Ramsey asked.

"Well, we did pretty good. He calmed himself down after a while and got right surly before I left him."

"Are you busy just now?"

"What do you need me to do?" Mr. Henry cut his eyes to the papers in Ramsey's hand.

"Would you carry this to Mr. Steele for me? I've got a lot to do today."

"Kinda need to git to my stand. Them taters ain't gonna sell themselves. But I'm going that way. I'll see Mr. Steele gits it." Mr. Henry put the copy in his coat pocket.

Relieved of his delivery duties, Ramsey set course for the telegraph office on Peachtree Street. He sent two telegrams: one to the Chicago police and the other to the War Department. The head telegrapher, a dyspeptic little man named Appleby, took the messages and payment without comment.

"So Tully was staying at The American Hotel," Ramsey said. "Did you find out anything else?"

"Not much. A fella named Jacob Brackman was registered there. He ain't paid his bill or checked out. I guess he damn sure ain't gonna pay it now. The desk clerk don't remember any visitors or messages. Don't mean much. The place is a beehive. Our man arrived Monday. Had his bags sent from the depot, so he probably weren't in town before then."

Sprague and Ramsey walked out along McDonough Street. The early spring breeze that freshened the morning was dying away. Ramsey halted, pushed his hat back, and loosened his collar.

"Anyways," continued Sprague, "I been talkin' to the railroad folks, and they said a train came by on that track 'round about an hour before the one that hit our friend. Crew didn't notice nothin'."

Sprague lowered his voice. "The engineer what hit the body was takin' it pretty hard, thinking he killed a man. I sorta let him know the truth. Put his mind at rest, ya know. Told him I'd stick him in jail if he talked, but ya never know. Had to tell Monahan too." Sprague looked away, ashamed of his kindness. "I had some men check with the folks around there" he continued. "Ain't nobody seen nothin'. Damn if we don't live in a city of the deaf and blind."

Ramsey and Sprague were searching for the ambush site. They reasoned that if Tully was dead before being placed on the tracks, he had not been dead long. That meant he must have been dumped there shortly after sundown. An earlier train had passed through without mishap, establishing a loose time frame. So if Tully was at Georgiana's before his murder and on his way back to his hotel, he was likely killed somewhere along McDonough Street.

It was just supposition, but they had further reason to believe this thinking was correct. South Butler Street forked off from McDonough Street just past Fair Street and angled east away from the city where it crossed the tracks. That was where the body had been found. If Tully were simply walking back to his lodgings, he would have continued down McDonough Street and ignored the change of direction. Logic suggested the murder occurred prior to Butler Street. The thinking seemed irrefutable earlier. Now, walking along the street in the light of day, Ramsey wondered if it was just wishful thinking.

The houses close to the city center had been built three or more to a block. Many were inhabited, though some derelicts awaited demolition. Not a good place for an ambush. Farther out, the houses grew sparser.

They walked on.

Sprague pointed at a large half-built house isolated from its neighbors by a bend in the road.

"Whadaya think?"

"Best bet yet."

A swarm of men were hard at work. The banging of their hammers filled the air as Sprague and Ramsey searched the grounds.

"What do you think you're doing? Get out of here!" a voice shouted from across the lot. A burly man strode over. "You'll get none of my timber, sir! None of my stone, neither! This stealing is damn well going to stop!"

Sprague held his badge in the man's face.

The man sputtered to a stop. "Maybe ya are the law, but you won't find anything of interest around here."

Sprague agreed that was likely the case. Still, what was the harm in them looking around?

"Well, just stay out of the way and mind you, be quick."

The lot was large and covered with brush, but eventually they found what they sought. The weeds behind a pile of stone intended for a root cellar were trampled. Unmistakable stains of dried blood lay on the ground. A trail of blood led across broken vegetation from the street.

That was that. They had the *where* of the murder. They looked around further but there wasn't anything more to find. Ramsey looked from the stone pile to the road and then let his eyes follow back up the street toward Georgiana's.

"You know, Ed, you've got to admire our murderer's audacity," he said.

"He's just goddamn lucky nobody noticed."

"Well, he had luck with him, certainly, but it was a bold move. The timing was perfect. Tully would be a hard man to surprise if he were on his guard. Until he got about here, he was probably alert, but as the houses grew more numerous, the road would have seemed free from threat. The killer struck when Tully didn't expect the blow—and in a place where the body could quickly be hidden."

Sprague walked to the pile of stone and surveyed the road from there.

"Still chancy."

"Yes, it was. Besides being seen, he risked the sound of an isolated gunshot. You hear guns being fired off all the time, but an isolated shot might attract notice. Still, he took his chance, and this pile of rock made a good place to hide. The workers were gone, and there was enough light to take the shot. Once Tully was down, our killer took another chance and dragged the body out of the street. Then, under the cover of darkness, he drove the corpse off in a wagon. I'm sure you saw the marks of wagon wheels. It took nerve to do all that."

"Okay, the killer is smart. He takes chances. He has guts. But answer me this: How'd he know Tully was gonna be strolling by at just that time, huh? You gonna tell me this wolf's a mind reader?"

"He arranged it somehow."

"He arranged it somehow? Don't know how that's gonna work, but let's say he's a smart one an' he done it. Now tell me this: How smart is it ridin' round the city with a dead man in your wagon?"

"How dangerous is it? He loaded the body after dark and drove back into town. When he crossed the railroad tracks, he—or someone with him—pushed the body off the wagon. Darkness disguised the moment. If anyone was near the crossing, the murderer would just drive on and look for another place to dump Tully."

"Maybe. Guess that explains the whiskey. It'd give us a reason to go thinkin' accident. It'd also cover having a man stretched out in the back of the wagon."

"Exactly. You stick a hat over the wound and toss a blanket over any blood on the clothes. Pour on some whiskey, and you no longer have a dead body—you have a drunk."

"But ain't our shooter takin' the long way round? Why not just leave the body in the street? Maybe hide it in the bushes so's folks wouldn't find it right away. Seems he went to a heap o' trouble dragging a dead body 'round the city."

"Maybe he was trying to buy some time."

"Then he woulda hid the body. That's all he needs to do, right? Something simple like that make any sense to you?"

"Maybe he was sending a message with the murder. Who knows. I don't have all the answers."

"Well why don't you go see if Georgiana's got any."

"Me?"

The deputy looked at the half-built house, avoiding Ramsey's eyes.

"I'd be obliged," he said slowly, "if you would take care of checking it out. That woman won't give me the time of day."

"Georgiana has a long memory, Ed. You're going to have to apologize."

"Apologize? She's lucky I let her stay open. Ought to shut her down just to jerk her into line."

"I think you tried that."

"Well, I may just do it again."

The deputy turned back toward the city, calling out over his shoulder, "I gotta go see 'bout Rafe Jenkins."

Georgiana Starlington operated her brothel and gambling establishment from a large house that stood on a low hill. It was a three-story structure with a veranda wrapped around the first floor. Behind four Doric columns, a second-story porch looked grandly down on all who entered. New paint and careful maintenance had largely redeemed the damage from the recent past. In a city denuded of trees by two armies, the beauty of the landscaping stood out. Innocent travelers took pleasure in viewing the tasteful grounds, not realizing they were admiring a house of sin.

For those whose tastes ran to something other than landscaping, Georgiana provided female companionship and ran reasonably honest gaming tables. Certainly she had the best clientele. Her contacts and money made her a force in local politics. She knew a great many things unlikely to pass before the eyes or ears of the more virtuous.

Ramsey had met her during Sherman's occupation in 1864. She was in a different location then, not so grand and with fewer girls. A search for an errant staff officer led him to question her. It did not go well. She informed him that gentlemen came to her establishment to escape their troubles, not to be hounded by the likes of him. Big Jake, her bartender, showed Ramsey the door and made clear what would happen if he came back. Sherman laughed when Ramsey returned empty-handed. It seems, the general had said, Southern whores defend their territory better than Southern generals.

But times change. The previous summer, the provost's guard arrested one of Georgiana's clients. Not long after, charges were filed against her. The city was forced to close her business. Ramsey had quietly used his connections to keep her out of jail and free from public humiliation. When she resumed her operation, the Army chose to turn a blind eye. She was grateful. Without a word passing between them, a deal was made: she provided Ramsey with the odd point of interest, and he kept her informed of the Army's intentions.

"Good morning, Captain Ramsey," said the elegantly dressed black man who met him at the front door. "I'm afraid we're not open for business at present."

"Nathaniel, could you take my card to Miss Starlington? It's important that I speak with her."

"Yes, sir. If you would wait here."

Ramsey took a chair in the front parlor. Though it was nearly noon, the smell of breakfast hung in the air. Through a window, he could see a black woman beating carpets. Big Jake strode down the hallway with a box of bottles in his massive arms. On the floor above, someone quietly sang a popular wartime song. A child's laughter rang out, followed by inaudible words calling after her.

Nathaniel returned and led him up the stairs to a sitting room. Its papered walls sported a stylish pattern. Bric-a-brac covered the shelves and tables. A rich oriental carpet lay beneath ornate furniture. An arrangement of flowers overpowered the room with scent.

They passed through to Georgiana's bedroom.

Nathaniel tapped, then opened the door. Inside the plain room, a brass bed sat near a bookshelf lined with carefully arranged volumes. Along another wall was an orderly desk, above which hung a large oil painting of Charleston harbor. A nearby stuffed chair had an open book resting on the arm.

Georgiana sat at a table in a bay window. She gestured for Ramsey to take the seat across from her and offered him a plate heaped with pastries and teacakes. She pointed to each and extolled its merits. An old black servant poured coffee and retired.

"Captain Ramsey," she said, leaning forward slightly, "it's wonderful to have you come to us. Nathaniel said you walked over. Is that true? Your leg appears to be mending."

It was said that Georgiana had been a great beauty in her youth. Now in her late thirties, her coal-black eyes were set in an oval face that featured more than one chin. The loss of her physical charms seemed of no concern to her. Perhaps she was grateful to be rid of them.

"Thank you for asking. My leg grows stronger. How are things with you?"

The answer, Ramsey knew, would not be brief. Georgiana relished conversation, and forcing her pace was a mistake. He sampled the pastries, sipped his coffee, and let her stories unfold.

Georgiana and her girls had gone for a picnic on the Chattahoochee River during the early days of spring. "Sorry, Captain Ramsey, but sometimes it's just nice for us girls when you men aren't around." The week before, she'd entertained some local politicians and northern businessmen. "For Yankees, they were uncommonly pleasant, though our own men could teach them much about gallantry." She spoke in a languorous, low-country accent, sometimes patting the table next to her plate for emphasis.

"Well, well, Captain, how I do go on. What brings you here? No problems, I trust?" The words came lightly, but she inclined her bulk forward, betraying interest.

"I'm afraid I do have some bad news. A man was found dead at the Butler Street crossing last night. It appeared he was run down by a train."

"Dear me! But it's not the first time there's been an accident there. No one's been killed before now, thank goodness. It's unconscionable that the city hasn't built more above-grade crossings." Her eyes snapped to his. "But you say *appeared.*"

"I fear the gentleman's death was not an accident."

"Quite regrettable. But how might this be a concern of mine?"

"Your poker chips were in his pocket. He'd likely been here the evening he died."

"My poker chips can be found in many pockets. I view them as a sort of advertisement. It tells you nothing."

"True. But there's more. Deputy Sprague and I discovered where Mr. Tully was murdered. It was on McDonough Street, not far from here."

"Describe this man."

"He was large and muscular. He wore gold-rim glasses, and his clothes were rather gaudy."

"Ah, I remember. Yes, he was here. He struck me as someone who might cause trouble, so I had Jake watching. He played blackjack for a time. He was a loud talker, but nothing untoward happened."

"Did he go upstairs?"

"Yes. I believe it was with Gracie."

"May I speak with her?"

Georgiana reached for the bell pull. The ancient servant reappeared.

"Marie, please ask Gracie to join us."

A girl came through the door a few minutes later. Barely in her twenties, she had wet hair and was obviously naked under a loosely tied silk robe. Seeing Ramsey, she made no effort to cinch it tighter. A woman in her line of work, he reflected, wasn't likely to make much of modesty.

Gracie answered his questions directly, sometimes glancing at Georgiana before she spoke. Her voice suggested education. Yes, she had been with Tully that evening and had watched him gamble. No, he didn't win, but he didn't lose much either. She was in hopes that he would take her upstairs again—he was rough but he was quick. The second tryst hadn't happened. A note arrived for the gentleman. He read the message, scooped up his remaining chips, and left without cashing them in. He said something rude when she urged him to stay.

Ramsey thanked her, and she left.

The pastries were gone. Georgiana reached again for the bell pull, and Marie cleared their dishes. She invited Ramsey to fill his pipe; she deftly rolled a cigarette for herself. The subject of Bill Tully was closed.

"Have you any other news, Captain?"

"There was a fire in town last Saturday night. Miller's Tavern burned to the ground."

"Yes, I heard. Hardly a loss. Only vermin will miss the place."

"That's not why I mention it. I was wondering if you've had any trouble with Rafe Jenkins. Sprague seems to think he had something to do with the fire."

Georgiana's eyes narrowed. Her pudgy right hand knotted into a fist. "Rafe Jenkins may very well have had something to do with that fire. Deputy Sprague, whatever deplorable qualities he may possess, is not a fool. Mr. Jenkins is a most tiresome man. I can assure you there are people looking into his activities. He is on very insecure footing. Whether he has the sense to know that, I cannot answer." The storm passed from her dark eyes. "Thank you for your concern, Captain. I'm afraid I must make my way in a hostile world. It is comforting to have a friend like you in my life. Another coffee, perhaps? We shouldn't, but since Lottie came to us from New Orleans, I have rediscovered the pleasure of good coffee."

Ramsey accepted the offer. Georgiana rolled another cigarette.

"How is Mr. Timmons doing?" she asked.

"He'll recover. The beating was only an attempt to chase him away."

"Mr. Timmons is not a popular man, though I know him to be an honest one." She puffed her cigarette and sipped her coffee. "Captain Ramsey, I hear things of late that concern me. I was a loyal Southerner throughout the late war, but when the war ended, well, reality is reality. I accept our defeat. I think most Southerners have. Our revolution and the country we might have created are things of the past. We have returned to the Union and slavery is at an end."

She shifted her large body and blew a cloud of smoke into the air above him.

"But where, I ask you, are things going? What are we to expect? Certainly we don't want a harsh peace, but the war has been over for a year and we still don't know what Washington expects. President Johnson has declared that we are reconstructed—whatever that means. He welcomes us back into the Union. Meanwhile, those in Congress talk of more stringent measures."

"I don't know what to tell you. President Johnson and Congress are at war with each other. No one knows how it will end. I've had letters from old Army friends who think Johnson's star is on the wane and the Radicals will have their day."

"So we're to be toyed with by fanatics? *'Boys throw stones at frogs for sport, but the frogs die in earnest.'* Who said that? Horace?

Ovid? I don't remember. But I hear talk, sometimes angry talk, about keeping the Negro in his place and running the Yankees out. The frogs may be running out of patience."

"The war might be over," replied Ramsey, "but the battle to shape the peace has only begun. During the conflict, many divisions in Washington were covered over, but they did not go away. With victory, fractures are appearing. Lincoln might have managed, but Lincoln is dead. There are those in Congress who see Johnson as an accident of history. They think him suspiciously lenient to the South and willing to throw away what four long years of fighting have won. They want harsher measures."

"They may get more than they wish. The defeated are prone to anger. There are those who would turn the situation to their advantage. Not everyone agreed with Lee's surrender, and many wished to fight on. That may happen if these fools don't come to their senses."

"Do you think the attack on Timmons was more than a personal matter?"

"I couldn't say." She leaned forward and spoke with care. "It is possible the attackers did not act on a whim."

"Do you know who's involved?"

Georgiana smiled. "One should never know too much. I only mention my concerns because, well, let's just say we both have friends on whom we can call. I know you still have the ear of powerful men."

"Georgiana, I—"

She raised her hand to silence him. "You don't admit it, of course. All I ask is that those men should know. Let's talk no more of these troubles. I have said what I have said. Now you will do what you will do. Would you join me on the veranda? It's a very fine day and we should enjoy the sunshine."

Duncan stood in the open door, leaning against the jamb in calculated defiance. The office was empty. His effort to impress his uncle had failed. He now realized that all they wanted him for was to watch the front door—"holding the fort" as Steele would say—so they could run around feeling important.

A wagon rolled by. Up the street at Johnson's Drygoods, two men gestured in anger, their voices lost in the distance. Nearby, a farmer methodically loaded boxes into his wagon. A Union officer looked in a shop window at a display of fabric. Across the street, a beggar missing an arm and both legs sat in a chair calling for alms from those who pretended not to see him. The air vibrated from the powerful piston thrusts driving a locomotive forward on nearby tracks. A black boy ran toward Duncan.

"I got a message fo' Cap'n Ramsey," he panted upon arrival.

"He's not here."

"Where he be?"

"He won't be back for a while."

The boy held up an envelope. "You know where he got to?"

"When he gets here, he'll be here! Go! Get along!"

If these words made matters clear to Duncan, they had little impact on the boy who held the envelope.

"You his friend?"

"Well . . . yes, I suppose. What do you have for him?"

"A message."

Duncan held out his hand. "Leave it with me, and I'll be sure that Captain Ramsey gets it."

The boy hesitated.

"That's my job," Duncan sighed. "I take messages until people come back."

Flashing a smile, the boy handed Duncan the envelope and raced off the way he had come.

The stationery was of superior quality. *Captain Allan Ramsey* was written in a feminine hand on the ivory surface. Duncan held it up to the light as he had seen Ramsey do, but the thick paper revealed no secrets. There was just the faintest scent of perfume. Did Ramsey have a woman in his life? Duncan didn't know, but there were lots of things he didn't know about Ramsey.

A train passed under the Broad Street Bridge and made its way out of the city. Like many structures in Atlanta, the bridge was newly rebuilt, crude, and serviceable. Ramsey watched the engine move slowly over groaning tracks. Cinders and ash floated down through the smoky air. Battered boxcars rumbled by. Ghostly figures lurked in the darkness of the empty cars, their few belongings clasped in their arms. He brushed the ash from his hat and shoulders and walked on.

A wagon, heavy with lumber from the planing mill, passed by. On Marietta Street, workers hauled a roof beam into place with ropes, pulleys, and profanity. A scant year ago, the business district was a burned-out shell. Now structures mushroomed on every street. Shacks and shanties became impromptu stores. Rents were enormous. People paid them. The religion of Atlanta was commerce.

Ramsey enjoyed the warm spring morning but was glad he hadn't much farther to go. Yesterday's walk to Georgiana's had been a trial for his leg. To spite his lameness, he tried to walk without his limp, tried to will it away, but the unnaturalness of his gait only aggravated the problem. He paused and looked at his pocket watch. Ten minutes until nine.

The evening before, Duncan had handed him a note from "a woman." The boy was obviously intrigued with what it might contain. He didn't hide his disappointment when Ramsey slipped it in his pocket and left without comment.

Despite the mystery that captivated Duncan, the note simply stated that a Mrs. Abigail Maynard wished to see Captain Ramsey on a matter of some importance. Would he be so kind as to call at nine o'clock tomorrow morning at her boarding establishment? If that was inconvenient, perhaps he could suggest a more suitable time. The note gave an address on Cone Street.

Chances were that Mrs. Maynard was looking for someone. Since the war had ended, a parade of people crisscrossed the South, searching for the missing and dead. Some were successful. Those with the means returned the deceased for reburial in family plots. The less fortunate mourned and carried their losses in their hearts. More often than not, the search was an empty trial; the dead were hard to locate and the missing rarely found.

But for a bit of luck, he might have been among the dead. The bullet that passed through his back and grazed his lung might have killed him. One of the shots that hit his leg narrowly missed an artery. There was no way to disguise or justify it. He'd made a mistake, made a bad choice for wrong reasons; he'd been a fool. Would anyone have searched for him? He doubted it. He took a deep breath, relished the sun on his face, and was grateful for the day.

Thirty-three Cone Street possessed modest frontage, but the house ran back from the street to a considerable depth. Several shutters were missing, and the paint was peeling—yet all in all an attractive house. The comings and goings of its tenants had worn the front steps.

The owner of the establishment introduced herself as Mrs. Hoehling and directed him to a small front parlor. A table with a vase of daffodils stood by a window, the yellow of the flowers reflected in its polished surface. Two matching chairs faced the divan along the wall. Despite his aching leg, Ramsey remained standing. He held his hat at his side and idly examined the gilt-framed landscape over the fireplace.

A woman swept through the door a few minutes later. She was young and slim. Her movements possessed an animal vitality, and her black dress was cut from the finest silk. A rich widow's dress. Brown hair nearly as dark as the garment was pulled into a bun over her high forehead. Penetrating blue eyes and a prominent nose dominated her features.

Mrs. Abigail Maynard took a seat on the divan. Ramsey gratefully lowered himself into one of the chairs. Unimpressed, his leg continued to throb.

"Thank you for meeting me, Captain Ramsey. I apologize for any inconvenience."

He couldn't place her accent. Ramsey demurred with a slight wave of his hand.

"I have a letter of introduction from Colonel Horace Porter that I believe will explain my situation." She offered the letter and waited while Ramsey read.

The letter said, in the concise hand that mirrored Porter's concise thought, that Mrs. John H. Maynard was the widow of a fine soldier and a man known personally to Porter. She was presently seeking the whereabouts of her sister, Susan Knowles (née St. Clair). She and her husband, Alfred, had run a boarding school about ten miles southeast of Decatur, Georgia. The school failed during the war and Alfred and Susan Knowles's whereabouts were unknown. At Porter's request, Major Wilhelm Havermeyer had made inquiries and found no trace of them. However, Porter would consider it a personal favor if his old friend would render assistance to Mrs. Maynard etc., etc.

Ramsey looked up from the letter.

"I would be eternally grateful for your help, Captain Ramsey."

"Mrs. Maynard, you have my profoundest sympathies."

"Thank you."

"However, at the present time I—"

"Colonel Porter has great confidence in your powers. He told me you handled unusual matters for General Grant and later General Sherman. He assured me that if anyone in Atlanta could help me locate my sister, it was you."

"I'm afraid Colonel Porter's confidence in my ability outstrips the resources at my disposal."

"Perhaps if I gave you some additional information, you would be in a better position to judge how we might proceed."

"Mrs. Maynard, I—"

"During the war, I lived with my husband's family in Boston. The last letter I received from my sister was dated July 19, 1864."

"There was no mail between Boston and Georgia in 1864."

"Obviously the letter did not come through the regular channels. My sister and I lived for many years in Europe, and we have connections there. Family friends in France helped us. Susan sent her letters by steamer to Nantes, and they were forwarded to me in Boston. I, of course, reversed the process when sending letters to her. It was a slow but reliable route."

"Steamer? I believe the term is 'blockade runner.'"

"Like many Europeans, our friends did not take sides. The Miannay family, for that was their name, owned a substantial interest in several such ships. One or another of them called at Wilmington every few months. I would get packets of Susan's letters periodically and she would get mine. It was all we had. I would spend days reading and rereading them."

"Is it not possible that later packets were lost in transit? As the war progressed, the Navy tightened the blockade and port cities were captured."

"I do not believe that was the case. M. Miannay told me that he received nothing from Susan after that July packet, and he and his associates did not lose a ship until September."

"So after July 1864, you heard nothing."

"That is the last time Susan wrote. However"—she removed an envelope from her pocket—"shortly before I left Boston, I received this letter."

Ramsey took it from her hand. The letter was an inquiry from Mr. Munford Coldwater. He inquired about the ownership of the Knowles's property. It was his intent to buy it, either from Mrs. Maynard or from the rightful owner if that were not she.

"Do you know Mr. Coldwater?" Ramsey asked.

"Not personally. Susan wrote in one of her letters that Alfred leased some land to him. He owns a nearby plantation and used the acreage to grow cotton. Susan and Alfred got a percentage of the profits. As you read in Colonel Porter's letter, my brother-in-law was using the house as a boarding school. He had no interest in working the land. However, as the school was new, he had a need for any money he could get." Frowning, she added, "It troubles me that a neighbor would make such an inquiry. Surely the question of selling the land should be put directly to Alfred, yet Mr. Coldwater applies to me as if I held ownership. Just as puzzling is how Mr. Coldwater would know about me or how to write to me in Boston."

"I'm sure Mr. Coldwater's letter has an innocent explanation. After all, he apparently knew your sister. Did Major Havermeyer contact the Dekalb County authorities?"

"I've been told that was done. I went to Captain Havermeyer upon arriving in Atlanta. He is very busy, and our interview was not at all satisfactory. That is why I have found it necessary to impose upon you."

Ramsey liked the woman's directness and energy. She had not tried to enlist his pity or pretend she was helpless. That made what he was about to say even harder.

"Mrs. Maynard, I hope you will understand. I am not *Captain* Ramsey. These days I am only Mr. Ramsey. My soldiering days are over, and I do not have the Army's resources at my disposal. I assure you that Major Havermeyer's reach is far greater than my own. If he was unable to locate your sister, there is nothing more I can do."

"Surely you are too modest. General Grant, I believe, wished you to continue in his service after the war. I doubt that offer was made to many others."

How much had Porter told this woman?

"It's difficult for me to disappoint you, Mrs. Maynard, but there is really nothing I can do. I'm very sorry. Perhaps if you returned to Boston, I'm sure—"

"I only ask for a bit of your time." Abigail Maynard's penetrating eyes caught his. Pain raged inside them. He looked down and turned his hat in his hands.

"I appreciate your concern, Mrs. Maynard—I truly do. If I should find myself in a position to help you, I will." He looked up at her. "At the moment I have neither the time nor the means to be of any service. It would be best if you returned to Boston. All may yet be well."

"I have come South to find my sister, Captain Ramsey!" Abigail Maynard's blue eyes flashed with anger. "I sincerely desire your help. My sister must be in trouble. If all were well, she would have written by now. I tell you, sir, I have no intention of returning to Boston! I have asked for your help, and you have refused it. Fine. You insist that you are powerless. Fine. You have declared my efforts a failure before they have been undertaken." She gave a disgusted flick of her hand. "So be it. I'm sorry to have wasted your time."

She fired her words like bullets. Her eyes never released his.

Ramsey desperately wanted to explain himself. He wanted to tell her that her search wasn't foolish—it was hopeless. It was a search not of the mind and eyes but of the heart. Her duty was to heal her life. Her sorrows were her own, and she must learn to bear them. If her sister was gone after two years, she was gone forever. Everyone in this life has lost something or someone; no one is whole.

"Good day, Mrs. Maynard," he said quietly. "I wish you well."

He stood to leave. Pain shot like an electric arc through his leg. He steadied himself clumsily against the back of the chair.

"Oh!" Abigail Maynard's hand flew to her lips.

"An old wound," Ramsey said with a weak smile, "terribly sorry." He slowly stood erect. "Sometimes my leg doesn't behave as it should. I'm quite all right."

He limped toward the door.

"Captain Ramsey . . . I've . . . I've had dreams," she said to his retreating back. Her voice was soft and distant.

He turned.

"Dreams," she repeated. "Your limp. It's just . . ." Her face was pale, her anger gone. "It's just that, for a long time, I've had dreams about my sister. Terrible dreams. There's screaming and blood. Blood running down over stones. And horses. So much blood. It's terrible. I wake up screaming." Tears filled her eyes. She looked away.

Ramsey was at a loss for what to say or do.

She cleared her throat and summoned her strength. "Just before I left Boston, the dream changed. In many ways it remains the same, but now, after the screaming and the blood, there is a mist . . . and there is a man . . . and the mist swirls around me, and the man comes toward me. There is danger, but I don't fear him. I never see his face, but he is tall like you, and"—she paused—"he limps."

They stared at each other in the long moment that followed. Tears streamed down her cheeks.

"I'm sorry, Captain Ramsey," she said, rubbing her eyes and trying to recover her composure. "You must think me mad. My life has not been easy of late. Goodbye."

She turned to the window.

Ramsey's thoughts lay heavy on him as he made his way back up Cone Street.

Deputy Marshal Sprague methodically put his chewing tobacco back into a leather pouch, which he stuffed in his coat pocket. The pouch created a bulge that mimicked the protrusion from his cheek. On the other side of the marshal's office, Officer Al Bates stared vacantly at a newspaper. It wasn't the *Intelligencer*.

"Did you read my story this morning?" Ramsey asked. "I said it was murder, but I said it as softly as I could. Steele changed some of it, made it more sensational than I wanted."

"Coulda' been worse." The wad in his cheek began to work down. "That fella Benson from the *New Era* been pesterin' the bejeesus outta me. He's pissed off 'cause he didn't find out about Tully till yesterday morning. An' anyway, he thinks we got it all wrong. Says the real problem is there ain't enough bridges over the railroad gulch. Broad Street Bridge ain't enough. Thinks we need a public campaign to get more bridges!"

"I guess he's going to get madder when he finds out you forgot to tell him it was murder."

"Benson can go to hell."

Al Bates wasn't looking in their direction but was grinning at Sprague's comments.

"Why don't we get out of here, Ed?" Ramsey said, nodding slightly toward Bates.

"Yeah, sure."

When they were outside, Ramsey told Sprague about Georgiana and Gracie.

"She tellin' the truth?"

"There's not much reason either one is lying. Tully was just another man for Gracie, and Georgiana had no reason to harm him. But there is one interesting point."

"Yeah, the note." Sprague's hound-dog eyes cut to Ramsey. "That musta been how they got him heading back to town. So if there's a note, where is it? I didn't miss it. Besides, when we took the body back to Doc Pierce's, I went over it again. Weren't no note."

"Well, if Tully kept it when he left Georgiana's and you didn't find it, the murderer must have taken it."

Ramsey paused to consider for a moment. "It takes a cool head to cover details like that, but somehow there seem to be stout nerves and cunning one minute and rashness the next. Why drag the body down to the tracks? Why take the risk? And as for throwing the body under a train, it mangled the corpse, but it wasn't likely to obscure a gunshot wound." Ramsey looked at Sprague. "Maybe there is more than one person involved."

Sprague spit into the dust and said nothing. Ahead of them lay the railroad tracks where the body had been found.

"I sent a telegram to a friend in the War Department," Ramsey said, "to find out what the Army knows about Tully. I hope to have the reply on Tuesday or thereabouts."

"Knew you'd do that, so's I didn't bother. Judge might as well pay for the information."

"Your notion of a free press?"

The Deputy blew into his handkerchief. "Damn nose runs like a river every spring."

"Where are Tully's belongings now?" Ramsey asked.

"Had the hotel lock 'em up in the room. You wanna take a look?"

"Sure."

"Well, I gotta get back to the marshal's office. Whit's gonna give Mayor Williams a report on the murder. Four o'clock at the hotel, okay?"

"Is Steele here?" Ramsey asked as he entered the *Intelligencer* office.

"He's with the Judge," said Jack Henderson in his I-don't-give-a-damn voice. "They've been up in his office for almost an hour. Said for you to come up as soon as you arrived."

Ramsey found Whitaker and Steele seated at a large table, talking earnestly. They stopped when he entered the room.

"Captain Ramsey, Mr. Steele told me about the murder. Do you bring us further news?" the judge asked. Despite open windows, the room was blue with cigar smoke. Ramsey pulled his pipe from his pocket and was soon adding to the haze.

"We know a bit more than we did last night."

"Tell us."

"Well, some of this you may know and some you may not, but I might as well start at the beginning." Ramsey knew that Whitaker, because of his legal training, liked his facts concise and unadorned. "A man named Bill Tully, calling himself Jacob Brackman, came to Atlanta for reasons unknown. He arrived on Monday and took a room at the American Hotel. That evening he placed a personal ad in our paper to run Tuesday.

We believe this personal ad was an encoded message. Its meaning is unknown to us. On Wednesday while he was gaming at Georgiana Starlington's establishment, Tully received a message. That was around seven-thirty. We do not have that note, nor do we know its contents. He left upon receiving it. As he walked up McDonough Street, he was shot dead. The bullet passed through him, but the weapon was large caliber and fired at close range. Later, after dark, Tully's body was dumped on the tracks at the Butler Street crossing where it was run over by an incoming train. Sprague said the engineer saw the body but was unable to stop. The conductor sent immediately for Superintendent Monahan and the police. Since another train had passed an hour earlier, the body must have been dropped there in the interval. Sprague and I have found the spot where Tully was murdered."

"Is Georgiana involved in any way?"

"No, she's not. I spoke with Sprague, and he confirmed that the note summoning Tully to his death was not found in his effects. As I told John, I knew Tully from my time in the Army and he was a bad character. I've sent a telegram to a friend in the War Department requesting any information they have on him."

The judge nodded his approval and puffed gently on his cigar. A stocky man with a fleshy face, he combed his dark brown hair straight back from his forehead. Though a secessionist, he was making his peace with the loss of the war and the new order of things.

"Thank you, Captain Ramsey," Whitaker said. "Mr. Steele and I were discussing the political side of the situation, and we feel we have done all we should in this matter. We intend to cooperate with the police and the provost. But," he added firmly, "I want you to continue looking into this matter. I know you are involved with some other things just now, but I want you to focus on this killing. We can let the rest of your work go to other hands." He checked a paper on his desk. "Mr. Clarke and Mr. Lowry are holding a meeting to reorganize the Board of Trade tonight, and"—he glanced down at the paper again—"the Atlanta Ladies Memorial Association is having its first meeting on the fifteenth. Mr. Henderson can handle the board meeting, and Duncan will see to the ladies."

Ramsey saw a smile flash over Steele's face.

"I've spoken with Marshal Anderson," Whitaker continued. "He feels the public must be kept informed of the efforts of the police. Your first two stories were correctly cautious, but from now on I want you to show that the police—the Atlanta police, not the Army—can deal with the problem. Mayor Williams and Marshal Anderson assured me you will have complete access to the investigation."

"Thanks."

Ramsey was certain the last thing in the world Whit Anderson wanted was a reporter in the middle of his investigation.

"I want you to look into things in your own way," Whitaker continued, guessing what was on Ramsey's mind. "Help Deputy Sprague as much as you like, but report to Mr. Steele and myself. Confine yourself to the investigation and leave the politics to us. If we feel we need to involve others, I will make the decision as to when and how."

Sprague and a young policeman named Dennett Wilson met Ramsey in the lobby of the American Hotel. They climbed the stairs to Tully's room. Sprague unlocked the door. The afternoon sun gave the room a cheerful appearance.

"Have your look around, Ramsey. Ya ain't gonna find much. Me and Wilson been over it already."

Ramsey opened the wardrobe doors and checked inside. Tully's clothes had Chicago shop labels. A cleaned and loaded .44 Colt Army service revolver lay on the side table across the room.

Ramsey nodded at the gun. "He didn't expect trouble if he left that behind."

"Has anyone been in this room since we were here this morning?" Wilson asked.

"Door was locked, wasn't it?" Sprague said.

"Yes, of course," Wilson said, "but I think someone's been here since this morning." He sighted along the edge of the table toward Tully's bag. "The valise has been moved. And the bureau drawers are closed."

"'Course they're closed. We done closed 'em before we left." Sprague grumbled.

Wilson shook his head. "They looked that way, but two of the drawers were just a bit ajar. They're shut tight now."

"So you sayin' someone's been in this room—someone who could get through a locked door. Someone who knew how to search without makin' a mess?" The deputy turned to Ramsey. "You wanna tell us about that?"

"I waited on you, Ed. I swear." Ramsey gestured toward the lock on the door. "But if you relied on *that* lock, you gave someone a gift. It could be defeated in well less than a minute."

"Less than a minute, huh? You wanna show us how ya did it?"

"Oh, for Christ's sake, Ed. Why don't you help me look."

"I done searched it," Sprague said and made no move to join in.

Ramsey examined the room in earnest. He ran his hand under the mattress. He lifted the small rug at the end of the bed, revealing a dead roach and a matchstick. Pulling out the bureau drawers, he looked on the backs and bottoms. He unrolled the window shades as far as they would go. One of them broke. Even with Wilson's help, his search of the room revealed nothing.

"Ya happy now?" said Sprague.

"I wonder who might have paid a visit? What were they after?" Ramsey turned to Wilson. "Did you notice anything missing since you were here before?"

"No, sir."

"Well, who knows," said Ramsey. "Maybe Whit Anderson or Willis Lanier came by. Thanks, Ed. Let me know if anything turns up."

Dennett Wilson was making a careful study of the lock as Ramsey left.

"Do you believe in dreams, Rabun? Do you think they actually tell us anything?"

"*Mon ami*, the dreams are the soul's truth. The dreams are the window through which our little mind sees the universe. We do not live in the only reality." Rabun nodded sagely and poured himself a small brandy. "Do you have the dreams?"

"Someone said she saw me in a dream," Ramsey said. "Actually, she said she saw a man that looked like me."

"Perhaps the lady is in love with you."

"God no. It's nothing like that. I only met her yesterday. She's never seen me before, but she described a dream in which there's a man with a limp who looks like me. I really don't think she was lying. She asked me for help finding her sister. I told her I could do nothing, and she didn't take it well. When I stood up to leave, I nearly fell because of this damn leg. That's when she told me about her dream."

"Perhaps she is a clever one. Perhaps she seeks to lure you with mystery. Perhaps she has already succeeded just a little?"

"Rabun, when she talked about the dream—it was frightening."

"Sometimes it is a strange path that the dreams take us on, but if they make us go, we have no choice. Do not fool yourself. You will fulfill what must be done because it will be your destiny to do so."

"I come here for decent liquor and good sense. I'm not looking for a spiritualist."

The bartender polished a shot glass. It looked like a thimble in his large hands.

"Try for one little moment to look beyond the end of your nose, *monsieur*. The cosmos is infinite. Beyond our wild imaginings, it is complex. You know no more of its workings than St. Clair, my cat, knows of Notre Dame. You think the logic, she leads you everywhere? *Non.* She leads you in circles on the floor like a blind beggar groping for scraps." He turned and headed back up the bar to tend to a customer. "No, no," he said, throwing his arms in the air as he retreated, "you must reach toward the stars."

Sprague climbed onto the barstool next to Ramsey. "What the hell is he goin' on about? He sounds crazier than usual."

"We are such stuff / As dreams are made on, and our little life / is rounded with a sleep."

"Drunk a little early, huh?"

"It's Shakespeare, Ed. Get yourself a glass and join me. The man we're waiting for isn't coming to a temperance meeting."

"You wanna tell me what you're up to and why you just had to git me over here?"

"Remember when I said Tully might have been in trouble when he was in Atlanta? Well, I went to see Havermeyer. He said there was a court-martial. The records have been sent to the War Department, but one of the officers who sat on Tully's court-martial is still in Atlanta. His name's Johnny Bass. During the war, I ran into him quite a few times. He's a good soldier but a hell of a drinker. He's just back from Jonesboro and agreed to meet with us."

"How long this gonna take? I ain't sure Whit's gonna want me drinkin' Rabun's whiskey all afternoon."

"It shouldn't be long."

Rabun served three men standing at the end of the bar and rejoined Ramsey and Sprague. "The back room—she is yours."

"Thanks Rabun. Could you set us up with a bottle of whiskey and three glasses."

Rabun moved off, and Sprague nodded toward the door. "That him?" he asked.

A dusty cavalry officer made his way unsteadily across the room toward them.

"Ramsey, you said you were going to buy me a drink, and I'm here to get it!"

Bass stood before them grinning, his hat pushed back on his curly blond head. An unlit nub of a cigar was clenched in his teeth. His bloodshot blue eyes wandered to Sprague and back to Ramsey. He stank of horses and whiskey.

"Johnny, this is Deputy Marshal Ed Sprague. Ed, Colonel Johnny Bass." The two men shook hands.

"It ain't *colonel* no more. It's *captain*." Bass gave Ramsey a mock salute. "War's over. I turned into a captain and you turned into a mister."

"Not bad ranks for either of us."

"If Stevenson gets his way, I'll be a mister too."

Ramsey pointed toward a door at the back of the bar. "Let's go back and share a bottle. There's something we'd like to talk to you about."

Bass followed them to the back room.

"Well, pour me a damn drink." He flopped into a chair and nearly rolled back out of it. "Damn," he muttered and caught the wall with an outstretched hand.

Sprague frowned.

Ramsey poured three whiskeys and took out his notebook. "Johnny, I need your help. Do you remember Bill Tully by any chance?"

"A bastard. What about him?"

"He got into some pretty serious trouble, didn't he?"

"Goddamn right! He pissed off the wrong man. Black Jack Logan gets down on your ass, you're gonna feel it." Bass finished his whiskey with a gulp and reached for the bottle.

Sprague's hand seized it. "Cap'n Bass, I ain't here to git drunk and I ain't here to watch you gittin' drunker. Tell us about Tully. You can do what you want with this here bottle when I leave. Otherwise me an' the bottle are leavin' together."

Bass glared at Sprague.

"Johnny, we really need to know," said Ramsey soothingly. "Tell us about Tully's court-martial. Havermeyer said you were there."

"Shit!" Bass slammed the table. "Shit!"

"Tell us about Bill Tully," repeated Ramsey, "as a favor to me."

Bass turned angrily to Ramsey. "I wasn't on any goddamn court-martial for Bill Tully!"

"But Havermeyer—"

"Havermeyer wasn't there. That little bastard doesn't know half as much as he thinks he does. There wasn't any goddamn court-martial—not then anyway." Bass slid his glass forward and glared at Ramsey. "You tell your friend to pour me a drink."

Ramsey nodded, and Sprague poured a finger of whiskey into the glass. Bass snorted with satisfaction but left the whiskey on the table.

"Why wasn't there a court-martial, Johnny?"

"Should have been a court-martial. We should have hung the son of a bitch. We should have cut his balls off first. And all that should've happened a long time before Sherman made it to Atlanta. Something funny was always going on with Tully. You know he disemboweled a man once? Left him tied to a tree, his guts spilling out, because he cheated Tully in some bullshit deal. Nobody could do a damn thing, 'cause the witness got himself killed too. Imagine that."

Bass took a small sip of whiskey, as if to wash a bad taste from his mouth. "Tully had an alibi. Tully always had an alibi. Mostly he had friends. Bullshit crooked friends."

"Who was his friends?" Sprague asked.

Bass answered but addressed Ramsey. "Nobody knew. Not at first, anyway. Hell, nobody's ever gonna know even a tenth of what went on with that bunch. Tully would do things, and no matter what charges were brought against him, they just never stuck. Like he was a greased pig or something. In Atlanta, General Logan—"

Rabun entered and placed a ham sandwich and a cup of coffee in front of Bass, who began to eat as if he'd expected the meal.

"You boys want something?" Bass mumbled through a mouthful of bread and ham.

Rabun gave Ramsey a slight nod and left the room. The sandwich rapidly disappeared, and to Sprague's surprise, Bass sipped the coffee.

"Well, now, where were we? You want to know about Bill Tully. Black Jack Logan found out Tully was trading stolen guns and ammunition to the Rebs for cotton. Can you imagine that? They're shooting at us and that bastard's selling them guns. I heard it was about a hundred bales. Some speculators in Chattanooga were gonna ship it north. You know how that cotton business was, Ramsey. A pain in the ass the whole war. Good men went bad fooling with cotton. We shoulda just burned all we got our hands on. In the end, it turns out Tully's got a friend higher up the ranks. A guardian angel, so to speak. More than one I suspect, but the one I'm talking about was

Major Simon Giles. You remember him, Ramsey? That quartermaster in the 98th?"

"I'm not sure. Describe him."

"An Englishman. Claimed to have served Her Majesty in the Crimea and all that palaver. Well, no one knew, but he and Tully were tight. They were both in the 98th. That was in Garrard's Division. Hell, Garrard was one slack son of a bitch. No damn wonder he had thieves riding with him. Of course, there were more than Tully and Giles, but they weren't much. Just troopers out for fast money."

"You remember any names?"

"Well, let me think." Bass closed his eyes. "I seem to remember it was O'Bannion, Hackett, Mason . . . Jesus, what's that other one? Oh yeah, a fella named Turney. Those are the names that came up in the investigation."

"Butt here weren't no court-martial?" asked Sprague.

Bass drained the last of the coffee. His puffy face was lined and weary. "Hell, no. Not then. The charges just got dropped."

Ramsey topped up Bass's whiskey. "What happened?"

"Who knows. The provost had given the investigation to Sam Potter. A good man, Sam. Showed Logan and me all his files when the bastards got off. God, he was mad."

"So they got away with it?"

"They did then. Logan stepped in after he saw Potter's files. The general had Tully and the rest put in the brig, but that didn't last either. You know how it was back then, Ramsey. Hood was moving up to the northwest towards Nashville, trying to get Sherman to chase him. We were in the saddle nearly twenty-four hours a day keeping an eye on him. Of course, Billy Sherman didn't take the bait. He turns and marches off to Savannah. With all that going on, the niceties of law and order got forgotten."

Bass reached in his shirt pocket, pulled out a small cigar, and lit it.

"When Sherman was about to march off through Georgia," he continued, "General Kilpatrick asked for them. He needed every trooper who could ride. That crew were reassigned to the 92nd Illinois. Sherman okayed it. I don't think he gave a damn. Kilpatrick said they'd fight, and that was true enough. God knows, there was nobody better for tearing up the countryside."

"So what did Black Jack do then?"

"Couldn't do much right away, but then the damnedest thing happened." Bass reached for his glass of whiskey. "Sherman wasn't out of Atlanta for more than a week. We were rearguard, chasing Joe Wheeler all over." Bass looked at Sprague and grinned. "And he was chasing us some too. All of a sudden, Tully's crew just up and deserted." Bass snapped his fingers in the air. "When Sam Potter found out, he sent some handpicked men from the 9th Illinois after them. I thought that was interesting. He did it without asking Kilpatrick or Sherman."

"Why was using men from the 9th of interest?"

"Because that unit wasn't under Kilpatrick's command. Potter didn't ever say anything outright, but I think he had doubts about Kilpatrick."

Bass drew on the cigar and sent a cloud of smoke into the air.

"Anyway, the boys from the 9th caught 'em. Guess what— the whole lot of 'em were headed back toward Atlanta! They got court-martialed properly that time. Charge was desertion— hard to sweep that under the rug. They went to prison. I heard some politician saved 'em from being hanged."

"Thank you, Johnny." Ramsey slid his chair back.

"Hold on. I ain't finished." Bass poured a whiskey and gulped it down.

"The Army wasn't gonna make any of 'em serve much time 'cause the war ended and no one cared anymore. I think there was some civilian pressure to let them go. I'm not sure. Sam Potter got Logan involved again, and Black Jack was happy to help. He makes a bad enemy. He was an Illinois Congressman before the war, and he can use the telegraph the way other generals use artillery. He found out about outstanding warrants against Tully and Giles in Chicago. They were from before the war, so they were old, but they were still in effect. Logan called some favors and clapped their sorry asses into state prison as soon as the Army let 'em loose. Last I heard, Tully and Giles were still in jail. And that, gentlemen, *is* the end of the tale. You can check with Sam Potter if you can find him, but I think I got it straight."

He stood and grabbed the bottle.

"I'll take this. I earned it." The cavalryman took a long pull on the bottle and lumbered out the door.

Sprague shook his head. "How the hell did you fellas ever beat us, Ramsey?"

"He wasn't always like that. He was once one of the best."

Sprague grunted.

Ramsey closed his notebook and lit his pipe. "I'll wire the authorities in Illinois and see what I can find out. Clearly Tully wasn't in jail if he managed to get himself killed in Atlanta. Maybe we can find something now that we know what to ask for. There was no reply to my first telegram."

Sprague drummed his fingers on the table. "Suppose Tully coulda come here lookin' for the folks he done the cotton deal with. Maybe he got cheated. Man like that'd want revenge. Could be he come for them and they got him first."

"Maybe, but don't you think it's odd that Tully was so interested in Atlanta? Think about it. He was here for a couple of months when Sherman held the city. By the fall of '64 he's in the brig. He gets out and what does he do? Fight on to Savannah? No. He deserts and heads right back to Atlanta. He nearly gets hung for his trouble, and he does wind up in prison.

Since the war is ending, it looks like his luck is changing. Someone pulls strings to get him out the brig early. Then sadly for Tully, Logan gets him locked up in Chicago, at least for a time. Then he gets out of prison. All time served, he's a free man. He can go anywhere he wants. What does he do? He heads straight back to Atlanta. This time he gets himself killed. Very strange."

"Yup. Damn strange."

The rain cascaded off the roof outside the window. Ramsey watched it splash on the ground and turn into a reddish-brown sludge. Two days of spring rain and the streets were a quagmire. Mud. Atlanta was the capital of mud. If the world were short of mud, Atlanta could supply it. He imagined a huge depot with an endless parade of railroad cars pulling in, being loaded with mud, and pulling out. The world demands mud! New York is fresh out. Rush the order! The Sahara has no mud—the Bedouin are crazy for it! Double the order! It's not just mud—it's *red clay mud*! Why, our mud is—

"It's beautiful, isn't it?" Duncan walked up beside Ramsey. "I mean look at the budding trees, the silvery rain, and the red of the earth. Atlanta is a godforsaken hole, but there are times when it can be so very beautiful."

The mudworks crumbled before Duncan's vision of beauty.

Ramsey resumed work on another follow-up story on the murder. The first one had been easy, revealing an accident on the tracks. For the second, he continued the theme of an accident but mentioned that the police had some suspicion of murder. He'd thrown in a few facts to highlight their efforts. The third, at Steele's insistence, was an editorial piece, taking a tougher, more civic-minded approach, using the incident to comment on crime in general. That one hadn't pleased Sprague. The *Intelligencer* had said nothing the day before. Ramsey hoped that would continue but it did not.

Steele wanted something fresh, but ideas just wouldn't come. POLICE BAFFLED—CONSTABULARY HOPES FOR LUCKY BREAK captured the truth but was decidedly impolitic. DRIPPING POLICEMEN SEARCH FOR SOGGY CLUES lacked the gravitas a murder investigation demanded. He set down his pen. Sprague. He would go see Sprague.

Grabbing his hat and coat, Ramsey plunged through the door into the storm. He pulled his hat low, cinched his coat tight, and tucked his head against the rain. Intent on his footing, he was slow to hear Sprague bellowing from a covered buggy on the other side of the street. He splashed his way to the deputy.

"For Christ's sake, get in!" shouted Sprague. The driver, Doc Pierce, sat patiently beside the policeman. Ramsey squeezed in next to Sprague.

"Piss poor day to get yourself killed!" Sprague said.

"What?"

"An' why the hell you out walking? I said I'd come for you."

"What are you talking about?"

"Didn't ya get my message? We got us another goddamn body!"

"What?"

"I sent Mr. Henry to get you. Some folks saw a hat in the bushes down in the Triangle. They went to grab it, and damn if they didn't find a stiff. Me an' the doc are on our way there now."

"You waited on Doc Pierce?"

"Well, I wasn't gonna walk all the way out there in this mess, was I? Ain't a fool like you. An' there's no rush. Body ain't going anywhere. Told the marshal the same goddamn—"

"Enough! Deputy Sprague, please, your language! If you can't avoid using profanity, you may leave this conveyance at once." Dr. Lucius Pierce was a godly man.

A chill crept up Ramsey's wet back. "There's a dead body in the Triangle?" he asked quietly. The Triangle was a patch of land bounded by the tracks of three railroads: the Western and Atlantic, the Macon and Western, and the Georgia.

"I got word about an hour ago," Sprague said. "What anyone was doin' out on a day like this beats me."

Doc Pierce pulled the reins and turned the buggy onto Thompson Street. "Maybe they have no place to go," he said in his soft voice. "That's railroad land, but there are plenty of people living in shanties down there. Many folks have very little these days."

Doc Pierce had worked to mend the carnage of Murfreesboro, Chickamauga, and a dozen other places during four years of war. Now he battled the smallpox that raged in the encampments of the poor, and healed the sick for whatever payment they could manage.

A policeman signaled to them. The buggy halted and the three men got out. Pierce opened his umbrella and started forward. Sprague and Ramsey pulled up their collars and followed him. They crossed the tracks and pushed their way through fifty yards of scrub, then continued down an embankment to the body. The rain slackened.

A man's bare feet protruded from a bush.

"Pull him out and roll him over," Sprague said to a nearby policeman.

A thickset corpse of a man in his late twenties emerged. Thinning brown hair framed his angular face and large ears. He had a shaggy untrimmed beard and wore no coat. A bullet hole marked his chest.

Sprague checked the man's pockets, then turned to the two men under the umbrella.

"Wanna take a look?"

Doc Pierce remained motionless as Ramsey stepped forward. The bewhiskered face told him little. The bullet hole was large. Doc Pierce leaned over his shoulder.

"It looks like a rifle," Ramsey said.

"Likely," Doc agreed.

Though the rain had washed the blood away, dark fibers matted the wound. Ramsey looked from the body up to the tracks on the hill above.

Doc Pierce mumbled a prayer. "You may remove the body to my surgery when you are ready, Deputy," he said when he finished.

Sprague sat at his desk, writing. Nearby, a potbelly stove made the room too warm, but neither man minded. Their hats and coats dripped small puddles on the floor beneath the rack.

"We got soaked for nothing," Sprague growled. "Them damn fools dragged that body to hell an' back. God only knows where he was killed. An' they took all they wanted off him when they got done with the draggin'. How am I gonna investigate if folks do that. Huh? They start out sayin' they seen a hat. Well, there ain't no hat. I didn't see no damn hat! You see a hat? And we don't even know where he got himself killed. It sure as hell weren't where we found him."

"I talked with the doc. He said the rain makes it hard to say, but he thinks the man was dead for less than twelve hours."

"Meanin'?"

"Meaning if Doc is right, the victim was killed in the middle of the night." Ramsey fished his pipe and tobacco from his coat pocket. "So if his body was thrown from a train passing on the tracks above, the people who found the body couldn't have seen who threw it down there."

"Well, it musta been like Christmas when they found it," said Sprague. "The stuff that's missing is stuff them folks want: hat, coat, shoes, wallet. Bet if we go back down there in a day or two, we gonna find one of 'em wearing a coat with a bullet hole in it. With all that's gone, we don't know who the hell this dead un is."

"The folks in the Triangle didn't take his shoes, Ed. They took his boots. The body still had on pants, showing he wore boots that came almost to his knees. And did you see the mark made by his belt buckle?"

"What about it?"

"It might have been a cavalryman's belt." Ramsey stopped warming his hands and turned his back to the stove. "You know," he said, "there's always people getting beat up, shot, stabbed, and robbed in this town. Things have gotten to the point where horse stealing is almost considered honest work. These last few days, we've seen something different. I think this dead man is tied to Tully's murder."

"That's a pretty big jump."

"Well, it's certainly possible the same gun was used. And it's possible our victim was once a cavalry trooper. What's more, the body was dumped just like the first one. It was thrown off the Western and Atlantic trestle. Whoever did it knew the body would be rummaged for anything useful. That would make our job harder and give those folks a reason to forget all they knew."

"Okay, but there's a lot of hard-luck ex-troopers are runnin' around," Sprague said. "They didn't all ride with Tully."

"True," replied Ramsey, "but the ad Tully ran was meant for people who knew its meaning. People who probably weren't in Atlanta. I wouldn't be surprised if one of them just joined him on the table over at Doc Pierce's surgery."

"You think we got some wolf pickin' off folks as they come to town?"

"I'll ask Johnny Bass to take a look at the body. Maybe he can tell us who it is."

"Maybe they can have 'em a drink together."

"It seems to me," Ramsey continued, "we need to know four things. One, the identity of our dead man. Two, who has come to Atlanta in the last week? Three, what does the ad that Tully wanted published say? And four, what did the folks in the Triangle see?"

"Well wantin' ain't gettin'. Maybe we can identify the dead fella, but finding out who's arrived in Atlanta is damn near impossible—unless I got the entire Army of Tennessee askin' around—which I don't. And you ain't gonna find out 'bout the ad 'cause you can't crack the code. You told me as much when you was in a saner frame of mind. An' it ain't worth the bother of talkin' to the folks in the Triangle unless we just want to hear 'em lie. We ain't gettin' too far here, boy."

"Okay, but ask Whit if you can have a few men to check recent arrivals. You might get lucky. I should think they'd be good at finding Yankees. As for the Triangle, I'll see if Mr. Henry will go ask around. Everybody talks to him."

"What about the message? You got a plan for that too?"

"I can't handle it, but that doesn't mean no one can. During the war there were a few men who could."

"Someone around here?"

"Heflin Sanbourne."

"My God, Ramsey, he's a nutcase! First you get me listening to some drunk telling stories 'bout your friend Tully, an' now you think the insane gonna help us out! Save the trip to Decatur; it's a waste a time. How ya gonna know if he does break the code, huh? Maybe he just sees visions and makes it all up."

Ramsey shrugged into his coat. It was still not dry.

"When you come up with more ideas than you have dead bodies, Ed, I'll listen. Until then, I've got work to do. My editor will want something on your latest unsolved murder."

"Well, you go tell your plans to Whitaker and he'll say you're crazy too. Probably get one of the other boys, Henderson or Isaacs, to write your stories from here on, huh?"

"We both lead complicated lives."

Ramsey left the deputy. As he walked along the wooden sidewalk, his boots made an irregular hollow rhythm. Perhaps it was the gloom of the day, or maybe the chill that was once again creeping up his spine, but he couldn't shake the feeling that events were far from over.

Johnny Bass looked at the corpse.

"It's O'Bannion."

Doc Pierce had been holding up the sheet that covered the dead man's face. He let it fall back into place and returned to the medicinal preparation with the sickly smell that grew stronger by the minute.

"You shoot him?" asked Bass.

"No, they found him over by the tracks near the Triangle yesterday afternoon. Is there anything you can tell me about him?"

"Not really. O'Bannion was an okay trooper if someone kept an eye on him, and a problem if you didn't. I don't know that he ever got in real trouble until he got mixed up with Tully."

"What can you tell me about the others"—Ramsey referred to his notebook—"Mason, Hackett, and Turney?"

"Let's get out of here, Ramsey. The smell is making me sick."

"So long, Doc," Ramsey called. Doc Pierce waved to them without looking up from his work.

Both men breathed deeply when they reached the street.

"So, Johnny, what about the others?"

Bass frowned. "Damn, Ramsey, it was a while back. I don't know how much I remember. Let's see. Mason. Mason was pretty much like O'Bannion—muscle that would do what it was told. I don't know about Turney. He was kind of a nervous fella. They called him 'Turnkey' for some reason—guess it was some joke with his name. Hackett was a real piece of work— mean as a snake and twice as deadly. You might say he was like Tully but with half the brains and twice as vicious. I wouldn't put anything past him."

"And Giles?"

"Well, he was an officer, and I knew him better than the others. He was English and sounded like it. Came across as a gentleman. I was told he served in the Crimean War, and it's probably true, because he knew soldiering. Early in the war, he won himself a commendation for bravery. He didn't seem like a man who would get mixed up with someone like Tully. Right up until his desertion, there wasn't much that could be said against him. Nothing specific, anyway. Odd things seemed to happen wherever he was, but those things always got explained away."

"Is there anything that could help me recognize any of them if I saw them?"

"God knows what they look like now. I think Mason was like O'Bannion in there, but shorter. Turney was a little weasel of a fella. Kinda skinny and nervous. Hackett was a big guy with wide-set eyes that didn't work quite right. They aimed in different directions. God only knows how he could hit anything he shot at, but he could. And he sure would beat it to death if he caught it."

Bass thought hard for a minute. "Giles was pretty average. Medium build. Brown hair. Closely trimmed beard. Well educated."

"That's plenty, Johnny. More than I expected. Thanks for meeting me on a Sunday morning."

"Well, the chaplain knows not to expect me. Where's the deputy?"

"He couldn't make it."

Sprague wasn't there, because Sprague didn't like drunks. But Johnny Bass wasn't drunk—at least not yet. He was washed and more like the officer Ramsey remembered.

"Ramsey . . look . . . well . . . I apologize about the other day. I'd got to drinking with a fella down in Jonesboro, and it took me a while to get stopped." Bass gave Ramsey a half-hearted grin. "Sometimes I just go howlin' at the moon."

Ramsey turned to go up the street.

"Do you miss it?" Bass called after him.

Ramsey turned back. "Miss what?"

"The war. I know it was terrible and all that. I know I'm supposed to be glad it's over, but soldiering was the only damn thing I ever got right. Here lately I kinda think the lucky ones are dead."

"Johnny, you can't believe that. Just give it time."

Bass straightened his hat to look more regulation. "Well we sure got a lot of that. I put in for a transfer. Stevenson will never sign it. He's bound and determined to make me a civilian. Can't say I blame him. I ain't exactly been a model soldier here lately. Garrison duty is bullshit. Havermeyer spends his days riding my ass about everything under the sun. That bastard never faced anything more dangerous than an inkwell his whole damn life. Staff officers can kiss my ass."

The two men shook hands and Bass strode off. Ramsey watched him go, wondering how much longer the cavalryman would hold together.

When Charles Appleby opened the telegraph office the next morning, Allan Ramsey was waiting at the window. Appleby produced an envelope.

Ramsey ripped it open and read the following unadorned facts: *William Albert Tully released March 17. Sentence complete. Simon Giles died in custody March 25.*

So Tully, Giles, and now O'Bannion were dead. That left Mason, Turney, and Hackett. Could they be in Atlanta? If the murderer was a member of the gang, and if Bass's recollections were reliable, the most likely candidate was Hackett. He would be a difficult man to miss in a crowd.

"You have a reply or are you just going to stand there?"

"No reply."

Ramsey dropped the message in his pocket and descended to the street.

"Hello, Allan. Here for a game of chess? Do you never tire of beating poor Rabun?" Jasper Dunlap shook his head in mock sympathy for the saloonkeeper. "Pity though. You playing chess, I mean. Such a waste. A man of your talents should play a more profitable game." He waved to the bartender. "Mr. Winks, a whiskey for my friend and soda water for me."

"Soda water, Jasper?" Ramsey looked curiously at the short heavyset man. "Not taking the cure, are you?"

"Ah, my lad, thankfully no. But tonight will prove difficult even without an early waltz with the bottle. One must drink to be social but still maintain a clear head in this line of work. We spend our nights at labor while others sleep. It's a hard life that God has decreed for me, but I endure." Jasper ended with his eyes downcast, looking at the glass of water before him. He waved at three men across the room. One hesitantly waved back, one nodded politely, and the third ignored him.

"I see that you and Bill Solomon are still on the outs," Ramsey said.

"I can't say he has much enthusiasm for my company, nor I for his. Still, if Bill and I are to play a decent game of poker in this town, we must not only endure the long hours; we must endure each other as well. Solomon's a hard man, but we have a detente at present. Let us say we cheat in judicious ways."

"No doubt you both win."

"That is often our good fortune. Say, there's a chair open in the game tonight. Why not join us?"

"I told Whitey I'd sit in on his table when I finish playing chess with Rabun."

"Good lord, that Three Card Monte shyster? His card skills are a disgrace to the profession."

"That's why I play him and not you or Bill Solomon."

"Really now," protested Jasper, "you just need to be more daring. Think big, win big. That's the ticket."

"Think big, die poor. That's the reality. Is that J. T. Porter with Bill Solomon?"

"Yes, it is."

"It seems our city treasurer has started keeping some pretty fast company."

"Illustrious company, my boy, illustrious. That man sitting with them is General John Gordon, late of the Army of Northern Virginia."

"Really now?"

It was impossible that someone at a table so far away could have heard Jasper's words, but at that moment General John Brown Gordon looked up and met Ramsey's eye with a look of calm appraisal.

"You're acquainted then?" asked Jasper, seeing the general's glance.

"Well, I know him only by reputation. We haven't been introduced."

"A most interesting man. I have the honor to be playing a hand or two with him this evening. You two old warriors should meet. Come with me."

Jasper tried to take Ramsey's elbow.

"Another time, perhaps," said Ramsey. "As easy as it is to say no to your invitation, it would be impossible to decline his. Besides, there isn't much meat in my wallet for you birds to pick on. I'm not a rich man."

"Ah, my boy, it's just a relaxing game among gentlemen tonight. And frankly, though there are wealthy men in this town, I am not among them. My wife and daughter consume my earnings like locusts ravaging a wheat field. Poverty haunts my every step, and I'm afraid the same must be said for the general. He's trying to raise money to start a sawmill operation down on the coast. He even queried me about buying an interest. I see your grin, but I assure you it's quite true. I was forced to decline the opportunity, but he accepted my offer to assist him in getting his backing elsewhere."

"Does this game have anything to do with his business interests?" Ramsey asked.

"Not directly. We're seeking funds in other quarters. I'm here to protect him from the likes of Bill Solomon."

"Then no doubt he's in good hands."

Dunlap saw his companions following Rabun to the back room. "I must run. No rest for the weary." He hurried away, sliding between tables and chairs with remarkable grace for a large man.

Rabun returned, put the chessboard on the bar, and set up the pieces. "So *Monsieur* Dunlap has not lured you into his poker game?"

"I'm not a fool, Rabun. Jasper and the general won't lose. God knows Bill Solomon won't lose, so you've got to feel sorry for Porter. He'll have to lose to everyone."

"Ah, it's not so bad as that. There are already two other soon-to-be-unlucky men in the back. Perhaps the good Jasper, he lets you win after all."

"I'll stick with chess."

"Then your fate will be sad."

Rabun poured them both a brandy.

"Speaking of fate," said Ramsey, "I've decided to give a little help to that woman I told you about, the one with the dream. She's accompanying me to Decatur to speak with Sheriff Powell about her sister."

"Ah, Decatur is such a hard place to find. She would never locate it alone."

"Don't be silly, Rabun. It's just that, well, I've got business there, and I might as well escort the lady. Besides, I didn't like the way things ended the first time we met."

"Surely there are many reasons for you to accompany her." Rabun shoved the white king pawn forward.

"I thought it was my turn to play white."

"It is. But I am punishing you for having deprived me of my victory in our last game."

Ramsey moved the black king pawn.

Rabun quickly moved a knight. "You say this woman, she looks for her sister?"

"Yes."

"And there is violence in her dream?"

"Blood and horses. But I really don't see what her dream has to do with anything. I'm just doing her a small favor in hopes that we can part on a happier note."

Ramsey responded with a knight move of his own.

Rabun's king bishop flew across the board to threaten Ramsey's knight. The saloonkeeper looked up at his friend. "Let us hope that will be so, my friend."

Abigail Maynard descended the stairs at nine o'clock to find Allan Ramsey waiting in the parlor. The day before, he'd sent a note saying he was going to Decatur. He proposed she accompany him so she might speak to the Dekalb County sheriff about her sister. She gladly accepted his offer. Now she wondered how awkward their meeting would be.

"Good morning, Mrs. Maynard. I trust you are well." Ramsey's formal tone and stiff nod reassured her. They were both on uncertain ground.

"Quite well, Captain. And you?"

"Very well."

"It seems we have a fine day for traveling," she said.

"Indeed we do, Mrs. Maynard. Shall we go?"

He gestured toward the door, but she did not move.

"Captain Ramsey, thank you for your kind offer to accompany me to Decatur. I had no right to expect it after our first meeting. I apologize for saying some unfortunate things."

"No apology is necessary. I'm sure the fault was mine."

She smiled. "Then let us make a new beginning. Since we are to spend the day together, won't you call me Abby? That's the name my friends use, and I hope I may count you among them."

"Thank you," he said, offering her his arm. "And you must call me Allan."

Strictly speaking, Atlanta didn't have a passenger station. Sherman had destroyed the old one, and a replacement was not yet finished. Passengers were compelled to wait at the Western and Atlantic freight depot, a squat stone building sitting along the tracks near Whitehall Street.

After pushing through the crowd of vagrants, beggars, thieves, and ne'er-do-wells who ringed the station, the two travelers purchased tickets for Decatur.

The platform was only slightly less chaotic than the street outside the depot. A harried woman struggled with three impatient children, her efforts growing more ineffectual as time passed. She repeatedly looked up the tracks as if to hurry the train along. Nearby, a commercial traveler held forth about the quality of his wares. He addressed all who would listen and many who tried not to. Specifically, he harangued a man in a dirty gray suit who was apparently too polite to walk away. The amiably drunk salesman occasionally took quick nips from a pocket flask.

Farther along, a crowd watched the antics of a small gentleman wearing a top hat and frock coat. The man stood behind a packing case and played a card game with a hulking creature dressed in tattered homespun. Each game lasted only a few moments, and the little man frequently lost. After each loss, he would say things that made the crowd laugh.

Abby strolled over for a better look.

"He handles the crowd rather well, don't you think?" she said.

"If we were closer," replied Ramsey, "you would see that he was drunk and being duped by the big man."

They reached the outer ring of the crowd as other people began to play in the large man's place.

"Drunk and duped. I think the man in the frock coat is neither of those things."

"There's no law against pretending, is there?" Ramsey asked.

"Certainly not, but that man is a confidence trickster."

The crowd continued betting. The little man was doing better now, not losing so often.

"A confidence trickster?" said Ramsey. "I doubt that's how Chatsworth White, known as 'Whitey' by the way, would describe himself. It sounds rather sinister, don't you think? I believe he fancies himself an entertainer. But money will change hands, and in the end it will flow toward him. How did you know what he was up to?"

"I've seen such things before. Is he someone you know?"

"He's a friend. Not such a bad fellow, really."

Abby briefly looked at Ramsey then back at the card game. Her expression was hard to read.

"Three Card Monte is Whitey's specialty," Ramsey said. "The big fellow, Joe Frank, is Whitey's half-brother—half-brother and half-witted. Whitey taught him his role, and he's gotten pretty good at it. When Joe Frank wins, it attracts a crowd. They also see Whitey sipping from a bottle, like that man over there"—Ramsey nodded toward the salesman—"and he appears to be just as drunk. In Whitey's case, the bottle contains cold tea. It's a convincing performance because he doesn't overdo it."

More people joined the circle of players. "There," Ramsey continued, "you see how Joe Frank has moved to the edge of the crowd? He'll wait around in case things get ugly. They rarely do. Whitey keeps everyone laughing, and he doesn't let anyone lose too much. He'll milk the crowd for a while, and even the losers will have a good time. If things do get rough, Joe Frank's strong as a bull. He can make a crowd back off."

A roar of laughter came as people pointed to a man who had just lost. Someone else stepped up to play.

"You have interesting friends, Allan."

"Interesting? I don't know. Whitey is just someone trying to make his way in this world. Besides, I don't have much sympathy for the losers. They're trying to take advantage of a man they see as an easy victim. In my opinion, they're getting what they deserve. But there's another way you might look at it, and I think it's how Whitey sees things. Life has been terribly difficult for so many people. Playing the game with him, listening to his silly remarks, may be the most fun many in the crowd have had for a long time. They're just paying for his performance."

Abby smiled and looked up the tracks. A smudge of smoke appeared in the distance.

When the train shuddered to a stop, the child-weary mother, the drunken salesman, and most of those waiting boarded the first two cars. Ramsey and Abby chose the third. The passengers already on board briefly noted their arrival, shifted themselves, and continued their naps or conversations. The seats were little more than hard wooden benches with backs on them.

The two travelers settled themselves for the trip and waited for the train to resume its journey. Decatur was only eleven miles away, but the condition of the rails meant an hour's travel—barring a derailment.

"You were quick to catch on to Chatsworth White," Ramsey said. "I dare say many in the crowd won't ever figure out what he's doing."

"My life hasn't been as sheltered as you suppose. My father was a writer and journalist. We traveled all over Europe. He was quite famous in literary circles. Famous but not prosperous. The bailiffs often nipped at our heels. My life as a proper Bostonian began only when I married John Maynard."

"You met him on your travels?"

"No. We met in New York. My father spent much of his life in Europe, but he was born an American. He returned to the United States and settled in New York a few years before the war. Susan and I made the hard decision to accompany him."

"Is he living there now?"

"Sadly, he died several years ago."

The train shuddered, clanged, shuddered again, and slowly moved forward like an old man stirring from a chair and shuffling away. Outside the window, Atlanta passed by at glacial speed. Ramsey looked back for Whitey's card game. Whitey and Joe Frank were gone.

"It's so awful." Abigail Maynard's eyes fixed on an earthen scar that stretched across the land. Exposed red clay, the color of dried blood, was still damp from recent rains. Along the undulating ground, *chevaux-de-frise* lay like the bones of dead snakes picked over by vultures. Indeed, they were being scavenged to satisfy Atlanta's insatiable need for wood. Behind them were breastworks and abandoned trenches. Rifle pits pockmarked the hillslopes. Here and there, a random tree or cluster of saplings stood as witnesses to the destruction. Vegetation struggled for life on the wasted land. If nature planned to heal man's insanity, she was in no hurry.

"I had no idea," said Abby.

"These defenses surround much of the city. Didn't you see them when you arrived?"

"No, the train down from Chattanooga was late. We must have passed through after dark. John wrote of such things."

She'd lost her husband in the war, but she hadn't had any direct contact with it. There had been bond rallies, of course, and work with Sanitary Committees. The wife of a socially prominent officer was a busy one, but such things were far away from war's reality. She knew of its pain, but she did not know its horror.

The experience of war is a personal matter; it doesn't survive time and distance. What do numbers like five thousand dead and eleven thousand wounded really mean? Do newspapers trumpeting battles won or lost really count for anything? The civilian world cares only for the few—fathers, sons, and brothers. Their suffering, their death is real; all else is abstraction. Though loved ones feel the emptiness of loss, they never know the terrible truth.

That truth lives in the hollow faces and the ragged wounds of the survivors. It remains with corpses rotting in shallow graves. Patriotic illusion begins with waving flags and cheering crowds; it ends holding a comrade spewing blood from a chest wound. Where is the glory when artillery rips ragged holes in a line of men, throwing their bodies and souls to the wind? Where is it when the hearty cheering for young men marching off to war turns into the moans of the wounded in "no man's land" or the screams from the surgeons' tent?

"Is this what it was like for John when he was with Grant?" Abby asked quietly.

"Your husband was at Petersburg?"

"Yes. That is where he was wounded."

"The works there were much larger and more elaborate, since the two armies faced each other for the better part of a year, but yes, I suppose it's mainly a matter of scale. They would not have been so different from what you see here."

"What are those people doing?" she asked. In the distance, figures were walking about, seemingly randomly. Occasionally one would bend and pick something up.

"They're searching for spent ordnance, *minie* balls mostly. They call it the 'lead mines.' They search for various projectiles, which they then sell to be melted down into other things. Some of them live in abandoned bunkers and dugouts." He pointed at a low hill in the distance. "That's where Hood tried to turn our flank. General McPherson was killed that day, but our lines held."

She did not reply. McPherson's fate held little interest as she stared into the battered landscape. The train slowly crept through the earthworks and entered woodland again. They rode in silence.

The town of Decatur perched on a gentle ridge that ran parallel to the train tracks. Houses and businesses clustered around a large neoclassical courthouse standing majestically on its highest point. During the war-torn summer two years before, Confederate General Joe Wheeler attacked the Union supply train encamped in the little town, and scars from the ensuing battle were still present. Broken or missing fences, dead or cut trees, and crude repairs made to damaged houses spoke of the violence. Few houses, even those otherwise unscathed, had all their windows intact. There had been looting, of course. First it was Garrard's Union boys taking what they wished. Then it was Wheeler's Southerners despoiling the locals and offering worthless Confederate script in return. As a final insult, the left wing of Sherman's Army came through as he marched off to Savannah and glory.

Yet if broken windows remained and damaged buildings waited on hands to repair them, the shops were open and the streets were clean and orderly. The residents, now returned from their refugee days, had taken up the sensible patterns of life. The little town was quieter and more healed than Atlanta to the west.

Abby's brisk stride up the hill to the courthouse betrayed her concern for her sister. If any records survived, she would find them there. Perhaps the sheriff could give her information too.

Ramsey feared for her hopes. Many civic records had been scattered by the war or had never been made at all. The sheriff she was about to meet was a different man than the one who'd held the post in 1864. But at least she was trying. He was glad she had that small solace.

The wait at the courthouse was a short one. Sheriff James O. Powell was a hearty man with a ruddy face weathered by days in the sun. Behind his wire-rimmed spectacles, he beamed out at the world like the satisfied father of a bride. His thinning hair lent emphasis to the fringe over his ears and his graying muttonchop beard. When Ramsey wired him concerning their proposed visit, Sheriff Powell had responded quickly. Now he ushered them into his office and, despite their protests, soon brought coffee for all.

Once they were comfortable, Powell was in no hurry to get to the matter at hand. His meandering preamble touched on the Atlanta City Council (sound policy, sir, sound!), the smallpox epidemic (terrible, terrible!), and finally the spring weather (far too rainy!).

Abby endured it all with steely patience, a chipped cup and saucer balanced on her knee.

When he finally addressed her, Sheriff Powell caught her by surprise.

"I understand you are Alfred Knowles's sister-in-law."

"Yes, I am."

"Sad thing, all that. I really don't know much about what happened. I wasn't the sheriff then. In fact, I wasn't even here. Got sent off with the Georgia State Line Militia. They made me a sergeant, you know, but I can't say much for soldiering. We spent some time in Macon digging earthworks. Then they sent us on a fool's errand to stop Sherman at Griswoldville. Ugly mess, that. We weren't properly trained and didn't have a chance. The Yanks just pushed us aside and kept going, why—"

"Is there *any* information you can give me, Sheriff?"

"Patience, Mrs. Maynard, patience. All things in good time. I have everything I could find right here."

He slid a paper across the desk to her and directed the tale of his war service to Ramsey.

The document was written in a spidery hand she read with difficulty. When she finished reading, she looked up to find the two men watching her. Her hand trembled as she handed the paper to Ramsey.

On July 23, 1864, I was summoned by Mr. Munford Coldwater's boy. Coldwater's note said there had been trouble at the Knowles plantation and we would find some dead Negroes. I rode out with Deputy Lemuel Carter. We arrived at about four in the afternoon. The house was badly burned and still lay smoldering. There had been repeated storms and rain during the day. The rain kept the house from complete destruction. The bodies of five dead Negroes, four males and one female, were on the cellar stairs. All had been shot. We searched the well and the woods, but nothing more was found.

We did not search the house, because of its unsafe condition. Most of the roof was burned and part of the upper story collapsed down onto the first. Mr. Coldwater and a servant rode up while we were investigating. He said he had heard shots around nine o'clock that morning and saw smoke about noon. He rode over later with his servant, Samson. He said that the rain had returned and the fire was going out when they arrived. Mr. Coldwater stated that the killings were the result of a slave uprising, as several of those owned by Alfred Knowles were missing and not among the dead.

The whereabouts of Mr. Alfred Knowles and his wife has not been determined.

Signed,
Oliver Winningham
X (Lemuel Carter)

"I'm afraid, Mrs. Maynard," said the sheriff, "that nothing has changed since that was written. Alfred Knowles and your sister have not returned. As far as I know, the house is just as it was left. I had cause to ride out that way a few months ago, and I can assure you that the place is uninhabitable."

"Susan called it Charlton. Where is it, Sheriff?"

Powell turned to a wall map behind him. His finger traced a ragged line. "It's down on Snapfinger Creek. Lovely place really. The creek gives you all the water you need, and the land is quite good. Don't know why Knowles wanted to turn it into a school, but he came here with strange ideas."

Ramsey looked at the map. "Covington Road runs that way?"

The Sheriff nodded. "Yes, you take a smaller road off the main one a couple of miles from the house. It's overgrown now and a little tricky to find. Then that branches off to an even smaller track that leads to the house."

"Did Mr. Knowles have any kin around here?" Ramsey asked.

"No. There's a Knowles family in these parts, but they weren't related. Franklin bought the place back in '54. Munford Coldwater wanted it. When old man Bentley died and his widow decided to sell, he thought he'd get it. Then up from nowhere came Franklin Knowles with a better offer. Made Munford mad, but he wouldn't meet Franklin's price, and that was an end to it. Widow Bentley went to Milledgeville to live with her daughter."

"What happened to Franklin Knowles?" Abigail Maynard asked.

Powell shook his head. "Sad story, that. Franklin knew farming all right, but he, well . . . let's just say he had a dissolute nature. Drank something terrible, he did, and he was a gambler. Some folks said he had other vices too. The decent people around here didn't think much of him and kept themselves apart. About the only one you could say was his friend was young Denton Coldwater. They seemed pretty thick."

"How did Franklin die?"

"In an accident. He'd been playing cards at Murphy's Tavern and left about dusk. Drunk as a lord, they say. They found him by his horse the next morning. He'd broken his neck in a fall. Munford Coldwater tried to get Charlton a second time, seeing as Franklin didn't have any family living with him. No one around here except Franklin's lawyer knew about his brother Alfred. Franklin left everything to him. Seems Alfred was teaching at a boarding school up in New England. Alfred and his wife arrived in '59. They were nice people, but they let the plantation go to ruin."

"I believe they started a school," said Abby firmly.

"Yes, of course."

"Had Franklin been winning or losing the day he died?" Ramsey asked.

"How would I know?" said Powell, a bit taken aback. The sheriff thought for a moment. "Probably won. He was good at cards. He could drink and keep his head, so they say."

Ramsey had his battered leather notebook out. "Was Franklin's wallet found on him?"

"I don't know."

"Who else was in the card game?"

"I don't know that either."

"How good a horseman was Franklin? Was he the kind of man who might fall off his horse?"

Powell's smile was gone. "From what I hear, anyone would fall off his horse if he tried to ride in that condition."

"No doubt."

"Mr. Ramsey, what has all this got to do with Alfred and Susan Knowles?"

Before Ramsey could respond, Abigail Maynard broke in. "I know we're asking too much of you, Sheriff," she said in a soft voice. "I thank you so much for your kindness. But I wonder, what were relations between the Coldwater family and Alfred Knowles like?"

"Good enough, I suppose. The war came along, and everyone banded together. I mean Munford is, well, Munford. And his son Denton isn't always an easy man either. They're both respectable, mind you, and remember it was Munford who summoned Sheriff Winningham the day the house burned."

There was little point in asking Powell anymore questions. Abby thanked him, he and Ramsey shook hands, and they left. The sheriff, his smile now gone, walked them to the door.

"Well what do you think?" Abby asked when they reached the street.

"I think it's possible that there's more to Franklin's death than we were told, but to be fair, Sheriff Powell isn't the man to ask. It was all before his time, and he doesn't know much beyond common gossip. The same goes for the events at Charlton. All we have is Winningham's report. I've met the man, and he's conscientious by nature. I mean, look at what he did. He checked out the events at Charlton, even though they occurred in the middle of a war. Not many lawmen would have bothered. Still, did he really investigate? He just rode out there and had a quick look around."

"Do you think Munford Coldwater was involved in Franklin's death and the disappearance of Susan and Alfred?" Abby shot an anxious glance at Ramsey.

"I doubt it. If Munford Coldwater and his son are killing people to get Charlton, they're not working very hard at it. Franklin bought the Bentley place in '54. He died in '59. Alfred and Susan arrived in '59 and disappeared in '64. Those are long gaps of time, and it's not like the Coldwaters lacked opportunities. With a drunk like Franklin, staging an ambush wouldn't have been difficult. As for your sister and Alfred, well, in the summer of '64 there was fighting all around here. If he intended violence, Munford could just ride over, shoot them down, and ride home. When their bodies were found, everyone would blame it on the war. But their bodies weren't found. The only bodies that were found were those of slaves. I can't see how that would benefit the Coldwater family."

"Who would do such a terrible thing? Certainly Susan and Alfred wouldn't kill people, and the notion of a slave revolt is patent nonsense."

"We may never know, Abby. Cruelty often has little explanation."

Ramsey stopped and looked around to get his bearings. A tree-lined track lay to the left. "That must be Sycamore Lane," he said, "and over there"—he pointed farther along—"is our destination. We shall speak more of your sister on our return to Atlanta."

Heflin Sanbourne was known in the scientific world before the war. Though a polymath with a deep interest in several disciplines, he was primarily a mathematician. Those few who understood his work said he possessed both creativity and precision. Various prestigious academic positions were offered to him. Shy by nature and of independent means, he chose a private life.

Twice before, his and Ramsey's lives had touched.

In 1857, through a prodigious feat of persuasion, Sanbourne was lured to Yale University for a scientific conference. Most of the notable men in that world were present. *The Hartford Courant*, Ramsey's employer, dubbed this meeting 'The Gathering of Genius' and sent him to cover the event. He managed to get interviews with Professor Bernstein of the Sorbonne and the Englishman Sir Russell Lowell, which resulted in shallow, understandable expositions of their work. While pleased with these efforts, his editor suggested something different—try the human-interest angle, he telegraphed. Wondering what human interest lay in exponents and square roots, Ramsey next interviewed the retiring Southerner.

Nervous and reticent, Sanbourne continually ran his fingers through his long brown hair and spoke in a barely audible whisper about matters utterly beyond Ramsey's comprehension. Uncomfortable with eye contact, Sanbourne focused on blossoms swaying outside the window.

Desperate to salvage something from their time together, Ramsey commented on the flowers.

"Yes, they are beautiful," Sanbourne said. "One doesn't expect them this far north. *Azalea arborescens*. It is one of the few such species that can handle the cold."

Ramsey gently pressed on the subject, and Sanbourne slowly opened up about his garden. He told of the candied scent of honeysuckle in the warm Southern air, the riot of color that came each spring, and the miracle of life that rose from the soil. He described dew sparkling in the sun. He conjured up the feel and scent of moist air in the stillness of late night. As Sanbourne's nervousness eased, he told of the loneliness of his long childhood illnesses and how that brought him to both his love of nature and his fascination with science.

A night of writing gave the *Courant* a story in which soil, flowers, and rain coexisted with the ethereal realm of pure mathematics. It was a great success. For a brief time, Heflin Sanbourne achieved a minor celebrity he found utterly appalling.

It would have been best if he and Ramsey's paths never crossed again.

In July 1863, after Vicksburg fell, Grant was placed in command of the Union forces in the west. The most immediate problem he faced was in Chattanooga. Rosecrans's army was trapped there after its defeat at Chickamauga. Braxton Bragg's Confederates held the high ground that ringed the city. From this dominant position, they choked off much of the food and munitions needed by the Federal Army, and without immediate action, that army would wither and die. Grant went to Chattanooga to take personal charge, with Ramsey as part of his staff.

An effort was made to create new supply lines to ease the situation. While this met with a degree of success, certain events caused Grant to suspect information was leaking from his headquarters. Either a traitor was at work, or the codes were no longer secure. An investigation ensued; no traitor was found, and the codes were strengthened. The matter was declared settled.

Grant had doubts and summoned Ramsey.

Spies were worked into the Southern camp. A local Unionist risked arrest, acting as conduit for their information. Eventually these efforts led to a tent where Heflin Sanbourne sat patiently deciphering the Union Army's encoded battle plans.

Ramsey devised a counter strategy: issue misleading orders by telegraph and send the actual ones by courier. The false communiques led Bragg to conclude that Grant would not attempt battle before spring. He split his forces, sending General Longstreet to attack Knoxville. In late November, Grant attacked. Union soldiers swept up Missionary Ridge. The weakened Confederate line broke. Bragg's siege of Chattanooga was over.

Humiliated and aware he would soon be relieved of command, Bragg unleashed his dyspeptic fury on all around him. He gave Major Heflin Sanbourne field duties. Watching soldiers fall broken and bloody in a minor skirmish, Sanbourne's mind snapped.

Ramsey knocked on Sanbourne's front door. A porch fronted all four sides of the large newly painted two-story clapboard house. Above the front door, a smaller second-story porch looked out across the yard. A sizable garden had been tilled in the back. Wartime damage had been repaired.

Ramsey had not received a reply to the telegram he'd sent Sanbourne, though he'd not mentioned that to Sprague or Whitaker. Now, as he stood before the door, the past lay heavy on him, and he hoped he would be turned away. Ruining a man is one thing; looking into his eyes, another.

The door swung open. A large, scowling, middle-aged black man stood before them.

"Yes?"

"Mr. Ramsey to see Mr. Sanbourne." Ramsey produced a card and passed it to the black man who took it without looking. He made no move to let them enter.

"Is Mr. Sanbourne in?"

"He's in, but he cain't be disturbed. He's been sick." The door started to swing shut.

"I sent a telegram. Perhaps you remember it?"

"We got it."

A young woman appeared behind the man.

"Father, Mr. Heflin says he'll see Mr. Ramsey. Mr. Heflin is finished with his rest."

The man opened the door and strode away, leaving them with the young woman.

"Don't take no offense," she said. "Father, he protects Mr. Heflin. You visit for just a little, then go. Mr. Heflin is sometimes troubled in his mind. We don't want no bother from you."

She looked at Abby.

"Ma'am, Mr. Heflin is expecting but one, you better stay down here. You can sit yourself over there." She pointed to a wingback chair.

Abby made no protest and sat down.

"Mr. Heflin needs his peace, Mr. Ramsey. You remember that."

"I wish Mr. Sanbourne no harm," said Ramsey. Then, perhaps for himself, he repeated softly, "No harm."

She led him upstairs, down a hallway, and into a bedroom. It contained a bed, a wash stand, and an untidy desk littered with books. They crossed the room to a door that opened onto the second-story porch. There in a rocking chair sat a thin man with long brown hair.

"Mr. Heflin, the man from Atlanta is here." The girl directed an admonishing frown at Ramsey before leaving.

Sanbourne made no effort to offer the second rocking chair to his guest. After an awkward silence, he spoke in a low voice. "I'm surprised Jeremiah let you in, Mr. Ramsey."

"He wasn't going to. The girl brought me up."

"Ah."

Sanbourne stared out into the yard.

Ramsey sat down and waited.

At length the mathematician spoke again. "Jeremiah is a good man. He and Cassie have cared for me since the war. Jeremiah planted the garden, you know. He works very hard."

Sanbourne lapsed again into silence.

"Perhaps I should go," said Ramsey.

"You mentioned in your wire that we are acquainted."

"Yes, we met at Yale before the war. You were there for a conference. I interviewed you."

Sanbourne glanced furtively at Ramsey. "Yes . . ."

"I'm sorry to trouble you, but I have two messages that I must get deciphered. I believe you are the only one who can help me."

Sanbourne's eyes flared with momentary wildness.

"I work for the *Intelligencer*," Ramsey continued, "the newspaper in Atlanta. These messages were left with us to publish as personal ads. We now believe them to be related to two recent murders. If the contents were known, perhaps further bloodshed could be avoided." He offered an envelope.

Sanbourne made no move to take it. "You are not with the police?"

"I am not a policeman. However, this is a police matter. I am aiding Deputy Marshal Ed Sprague."

"Why come to me?"

The question carried in its belly memories of wartime terror.

"I believe you possess the skills necessary for this work. Even if unsuccessful, your efforts would be much appreciated."

Sanbourne looked at the sway of the leaves.

The request had always been a gamble. Ramsey had no way to know how much of the former Heflin Sanbourne was left on this earth. Ramsey shifted uneasily in his chair.

Sanbourne finally spoke in a soft voice. "I am tired now, Mr. Ramsey. If you will leave the messages with Cassie, I will do what I can." He suddenly looked hard at Ramsey, searching his eyes.

Ramsey looked away, unable to bear the scrutiny. "Thank you, sir."

Cassie appeared in the doorway and held out her hand for the envelope. She made no effort to hide her eavesdropping.

Ramsey rose to go to her. "Please let me know how your work progresses," he said to Sanbourne, "You may wire me at the *Intelligencer* office."

Sanbourne was again looking out into the yard. "I will do what I can. Jeremiah goes to the city for us. He will bring any results."

"That will be quite satisfactory."

Ramsey had just left the bedroom when he heard Sanbourne's voice, high and loud.

"Bragg was an ass, Captain Ramsey! An ass and a fool!"

Rabun Perdido shoved a glass in front of a patron. A few feet away, Ramsey bent over the chessboard, staring at a problem of his own making. Rabun, a clever attacker, was often in trouble against patient defense. Tonight Ramsey wasn't in the mood for defense. He met Rabun's attack with a counterattack of his own. The game was a free-for-all. The barkeeper was delighted.

Rabun walked over and impatiently surveyed the game. "*Monsieur*, the pieces do not move themselves, you must think for them."

Ramsey remained silent and Rabun left to serve another customer. Finally, with a decisive gesture that overstated his confidence, Ramsey sent his queen pawn forward to secure the center.

Re-lighting his pipe, he considered the board. What was Rabun up to? His play was vigorous—it always was—but tonight's effort appeared haphazard. Some of his pieces were doing all the work, while others remained at or near their original squares. It wasn't like him.

Rabun returned and looked at the board.

"Ah, the pawn. I thought as much. Mere annoyance is not defense."

He moved his king rook. Ramsey responded by pulling his remaining knight back to consolidate his position.

Rabun's attack won't carry, he thought. The forces engaged are insufficient.

Rabun arched an eyebrow, following the move. He immediately moved his knight. Ramsey moved the rook pawn to create an escape for his king.

Rabun's dark eyes flashed. "You have counted the moves, *Monsieur le Commandant*, but you have not counted far enough. The game is bigger than your mind tonight."

He flung a pawn forward, and the attack began in earnest. A man at the end of the bar called for a whiskey. Rabun stood with his eyes closed, lost in thought. Then nodding decisively, he strode down the bar to answer the customer's third summons.

Ramsey parried the blow. And the next. And the next. Rabun's king bishop fell. His king rook was gone. A pawn, too, played its role and was swept from the board.

A move or two more, thought Ramsey, and it will be over. Just a move or two more.

Suddenly, Rabun's queen bishop swung forward in attack. Overlooked, forgotten, and now all powerful, it swept aside the existing equations on the board.

Ramsey tipped over his king.

"Good game, Rabun."

"*Oui.*"

Rabun returned with a bottle and poured two glasses.

"A great victory requires the great opponent. I salute you, *mon ami!*"

Ramsey sipped. "I should lose to you more often, Rabun. You serve me rotgut when I win."

"When you win, you get justice. As the defeated, I give you mercy."

"You are a kind man."

"Do you know where you first went wrong?"

Ramsey waited for the answer.

"When you dared to play me!" Rabun roared with laughter.

"No, my friend, I went wrong when I played your game and not mine. Still, I congratulate you." Ramsey raised his glass in salute. "As they say, many risks are nothing in the hands of a master."

As Ramsey left The Isle of Capri, the night air was stirring with a coming storm. Debris, flung by the wind, danced along the boardwalk. Not wanting to chase his hat up the street, Ramsey pulled it tighter on his head. A moment before, too much brandy had dulled him; now he was alert and alive. The air smelled of the coming rain. He looked up to see the moon break through the scudding clouds and then disappear again.

Farmers were saying the rain was too much of a good thing. If it continued, the crops would rot in the ground. Worry was a farmer's life. He lives at the mercy of the weather and has little except hope to protect him. The materials of the reporter's trade were more dependable: corruption, venality, and greed. All were in abundant supply. As long as people walked the earth, somebody would cheat, kill, or slander someone else—and the rest of the world would want to read about it.

The Broad Street Bridge loomed darkly ahead. Sprague might have laughed at Benson, but Benson and *The New Era* were right. Without enough bridges, men, women, and children had to dodge their way through the railroad yards. Everyone had a close call to talk about. Ramsey thought of Pacific Island tribes who sacrificed victims to a volcano god to preserve their homes. Perhaps Atlanta sacrificed the occasional citizen to the railroad god to appease the iron creatures that had created the city.

He stopped on the bridge and removed his hat. The wind played in his hair, and he thought back on the day. He'd enjoyed the trip with Abby. A man ought to find a woman like her and settle down. Maybe live in a little town like Decatur. It was quiet there. All over the country, North and South, men and women were seeking a sense of peace. Maybe some of them were finding it. Maybe some of them were learning to forget the war, letting everyday life turn the past into mist.

Ramsey liked cities, but if the Bible were to be believed, God certainly didn't think much of them. The Deity often seemed to be destroying one or giving serious consideration to it. Maybe it reflected a certain queasiness He felt toward His human creations. Ramsey looked at the darkened buildings jutting saw-toothed into the sky, their windows decorated with the sparkle of lamplight. A city didn't have much to do with God. It was made in the image of man. It was where people rubbed against each other. Where they piled up their schemes and desires, dreams and illusions, into a great heap. The city was the residue of what men and women really were; it defined them because they, not God, had made it.

The wind grew stronger. Ramsey filled his pipe and cupped his hands around the bowl to light it. Lightning erupted in the sky. From the distance came a long roll of thunder. He wouldn't make it back to his room before the storm broke. He wasn't going to try. He remained on the bridge, drinking in the violence in the air around him.

He turned his back to the wind and leaned against the railing. Much had happened. Two men were dead. No motives and few clues offered themselves. All he and Sprague knew was that the victims had been together during the war. Whatever drew Tully and O'Bannion to Atlanta must have been important; they kept returning. But why had they been killed? What drew them back despite the danger? Danger from where? From whom? The Army no longer cared about these men, and the law had done what little it was ever going to do. Perhaps he and Sprague would never know. Not all questions get answered. The killer had the initiative. All they could do was wait for a mistake. It was someone else's game to win or lose. Waiting for an adversary's blunder is a sorry strategy. He doesn't always make one.

And what of Mrs. Abigail Maynard—a dead soldier's wife? Her dream bothered him. Just foolishness, no doubt, but why would she tell him such a thing? Was her mind weakened by the strain of her husband's death and the loss of her sister? Perhaps it was the need to believe in a life beyond this one. Certainly she had the courage to search for answers. Would she want the ones she found? The truth cares nothing for us. It can heal and it can destroy. She had suffered the death of her husband. Despite her hopes, she would likely have to face the death of her sister. Would she be strong enough for that truth as well?

Death. It had come to claim him during the war but was denied. He'd fallen into the Reaper's cold clutches and was destined for an early grave. Yet Sadie, an ancient root doctor, had seen in her visions he would live. She nursed him to health against impossible odds. Mr. Henry said she wouldn't have bothered without the vision. "She don't waste no time on dead people."

Ramsey heard footsteps.

"Evenin', Mr. Allan," a familiar voice said. Mr. Henry and a young man joined him on the bridge. "Rain's comin' soon. Best to get under cover."

As if to underscore his words, the wind whipped their coats, and several large wet drops splattered on the bridge.

"This is my nephew, Gideon, Mr. Allan." Mr. Henry indicated a figure who stood slightly behind him. The young man nodded respectfully and removed his hat. He was no more than nineteen or twenty, solidly built, with a pleasant intelligent face. Even in the poor light, there was no mistaking the family resemblance.

"Pleasure to meet you, Gideon. Mr. Henry tells me you've been a help to him in the business."

"I does what I can, suh."

"Mr. Henry," said Ramsey, "I was planning to come see you tomorrow. I wonder if you'd speak with the folks down in the Triangle about the dead man they found. They won't talk to me or Sprague, but they will to you. I don't want to cause them harm. We just need to know what really happened."

Several more drops spattered on the bridge.

"I'll talk to 'em, but now we best be gittin' in or we be gittin' wet."

With that, Mr. Henry and Gideon hastened across the bridge. Ramsey followed slowly after them.

Ed Sprague sat at the table in Ramsey's room eating a lunch of cold ham, biscuits, corn casserole, and a plate of sliced apples that Mrs. Carraway had sent up. Ramsey poured a cup of coffee. Sprague read over the telegrams that Ramsey had given him, then flipped the messages on the table.

"So Giles is dead, huh? Guess the son of a bitch deserved it. How'd you make out with your lunatic? He gonna work out that code for us?"

"I left a copy with Sanbourne. He said he'd send the results back with his man, Jeremiah."

"I ain't gonna hold my breath. Had another meeting with Whit Anderson and Mayor Williams this morning. They're on my ass real hard. They want progress. Shit, I want progress, you want progress—there just ain't no goddamn progress. So far the Army's stayed out of this mess. Ain't nobody takin' bets on how long that'll last."

Sprague popped a slice of apple into his mouth and wagged the empty fork at Ramsey.

"This bullshit makes me wanna just go off and raise chickens."

Ramsey pitied the chickens.

"Have any luck with the new arrivals?" he asked.

Sprague shook his head. "They's a hell of a lot of folks come and go in this town, an' none of 'em look like the them fellas Bass was talking about—at least not Hackett or Turney. They're the easiest to ask about."

"It was a long shot. No reason for them to check into a hotel or boarding house and wait for you to come round. The message was meant to run three times. We haven't run it since, but there's been something in the paper about the murders most days. They'll lay low if they know Tully is dead."

The deputy pushed his empty plate away. "Well, there's one damn thing you can take to the bank. We got at least one murderin' wolf running loose. Maybe he skipped town, maybe he didn't. But if there's some connection between the murders and the war, then we're left with Mason, Turney, and Hackett, 'cause everybody else is dead. Now, why would one of them want to come to our fair city and start in killin' the others? If Bass is right, Hackett's our man, but ain't nobody seen him."

"I don't see there's too much more we can do," Ramsey said. "Maybe Sanbourne solves the code, or maybe you get lucky, or maybe Mr. Henry finds something."

"Piss poor place to be. Waitin' on dumb luck to snatch the bacon outta the fire." The deputy fished a stub of a cigar out of his pocket. "How things go with your widow? She find her sister?"

"Well, she talked to Sheriff Powell, but he couldn't tell her much. Apparently the Coldwaters, father and son, have tried to buy Knowles's land in the past. They've approached Mrs. Maynard about selling, since her sister and brother-in-law have disappeared. I can't say if there's anything in that."

"I know them Coldwaters. They bastards, all right, but they ain't been murderin' bastards. She headed back to Boston?"

"She should, but she won't. She's not ready to turn it loose."

Sprague rose to go. "Oh, I been so worried 'bout these murders, I almost forgot. Lovick Thomas arrested Rafe Jenkins this morning. Seems ol' Rafe had stolen goods hidden in his storeroom. Stuff was stuck under some rags in a barrel. 'Course Rafe says he ain't never seen none of it before, but that ain't gonna wash in court."

Sprague's eyes were lit with a mischievous glow. "Thing was, Lovick didn't know about any stolen goods. Whit

Anderson was called over to the mayor's office, and when he comes back, he tells Thomas to take some men over to Rafe Jenkins's place and search it. The marshal already had the warrant made out. Whit told Lovick to pay close attention to the back rooms."

"Marshal Anderson's quite a lawman."

"Yup, he sure gets the jump on crime. Rafe's gonna do time on this deal. Looks like he pissed off some folks he shoulda let alone."

"There may be a lesson in that."

"Shit, I ain't afraid of that fat whore."

That a person faced with compelling problems will often busy himself with meaningless tasks is a curious truth. Two men had been murdered, pressure for results had grown exponentially, and the investigation was making no headway. Ramsey went to the *Intelligencer* to sort out his desk and files.

His effort was modest at best. Mostly he regaled Duncan and Mr. Henry with stories of politicians stupid or clever and women virtuous or otherwise. He was now well along with a story of a drunken councilman and a prostitute. Mr. Henry suddenly looked at the front door. Ramsey followed his gaze as Abby Maynard entered the room.

"Abby, what a pleasant surprise," Ramsey said. "May I introduce Mr. Duncan Moore and Mr. Henry O'Neill."

"It's very nice to meet you, Mr. Moore," she said, "and, of course, Mr. Henry and I are friends already. How are you?"

"Jist fine, ma'am."

"I fear I've interrupted you, Allan. Perhaps I should come back later."

"Not at all. What can I do for you?" Ramsey said, feeling somewhat self-conscious about his appearance. His shirtsleeves were rolled to the elbow and his shirt was smeared with dust.

"I wonder if I might have a private word."

"Of course." Ramsey looked around him.

"What about the judge's office?" said Duncan. "He's out of town and it's quiet up there."

Ramsey nodded and Duncan went for the key. They ascended the stairs, and Ramsey unlocked the door. Abby took a seat in one of the plush chairs across from the judge's desk. Ramsey rinsed his hands at the washstand.

"I'm afraid you caught me in the midst of a little spring cleaning," he said. "My pile-not-file method catches up with me. What can I do for you?"

"Allan, let me thank you again for accompanying me to see Sheriff Powell."

"I was glad to do it. Wish we'd had better luck."

"Well, perhaps there is some progress still to be made. Do you remember the letter I received from Mr. Munford Coldwater requesting information about my ownership of the Charlton property?"

"Yes."

"After Sheriff Powell told us how Mr. Coldwater was involved in the events at the time of Susan's disappearance, I felt I had to talk to him. I sent a note and asked to meet him. I did so when we returned from Decatur, and this morning I received his reply. He suggests that we meet tomorrow afternoon at his son's place of business, Howell and Coldwater." She hesitated before adding, "I didn't tell him I'm not the owner of the property. I merely said I wished to discuss its sale."

"How can I be of assistance?"

"Allan, I was wondering if you would escort me to that meeting."

"That might not be wise, Abby. Denton Coldwater is a cotton factor. I've written about shady dealings in the cotton market. Though I didn't call anyone out by name, I believe Howell and Coldwater is one of the firms involved. Denton is aware of that. He's avoided a tangle with the law so far, but that says more about justice in these parts than about his innocence. I wouldn't be welcome at your meeting."

She thought for a moment. "I'd still like you to come with me. Munford Coldwater said nothing about his son attending our meeting. Even if the son is present, Mr. Coldwater is so anxious to get Charlton, I doubt he would let his feelings get out of hand."

The chance to unpleasantly surprise Denton Coldwater had its attractions. "All right then. If you want my company, I would be delighted to escort you."

"Thank you, Allan. Mr. Coldwater is my best hope now. I went to see Captain Havermeyer again yesterday. The man is impossible."

Duncan burst into the room. "Ramsey, quick! There are two men downstairs looking for a back issue."

"Just take care of it."

"Ramsey, they want the one for April 10th! That's the one with the code!"

"Have you gotten the newspaper yet?"

"No, I came to get you, and I sent Mr. Henry for the police."

Ramsey was amazed by the boy's good sense. "I need to deal with this, Abby."

He descended the stairs to find two men standing at the front counter. "Good afternoon gentlemen," he said brightly. "The *Intelligencer* is always happy to be of service. Mr. Moore will get your back issue from our files." He crossed to his desk where he busied himself with the mess that lay around it. "You gentlemen just get to town? You've come at a very nice time of year."

No answer. The two men looked at each other and then at the door Duncan went through.

Ramsey walked idly to the counter. "Can't say it hasn't been wet lately, but I believe we're in for a dry spell. How are you gentlemen doing today?"

The smaller of the two men was wearing a shabby coat and a slouch hat. He had a hatchet face, and he nervously bit his thin lips. The other man was big, over six feet tall, and wore a torn checkered shirt. Suspenders held up his dirty brown pants. Only one eye focused on Ramsey—the other aimed off to the left.

"Yeah, good weather," the smaller man agreed in a nasal voice.

The big man pushed in front of his partner. "We gonna get that paper or not?"

"All in good time," said Ramsey. "All in good time. No need to be hasty. Mr. Moore will return in a moment." Where the hell *were* the police? "I don't believe I've seen you fellas around. My name's Allan. Allan Ramsey. Are you gentleman in—"

"Goddamn!" the small man gasped in amazement.

Ramsey followed their eyes to where Abby Maynard was coming down the stairs.

"Holy Goddamn!" the little man said again.

The big man pulled the smaller man's arm, and they bolted for the street.

Ramsey reached the door in time to see them disappear around a corner.

He slammed his fist against the doorjamb. Abby joined him in the doorway.

"Who were those men, Allan?"

"They're wanted by the police." And where the devil *were* the police?

Moments later Mr. Henry ran up with a puffing Sprague trotting behind him.

"You get 'em?" the deputy gasped.

"No!" Ramsey said.

"Gone?" Sprague panted.

Sensing the coming storm of Sprague's profanity, Ramsey turned to Abby. "I'll need to speak with Deputy Sprague alone. I'm sorry."

"Of course, Allan. I'll see you tomorrow."

A moment later John Steele came through the door, his eyes bright with excitement. "What's going on? I saw the deputy come running in."

Duncan stepped forward. "Some men were asking for the back issue containing the coded message."

Steele looked to Ramsey and then to Sprague, but Duncan told the story in an excited rush. He didn't do a bad job, all things considered.

"Did you recognize these men?" Steele asked.

"From what Johnny Bass told us, it was Turney and Hackett."

Steele turned to Duncan. "You said these men recognized Mrs. Maynard?"

"Well, sort of."

"Did they or didn't they?"

"They reacted when they saw her," said Ramsey, "but it's impossible she would know them."

"You couldn't think of any way to stop them two?" asked Sprague.

"It was just me and Duncan. We had no chance against the big one."

"It's not the newspaper's job to apprehend criminals, Deputy," said Steele. "We would have had an arrest if the police were quicker."

"Now wait a minute, John."

"I'm telling you—"

"No! I'm telling you—"

"Gentlemen! Enough!" Ramsey snapped. "Arguing gets us nowhere. Now that we know they are here in Atlanta, we need to find these men. They may very well be involved in the murders, but"—he held up a hand to quiet both Sprague and Steele—"if they killed Tully and O'Bannion, why are they only now trying to get a copy of the paper with the code in it? It ran once. Tully was killed the next day. Now these men show up and ask for the paper that includes the code. If they were in Atlanta long enough to kill those two men, they wouldn't need to buy the back issue. My guess is that they probably don't even know Tully and O'Bannion are dead."

Sprague made a noncommittal grunt.

"Look, John," Ramsey said to his editor, "we might still have some luck on our side. They'll find a paper with the code somewhere—I don't doubt that—but it will take them a while. We might still be able to lay our hands on them. I have a man working on breaking the code. We might get the deciphered message in time to use it against them. In the meantime, the police can be searching the city."

"The coded message? You said it was impossible to break."

"Not for everyone."

"Who can do it?"

"Heflin Sanbourne."

"Lord, Ramsey . . ." The editor shook his head in disbelief.

"Yeah," said Sprague, "my thoughts as well."

"Say what you will. He's the only man in these parts who has a chance of success. He did such things during the war."

"John," said Sprague, "we both know Sanbourne's crazy. But now we know who we're after, and we know they in Atlanta. My boys'll be after 'em day and night. Whit and me want this thing finished more than you do."

"It would be good if you catch them before more bodies turn up," Steele said.

"Damn," Sprague muttered as he strode out the door.

At two o'clock, Ramsey opened the front door of the Hoehling boarding house and entered the foyer. Voices came from another room.

"He's shiftless and has no business hanging about taking everything we have."

"Mrs. Hoehling, I assure you—"

"You'll assure me of nothing! You don't know these people as I do. They lay about and steal as if it brought them God's grace. I will not have that man in my house!"

"Mr. Henry is no thief. You have no right—"

"I have every right! If you have use for him, arrange to meet him elsewhere."

A red-faced Mrs. Hoehling emerged from the parlor and disappeared down the hall. Moments later Abby appeared.

"A problem?" Ramsey asked.

"It's so ridiculous. Mrs. Hoehling thinks Mr. Henry has stolen eggs. He was here a few days ago, and she told him to go away. He returned today at my request to run some errands. About that time, she discovered eggs were missing and blamed him."

"Mr. Henry is no thief. Your landlady has the wrong man."

"You wouldn't have sent him to me if you didn't believe him to be reliable. Mrs. Hoehling just won't hear reason."

"I sent Mr. Henry to you?"

"Of course, the day after our first meeting. He showed up and said Mr. Allan sent him to see if he could be of any help."

"I'm sure you find him useful," Ramsey said, making a mental note to ask Mr. Henry.

The offices of Howell and Coldwater, 35 Peachtree Street, occupied a newly built two-story brick building. The masonry walls gave a sense of stability. The trim around the windows showed clean and white. A well-dressed black boy met them at the door and escorted them up a carpeted stairway to a second-floor suite of offices. He showed them into a small anteroom and left. The elegant Second Empire furnishings were calculated to impress.

Such are the wages of crime, thought Ramsey.

Across the small room, a door opened. The man who entered looked at Abby and staggered in surprise. "Mrs. Knowles! I—had I known, I—Denton!"

"My name is Maynard. Susan Knowles is my sister."

"But you—you are she! Denton!"

"I apologize if I surprised you. Susan Knowles is my twin sister. Are you Mr. Coldwater?"

"Yes."

A younger man entered. His eyes widened in surprise. "Is there a problem, Father?"

"Son, this is Mrs. Maynard. Says she is Susan Knowles's sister."

The younger man looked hard at Abby, his expression difficult to read. He said nothing.

The old man struggled for composure. "I am Munford Coldwater, and this is my son, Denton," he finally managed. "And you must be Mr. Maynard." He offered his hand.

"No, Father, this is Allan Ramsey. I believe I have spoken to you about him."

"Yes, Son, yes you did."

Munford Coldwater withdrew his hand and addressed Abby. "I'm afraid you've given me quite a shock, Mrs. Maynard. Please forgive me. I'm delighted to make your acquaintance." An awkward little bow followed.

"As am I," said Denton. He smiled reassuringly at her. "Surely, Mr. Ramsey has no business here. Our meeting is with you, Mrs. Maynard." He had the modulated voice of a well-mannered bully.

Denton Coldwater wore a stylish white linen suit. The family resemblance was clear, but Denton was taller and his features were less coarse than his father's.

"I apologize for any confusion," said Abby. "I've only recently arrived in Atlanta, and I wished to be escorted to our meeting. I'm sure you don't mind that I asked Mr. Ramsey, a friend of my late husband, to accompany me?" She imperceptibly cocked her head in a way that said, *So, that's settled.*

The elder Coldwater aimed a smile at Abby. "Yes, yes, of course. Come Denton. This way everyone." He led them into an adjoining office.

Ramsey glanced at Abby. She followed quickly and did not return the look.

An impressive performance. She was prepared to encounter Denton, and her calculations concerning Munford had been correct. The old man had no intention of doing anything that would be offensive to her. Had she also anticipated the surprise her likeness would cause the father and son. Had she planned on throwing the old man off balance from the beginning? Funny she hadn't mentioned earlier her sister was a twin.

Munford urged them to seat themselves near the window at a table set with plates of fruit and pastries. A servant appeared with coffee.

"Best coffee in Atlanta," said Munford with an attempt at affability. Ramsey doubted they'd gone all the way to Georgiana's to get it. He took a sip. The characterless brew revealed itself as a fraud.

Munford Coldwater's thickening middle-aged body stood well below six feet. He'd combed the graying remnants of his hair over his crown in an ineffectual display of vanity. His prewar coat was far from stylish, and his boots were scuffed with hard use. Cold blue eyes, nested too close together, viewed the world with appraisal. He smiled reflexively with no apparent joy.

Perhaps because of social uncertainty, he bombarded Abby with a stream of solicitations and concerns for her welfare. Was the chair comfortable? Any drafts? Were the pastries to her liking? The coffee? His concern became no less urgent as it became utterly trivial.

"I'm sure we've done what we can for Mrs. Maynard's comfort, Father," Denton said at length.

Munford sat back, letting Denton command the meeting. The younger Coldwater inquired about Abby's trip south, then added an amusing, though brief, travel story of his own.

Ramsey remained silent during these social pleasantries, carefully examining the contents of the room. Munford Coldwater sat across the table intently observing him.

The pleasantries over, Denton said, "Let me thank you, Mrs. Maynard, for agreeing to meet with us."

"Yes, it's time we spoke of what brings us together," said Munford. He flashed his smile and plunged into the matter at hand. "Would you be willing to sell us Charlton? Our properties lie together, and only the land Alfred leased us is being worked. Idle fields benefit no one. We could make you a fair offer."

"Acquiring this property must mean a great deal to you, Mr. Coldwater," she replied evenly.

"Well, strictly speaking," Munford said, "it doesn't." He was at ease now that the social amenities were over. "I was anxious to buy the land a while back. Tried to buy it several times, in fact. I was a younger man then, but I'm getting older. Denton might want it, though God knows cotton ain't easy now. Where he'll find the hands to work a crop is beyond me. Contracts with the darkies are worthless. They work for a while and then they're gone. We don't own them, and you just can't get a darkie to work for himself. Why they—"

"We needn't discuss that, Father. I'm sure it doesn't interest Mrs. Maynard."

Ramsey wondered at the interruption. The old man seemed to be doing just fine. He'd made his desire for the land apparent, but tempered his feelings with indifference before revealing the problems Abby would face if she tried to work the land herself.

"The truth is, Mrs. Maynard," Denton continued, "I have been fortunate enough to make some money in my business dealings. As I look to the future, I wish to invest in land. God only made so much and no more. I'm sure I speak against my own interests in saying this, but your land suits perfectly." His smile appeared as sincere as his father's rang false. "It makes sense to join Charlton to our existing holdings if only for convenience's sake. May I ask you if you intend to farm the land, or might we make you an offer?"

Ramsey reconsidered. The father and son played well off each other. Polished and assured, Denton wrapped himself around his father's tactics like a snake.

"Mr. Coldwater, I don't want to mislead you," said Abby. "I am not the owner of the Charlton property. It belongs to Mr. Alfred Knowles. I understand that he and my sister are not in residence at the moment, but it is their property. I have come to Atlanta to locate them. Their welfare is of great concern to me."

The father and son shared a quick glance.

"I believe I understand your situation, Mrs. Maynard," Denton said. "We have reached out to you because we, too, have been unable to locate Mr. and Mrs. Knowles. If my father and I can be of service to you, we would be happy to do whatever we can."

"Thank you. Would you tell me what you know about my sister and Alfred?" The slight rush in her words betrayed her anxiety.

"I don't know if we can add much to what is generally known. Alfred tried to start a boarding school at Charlton after his brother Franklin died. He made a good start, but only a start. The war ruined him. Families couldn't afford to send their children, and the two teachers he hired went off as soldiers. The school was finished long before the end of the war."

"Did Franklin encourage his brother Alfred to come south?" Ramsey asked.

"I wouldn't know," Denton said, a slight frown creasing his face.

"I just thought Franklin might have mentioned it."

"I hardly knew the man."

"You knew Alfred and Susan, though, didn't you?" Abby said quietly.

"I saw them occasionally. Father saw them much more than I did. Alfred had no interest in farming, so he leased some of the Charlton land to us. In fact, we still plant that parcel as the agreement has not been terminated."

"To whom are the payments made if the Knowles are not in residence?" Ramsey asked.

Munford's face reddened. Denton, ignoring Ramsey, addressed Abby. "Of course, all rents have been placed in escrow and will be paid when proper ownership of Charlton has been established."

"I'm sure they will, Mr. Coldwater." She took a breath and addressed Munford. "Sheriff Powell said it was you who sent for the authorities the day the house burned."

The sun flooded through the window, making the room grow stuffy. Munford patted his forehead with his handkerchief. "We need some air, son."

Denton rose to open the window. "Perhaps you should tell Mrs. Maynard what you know, Father."

Munford gathered his thoughts.

"Well, ma'am, it was towards the end of July in '64. It was a terrible time. Yankee cavalry and soldiers were everywhere. They stole us blind, ma'am, robbed us of everything but our hope of salvation. I think they even got that from some folks. It was terrible. Of course we hid things, but the Yanks made the darkies tell them where it all was. You just couldn't trust your own people. After all we done for 'em, they just told the Yankees everything." He shook his head sadly. "The Bluebellies even stole from your sister and Alfred. Them being for the Union and all, well, some folks thought it served them right, but that didn't matter to us. We did what we could for your family. And they did for us too. We were good neighbors, we were. Your sister may have been a Yankee and all, but she spent a lot of time over at the hospital in Covington nursing our boys. She was a good woman."

Abby's eyes grew moist. Munford stopped and glanced at Denton. Denton nodded.

Munford continued. "The last time I saw your sister was the morning of the fire. She rode over to our place and asked us if we could spare any cornmeal and eggs. Just like her to be riding around the country by herself, bareback and no saddle. She said Alfred was sick and she had to get back. We gave her some meal and a couple of eggs."

Munford adjusted himself in the chair and looked away as his memories returned.

"That was the last time I saw her. Later that morning we heard gunfire from the direction of Charlton. Not so much as a real fight but a whole bunch of shooting all at once. We didn't know what was happening, so I took my wife and we ran into the woods and hid. Samson came with us. After a while, when no one came around, we went back down to the house. We'd just got to where we thought it might be safe to go check on Alfred and Susan when there were more shots, but not so many as before. We waited a bit longer."

Munford stopped and appeared at a loss as to how to continue.

"What did you find when you went over?" Abby prompted. Her eyes were glassy, and her hands worked nervously in her lap.

Munford looked at his son. "I don't think I should say. Some things ain't fit for a woman's ears."

"I truly want to know." Abby's voice was almost inaudible.

"Continue, Father. I believe Mrs. Maynard wants us to tell her all we can."

"Well, I figured the Yanks wouldn't find me if I went the back way. They kept to the main roads 'cause they didn't know the country. I took Samson with me, and we were both armed just in case. Even before we got there, we could see the house was afire. We tied our horses in the woods, and Samson crept down to see if the Yankees were gone. That took a little while, but it didn't matter. There wasn't anything we could do to save the house. Then it started to rain right hard. We went out in the storm and looked for Alfred and Susan. We called out to them, even rode 'round the woods calling, but there was nobody. All we found was darkies laying dead on the cellar stairs."

"But there was no sign of Susan or Alfred?"

"They weren't there, ma'am. Samson and I called and called. We figured they'd run off into the woods like we had, thought they'd come back if they heard us. No one came, so we rode back home. Seeing as how we found the dead on the stairs, I sent Samson for the sheriff. Don't know if that made any sense, but I thought somebody should know about it."

Denton handed Abby a crisp white handkerchief, and she wiped the tears.

"What do you think happened?" Ramsey asked.

"Don't rightly know," said Munford, lost with his memories. "There must have been a fight between our boys and the Yankees. Then the darkies went wild, I guess. Knowles never kept them in line like he should have. They probably went on a killing spree just shooting one another. The Yankees stole, but they didn't usually kill for sport. Besides, the slaves were supposed to be their friends. As for Alfred and Susan, I don't know where they could have got to or what happened to them."

"Might Susan and Alfred have been in the burning house?" Ramsey asked.

Abby's face drained of color.

The older man shook his head. "I don't think so. It started to rain not long after Samson and I got there. A hard rain. The fire was going strong by then, but that ended it pretty quick. Only part of the house was destroyed. It ain't worth fixing up, and you couldn't live there or anything, but it's not all burned up. Even though some of it collapsed this past year, there are walls that still stand. Part of the roof hasn't fallen yet either. When Sheriff Winningham came out a few days later, the fire had cooled down. We went up into the house as far as we could and we didn't find anything, er . . . unusual."

"Would you tell us exactly what you saw on the cellar stairs?" Ramsey asked.

"I've told you that, sir," said Munford sharply. "There's a lady present! I won't go on about it."

"Thank you very much for all you've told us, Mr. Coldwater," Abby said. "I know it's been very difficult for you. As a personal favor, would you answer Mr. Ramsey's question?" She leaned forward and patted Munford's arm as she spoke. He couldn't refuse.

"There were five bodies on the stairs. They were down near the bottom. There were picks and shovels piled down there next to them, but I know why the tools were there."

"Why?" asked Ramsey in surprise.

"Well, I found some fresh digging out in the garden. Since it wasn't a time you'd start planting, I came back with a couple of field hands and had them check what was buried. I thought it might be something Alfred had hid, you know, maybe some china or silver or something. We were going to keep it safe for them until they came back. But it wasn't silver." He looked at Ramsey. "It was some dead soldiers. Our boys. I was sorry for disturbing them. Wouldn't have done it if I'd known."

"Had the bodies been buried long?" Ramsey asked.

"No, they must have been from the fight that morning— the first shots I heard. I suppose Knowles had his coloreds bury the dead. What happened after that I don't know."

"I hope my father has satisfied your curiosity, Mrs. Maynard," said Denton.

The meeting was over.

"Thank you for all you did for my sister and Alfred, Mr. Coldwater. It was very brave of you to go to Charlton that day. I'm sorry I asked you to recall such a terrible time. Is there anything else you can tell me?" she asked.

Munford and Denton exchanged a quick look.

"I think that's all," Denton said.

"Then I thank you. You've both been very kind for sharing what you know, but you've told me things I find distressing. I must ask Mr. Ramsey to accompany me back to my lodgings."

She rose. "When I find my sister, I will inform you if her property is for sale. I'm sure she and Alfred will be happy to discuss the matter with you if they are interested."

"Of course," said Denton, walking them to the door.

Abby and Ramsey walked back to the Hoehling house in silence. They hadn't gone far when Abby started to sob. She fought it at first, but her tears were uncontrollable. She crushed her face against Ramsey's shoulder and held him tightly. He put his arms around her and rocked her gently. No words of comfort came to him. In time, her tears subsided, and he gave her his handkerchief. It was clean but neither crisp nor white.

"That must have been awful to hear," he said.

"It was necessary." She wiped her tears away. "I think Colonel Porter was right. You are a good man."

II

Ramsey gathered his hat and coat from the rack in the front hallway. Katie and Elijah were struggling out the back door with a rolled carpet. Furniture was missing from the front parlor, and the floor was bare. At one end of the room, Mrs. Carraway stood, her arms folded under her ample bosom, surveying the house like Genghis Kahn on the field of battle. Spring-cleaning had arrived. Furniture would be moved and cleaned under. Carpets would be beaten free of the winter's dust and soot. Floors polished. Drapes taken down and aired. Windows washed. No inch of the house would remain untouched. A good time to be elsewhere. Ramsey slipped out the door.

Arriving at the *Intelligencer,* he found a black man sitting straight and holding his hat in his lap. Willie Isaacs nodded toward the waiting man.

"Says his name's Jeremiah and he's got a message for you. Wouldn't leave it with me. You know him?"

"I do."

Jeremiah rose at Ramsey's approach. "A message from Mr. Heflin."

He held out a small envelope sealed with red wax. The seal was intact. Ramsey tore it open and found three sheets of paper. The first was a short letter.

Capt. Ramsey,

Enclosed you will find the translations you requested. I have every reason to believe they are accurate. You were correct in assuming the Vicksburg Code was used. I hope this information is of service to you.

I must apologize for your reception at my home and assure you that you will not find my manners wanting on subsequent visits, which I sincerely hope you will make. Though I have been ill for some time, my health continues to improve, and I thank you for requesting my help in a matter of public interest.

Respectfully,
Heflin Sanbourne

The handwriting, small and almost feminine, had a surprising vigor.

The second sheet read:

"I could be bounded in a nutshell, and count myself a king of infinite space, were it not that I have bad dreams." (The key word is Bard).

Ramsey chuckled. There was no question that Sanbourne's mental capacities were intact. To test the accuracy of the translations, Ramsey had encoded a quote from Shakespeare's *Hamlet*: *For there is nothing either good or bad, but thinking makes it so.* Realizing it was a test, Sanbourne had turned his reply into a teasing joke referencing his illness with a different bit of dialogue from the same play.

The third and final sheet read:

Assemble at the Decatur Rd house as agreed. Attract no attention. Interference is possible. Will join you soon. Tully. (The key word is 'Covington').

"Are you going back to Decatur now?" Ramsey asked Jeremiah.

"There's errands first."

Ramsey scribbled a quick note of thanks. "Please see that Mr. Sanbourne gets this."

Jeremiah took the folded paper and left without comment.

Sprague saw the problem immediately.

The message read "Decatur Rd house."

Decatur Street, as it passed the Atlanta city limits, became Decatur Road. The house, when they found it, would be outside Sprague's jurisdiction. The proper course of action was to inform Sheriff Powell and ask him to investigate.

"What are you going to do?" Ramsey asked.

"I know what I oughta do. What I oughta to do is tell Whit Anderson and the mayor. What I oughta do is send word to Powell. That's what I oughta do. But it ain't what I wanna do. No sir, it ain't what I wanna do."

Sprague opened his pocketknife and sliced some tobacco. "We should send us a note to Powell," he continued, "Yes sir, that would be the thing to do." Sprague put some tobacco in his mouth and chewed, slowly, thoughtfully. "On the other hand, it's a nice day for a ride, ain't it? Kinda get away from our troubles. A ride in the country—that'd be a fine thing."

"Just you and me?" said Ramsey doubtfully.

"Yup."

Sprague reached into his desk drawer and pulled out his Colt revolver.

"'Course, if we do run up on Turney and Hackett, we only gonna ask a few questions, right? Maybe bring 'em back here and just talk to 'em. I can't see botherin' Sheriff Powell 'bout a little thing like that."

The deputy examined the gun and carefully lowered the hammer back onto the empty chamber. "And if we did have some problems, we could always just make a citizen's arrest an' hold 'em till we can go get Powell."

"Sure you want to do it that way, Ed? It could go sideways pretty fast."

Sprague pulled on his hat and coat.

"I been jerked around enough. I ain't giving this goddamn investigation away. You wanna come along?"

"Have you thought—"

"I asked if you was comin'."

Ramsey sighed. "I suppose somebody has to keep a fool like you from getting lost."

"If you got a gun, better bring it," Sprague said. "We might not want trouble, but them folks could have other ideas. Can you ride with that leg?"

"A hell of a lot better than I can without it."

"Then go get you a horse. Meet me back here. I'm gonna check an' see if anybody around here knows anything 'bout abandoned houses on Decatur Road."

Ramsey hadn't ridden in a long time. He was delighted to find he could do so with little discomfort. The chestnut mare from Murray's Livery Stable handled easily and had a bit of spirit to her.

Sprague, anxious to get on with the search, kept a quick trot through Five Points, an intersection more or less at the heart of the city. There they turned onto Decatur Road and soon found themselves passing through Smoky Row. A motley collection of shanties and saloons the freedmen created. Whatever might be said about the races, vice was wondrously colorblind. Some along the street waved as they passed. Most ignored them. A few took to their heels.

Sprague slowed his pace.

A saloon door swung open, and a giant of a man, his ebony skin stark against his crisp white shirt, stared at them.

"Morning, John," said Sprague, tipping his hat.

The black man spat.

A drunken prostitute waved and started toward them. Her companion drew her back. With whispers and sidelong glances, the two women hurried away. Music from a piano poured out of a liquor shanty along with drunken voices.

Buildings became fewer when the road took a slight turn and headed east. The sky was blue and cloudless, and the warm air carried the spicy scent of spring.

They rode side by side.

"Damnedest weather I ever seen," Sprague said. "We got rain, rain, rain, then just before ya think an' ark would be useful, it goes clear." He launched a stream of tobacco juice over his mount's ears. The horse, accustomed to Sprague's habits, was unperturbed.

"So you think there are six possible houses they could be using?" Ramsey asked.

"Who the hell knows? Wilson, Reynolds, an' me went over the map. They know what's along the road better'n I do. Showed me six places Tully mighta meant. Doubt if any of 'em is vacant now. Folks is stayin' any place outta the rain. What's more, they lots of shanties been put up."

"We don't need to worry about anything built since the war. Turney and Hackett wouldn't know about them."

"I see you're carrying a proper gun like I said to. Ain't seen you carry nothing but that little peashooter before," Sprague said.

"Ah, the derringer. Makes no sense to bring it today. Can't hit anything more than three feet away with it."

"Well, like we was saying earlier, there ain't gonna be no trouble."

They came to the barren earthworks east of the city. Stripped of much of its vegetation, the eroded red soil formed miniature plateaus and canyons. A soldier's boot, torn and weathered, lay in a nearby ravine. Farther on, a battered canteen and some broken cartridge boxes lay scattered on the ground.

This wasted world, Ramsey thought, is the true monument to war.

Nothing the Ladies Memorial Association commissioned could ever come close. Society might memorialize the men, the cause, or the outcome of a war. But the awful wantonness of destruction could only be felt in a place like this. In time, life would triumph even in this wasteland; grass would grow, bushes and trees would appear, and wildlife would return. Then this monument to destruction would be gone. Men, forgetting the horror, would fight again.

When they reached the wooded land past the earthworks, Sprague drew up his horse. He pulled a hand-drawn map from his pocket and pointed to a small track that led into the woods on their right.

"The old McKay place. Wilson says it's been fallin' down since before the war."

They rode single file down a badly overgrown path, saplings slapping at their thighs. Years of fallen leaves muffled the horse's hooves. Ramsey drew out a pair of field glasses and trained them on the house. The air was heavy with the scent of pine. Their presence quieted the birds, but a slight breeze moving through the leaves broke the silence. He watched the house for some time. It was still standing, but little else could be said for it. Rough-hewn weathered walls barely supported a sagging moss-covered roof. The windows were broken. A red cloth, the sign of smallpox, hung by the door.

"Thought I saw movement," Ramsey said. "No sign of horses. Smallpox flag could be useful to keep people away . . ."

Sprague's horse moved restlessly.

"Wait," Ramsey muttered, "There's a woman." They heard a baby's cry.

Ramsey lowered the glasses. "Let's move on, Ed."

The next house, in better condition and closer to the road, told much the same story—destitute people eking out a half-starved existence. At least they'd escaped the smallpox.

They returned to Decatur Road and continued on.

Sprague checked his map and pointed to the left. They turned and hurried along a washed-out rocky path that led into the woods toward the north. The afternoon sun dipped lower in the sky. A house stood in a clearing about fifty yards off. Ramsey again raised his field glasses.

No movement around the building. Behind him he could hear Sprague eating an apple. Ramsey's back ached from the riding. He arched into a stretch. Near the house a large pot stood above a smoky fire. A couple of chickens pecked relentlessly in the dirt.

"Ed, someone's living there, but I don't—"

"Get your hands in the air!" a voice barked behind them.

Sprague and Ramsey raised their hands.

A tall gaunt man dressed in tattered clothes walked around where they could see him. The dark spot on the arm of his faded shirt showed where an insignia of rank had once been.

"Let's suppose you tell me who you are and why you're snooping around."

"No cause for alarm," Ramsey said. "Lower the gun and we'll explain ourselves."

The man walked closer. His Enfield rifle pointed at Ramsey's chest.

"You start talking, and I'll decide what to do with this here rifle."

Sprague answered. "I'm Deputy Marshal Ed Sprague, and this here is Allan Ramsey. We're after some men said to be out this way. We got no quarrel with you."

"If you're law, prove it."

The rifle now turned its attention to Sprague.

The deputy slowly pulled his badge from his vest pocket and gently tossed it on the ground. The badge landed at the man's feet. He picked it up, careful to keep the rifle trained on Sprague. He looked the badge over carefully, then lowered the rifle and flipped the badge back to the Sprague.

Ramsey dismounted. His leg had grown stiff, and he struggled with his balance upon reaching the ground. A moment later Sprague was standing beside him.

"You live here?" asked the deputy.

A curt nod by way of an answer.

"We're looking for two men, maybe more," Sprague said. "Been around a few days or so, maybe less. They rough uns."

"Lot of them kind around these days," said the man with the rifle. He studied Ramsey and Sprague a moment longer, then tension left his spare frame. He balanced the rifle across his shoulder. "There's been some like that around here," he said. "If they come back again, I'll kill 'em."

Ramsey saw no reason to doubt that.

"Sorry 'bout the greeting you got," the man continued, "but I can't be too careful here lately. Name's Cecil Waugh. I'd be right pleased if you'd come to the house. I'll tell you what I can."

He led them to a structure built with crudely squared logs. The spaces between them were chinked with mud. Straps of wood secured tar paper to the roof. Two barrels of rainwater stood near the door. A tripod suspended a large cast-iron pot over the fire that smoldered in the front yard.

"This here's Sarah, my wife." A woman in a faded dress that hung loosely on her body nodded to them. She was as raw and bony as her husband.

Inside were two chairs and a table fashioned out of hewn wood. A meager assembly of cooking and eating utensils sat on top of some freight boxes along the wall. Inside a second room, a straw mattress lay on the floor. It was the only thing there. Chickens clucked in the yard.

The deputy accepted one of the offered chairs. Ramsey chose to stand and stretch his bad leg. Sarah poured them all some water while Cecil stood warily near the door.

"We had us a farm up near Marietta before the war," he said. "Sarah here, she ran it real good while I was gone to the army, but them Bluebellies come and burnt us out. They said bushwhackers was in the house, but it weren't true. They took everything they wanted and burnt the rest. Didn't leave Sarah and the baby a damn thing to live on. When I came home last spring, there wasn't no home to come to. We moved on. Wasn't any reason to stay up that way, an' Sarah's got kin down here."

Ramsey saw no evidence of a baby in the cabin. Her home and her child gone, Sarah sat in silence, listening without emotion as if hearing someone else's story.

"I worked a crop for Homer Haskins last summer," Cecil continued, "and took my share mostly in land. He had more'n he could plant anyways. Now I'm working what you see. Some of it I own, and the rest I'll pay off when my crop comes in. Cotton fetches good right now, and we got some corn and such like."

"The place shows promise," Ramsey said. He looked out at the lengthening shadows.

"You say there's been trouble lately?" he asked.

Cecil nodded. "Never had no trouble since we come down here, not till now, anyways. I was out hunting when I saw men down at the old Rowley place. You see folks over there now an' again, but these was different. They looked like trouble."

"What do you mean?"

"I mean they had horses an' guns and not much else. They weren't planning to work the place—you could tell that, sure enough. I thought they'd go robbin', so's I watched 'em."

"How long they been there?" Sprague asked.

"No more'n a few days. Yesterday one of 'em come up here while I was off in the field.

Wanted to buy some eggs, but Sarah seen he was drunk and up to something. She sent him off. He came back and tried to . . . to bother her."

Ramsey looked at Sarah. She glanced back but made no comment.

"Sarah's a good woman," Cecil nodded at her, "and she cuffed him. He wouldn't be put off, an' he hit her. Just lucky I came back for lunch round then. I grabbed an ax and woulda killed him on the spot, but he run off. Took a shot at me from the woods."

"Tell me," Ramsey asked, "was the man who attacked her a big man with wide-set funny looking eyes?"

Cecil nodded.

So that was that.

"You gonna take 'em?" Cecil asked.

"Thought we'd look in on 'em," Sprague said vaguely.

"Well, if you're going over there, I better show you the back way. Hope you fellas both brought guns."

Cecil directed his question at Ramsey; he could see Sprague's Colt jammed in his belt. Ramsey pulled an Adams .32 revolver from his pocket.

"We're both armed," he said.

Cecil eyed the pistol. "Horse, field glasses, little ol' sidearm—you musta been an officer."

"That doesn't matter anymore," said Ramsey. "We'd best think about what we're going to do."

"You sound like an officer too." Cecil turned to Sprague. "It ain't much more than a mile if we go on foot through the woods. Won't hurt to surprise 'em. If we don't hurry, we gonna lose the light."

He picked up his Enfield and headed toward the door. Sprague and Ramsey had little choice but to follow.

The sun sank toward the horizon, but they waited. Almost a half hour passed as they sat watching a large ramshackle house at the center of a large clearing. Surrounded by weeds and scrub pine, its masonry chimney had pulled away from the structure and tilted drunkenly. Nearby were the charred remains of a barn. Horses had trampled the brush close to the house, where a blanket and saddle rested on the porch railing.

The three men moved around to the west face. A horse aimlessly munched what grass it could find. A woodpecker hammered. The birds became accustomed to their presence, and the song of wrens and sparrows returned. Golden sunlight fell on the clearing, but the woods beyond grew darker.

Sprague lowered the field glasses and handed them back to Ramsey.

"Light's gonna fail," he said. "I suppose we oughta git on in there."

"How do you want to handle it?" Ramsey asked.

Sprague spoke to Waugh first. "Cecil, we're gonna need your help. I'd be obliged if you'd cover us. You see anything that don't look right, you shoot."

Waugh nodded his assent.

"You got any reloads?" Sprague asked.

"Three in my pocket."

"Good. Once we make the house, you swing 'round an' cover that little path. You know, the one on the other side. We'll try to take them that's in the house, but if one of 'em gets by, he's yours. Don't kill nobody if you can help it. A leg shot would be just fine."

Waugh nodded again.

"Ramsey, you go in the back. I'll swing round an' go in the front. For Christ's sake look before you go shootin'."

"And you remember I'm coming the other way."

Sprague pulled his Colt from its holster and examined it for a moment, then spoke to Waugh. "I think you oughta' know, Cecil, I ain't exactly got jurisdiction around here, so there ain't no point in me swearin' you as a deputy or such like."

Waugh accepted his unofficial status without comment.

Pistols drawn, Sprague and Ramsey made their way into the clearing. Sprague was swinging wide to the right of the house, moving toward its front. Ramsey picked his way through the brush and made for the back door. The exertion of moving low to the ground left his leg screaming in pain. A clammy knot of unease gripped him. He broke into a cold sweat and his heart pounded.

Ahead lay a rotting woodpile. A nightmare reality danced in his mind. He dropped to the ground, the smell of earth filling his nostrils. Breath came in shallow pants. Sweat stung his eyes. Forcing himself into a final rush, he threw himself down on the back steps.

The desire to flee was overwhelming. He slammed the cold metal of the pistol against his forehead. The pain was good. He hit himself again. A vision of a river came into his mind. He grabbed for it, tried to hold it, longing for it to draw him past the fear. Sweat and tears blinded his eyes. Closing them, he held his breath for what seemed an eternity. The house was silent. Panic returned on a wave of nausea.

He hung his head, wiped his eyes, and stared at the ground. Was fear all he had left? Had the ambush withered his soul just as it had damaged his leg? Had it lurked deep within him like a malignant seed, patiently biding its time until this moment to finish its work? His thoughts called out to his younger self, to a time before the ambush. He longed to embrace that younger man, that purer being, but he did not find him. Frozen and useless, crouching against the steps, he knew he never would. Never again.

His empty desperation banished thought from his mind. In its place a fury began to grow, roiling up like a thundercloud from the darkest part of his soul, and flashed into rage. He wanted to kill. He wanted to destroy everything and everyone around him. He wanted to die. He wanted to smother his fear in death and drop forever into emptiness.

Then as quickly as it had come to him, his rage was spent. It collapsed into the emptiness, and out of the emptiness rose a profound calm. Crystalline clarity filled his mind. He looked up at the house as if he were seeing it for the first time. The door above him was ajar. He reached out and eased it open a few inches. The hinges creaked and then silence returned. In the calm that embraced him, only the silence of that moment mattered. Only that small slice of eternity meant anything. Not his life. Not his death. Not his fear. Just the immensity of the moment.

A second passed . . . A minute? An hour? He saw the cracked and weathered wood of the door. A rusty nail protruded from a beam a few feet away. Its reddish-brown stain ran down like blood. His forehead ached and his hand trembled. He gently pushed the door fully open. Once again its hinges creaked. His eyes strained to see into the darkness beyond as he waited for a gunshot.

Silence.

He swung himself inside and dropped to the floor.

From the front of the house came quiet footsteps.

Sprague?

Ahead was an empty hallway. Ramsey crept forward. He stayed near the wall, trying to lessen the noise of his steps, but the floor groaned and popped under his weight. Dust motes danced in the sunlight that streamed through a broken window. The air was stale, musty with the odor of moldering wood and plaster.

And gun smoke.

In the half-light he saw it. Blood. Beginning at a door, a trail of blood ran up the hallway past where he was standing.

Sprague appeared at the end of the hall. The two men nodded to each other. Ramsey looked quickly into the room on his left. Empty. Sprague gestured toward the doorway that lay between them. The trail of blood passed under its closed door. Ramsey stood against the wall and raised his gun. Sprague moved off-line, and with a huge thrust, kicked in the door. Splintering wood shattered the silence. The door stuck three-quarters open against the rain-warped floorboards. A large bluebottle, startled by the noise, buzzed around the room before settling again by an eerie red lake. A whiskey bottle lay on its side, the contents forming a puddle. Playing cards lay scattered. One floated in the spilled liquor.

Sprague walked to the backdoor and signaled to Cecil Waugh that all was clear. The farmer stepped out of the shadows and trotted toward the house.

"Ed," said Ramsey, "have a look at the back stairs while there's still some light and tell me what you think."

Ramsey looked around the room. Someone had been sitting on the floor, drinking, maybe playing cards. That someone had been shot from the doorway. The body had been moved down the hall and out the door not long before they'd arrived.

Why move a wounded man? A seriously wounded one judging by the amount of blood.

Sprague returned. "Body been dragged out that way."

There was a bullet hole in the wall. Using his pocketknife, Ramsey dug out the slug and examined it. He flipped it to Sprague. "Ever seen one of these?"

Sprague held it close to his eyes and turned it slowly. "Nope."

"Spencer rifle," said Waugh, looking over Sprague's shoulder. "We captured some towards the end of the war. A repeatin' rifle, it is. They was awful to fight against. Ten men could hold off a hundred with 'em. We couldn't get enough ammunition for the ones we captured, so's they weren't worth carrying. Damn Bluebellies had all the ammo they needed."

Ramsey nodded. "I'd say you're right, Mr. Waugh. It looks like a Spencer to me too."

"What the hell happened to your head?" Sprague gestured to the bruise on Ramsey's forehead.

"Hit it coming in."

A quizzical look played over Cecil Waugh's lean features, but he said nothing.

"Why the hell shoot a man and drag his ass off?" said Sprague looking at the drying blood. "Jesus! Anybody who gets himself shot here lately gets toted off somewheres."

"Cecil, did you hear shots earlier today?" Ramsey asked.

"Can't say as I did, but me an' Sarah walked into Decatur and didn't get back till just before you fellas come along.

Ordinarily she'd a stayed behind, but what with that varmint being around, she wanted to come with me."

They hurried to inspect the old house before the light failed. The search revealed a leather valise, a worn carpetbag, saddlebags, and a Henry rifle: the belongings of two men. They took those and the horse back to Waugh's house.

They were about to leave when Sprague said, "We gonna need to take most of this stuff with us, but I appreciate what ya done for us back there, Cecil. Can't pay nothing, but I was wonderin' if you'd hold the rifle and the horse as evidence? If I need 'em I'll send for 'em, but you can use 'em till then. Don't know as I'll ever need 'em though."

Cecil Waugh's dour face achieved something close to joy.

Ramsey and Sprague rode in silence on the way back, accompanied by the occasional call of a night bird and the sound of the horses' hooves on the road. There was enough of a moon to find their way.

At length Sprague broke the silence.

"Ain't gonna be easy to tell the marshal about this. When he finds out we missed them wolves again, he ain't gonna be happy. Probably gonna replace me with Willis."

"He'd be a fool if he did."

"Could be, but we got us a city full of nervous folks. You kept some of this stuff out of the newspaper for a while, but two men are dead. Now we got a third stiff around somewhere if we can ever find the son of a bitch. He was carried off, and that's probably gonna bite us in the ass too. Hard to argue things ain't outta hand. Folks is worried. Some say blacks is doing it. I hear the boys in blue is sayin' it's Reb soldiers turned outlaw. That's what Whit told me. The Army, the mayor, the marshal, Whitaker—they all want an end to this killin'. Me? I just keep findin' more dead bodies. I'm about as popular as daddy's whore at the family picnic."

Willis Lanier was a good man. The people of Atlanta knew and trusted him. He was certainly better than Sprague at dealing with the public. Ramsey had seen Lanier's quick thinking and diplomacy defuse situations that might have turned ugly. But Sprague was the better investigator, even if his personality was an acquired taste.

"What happened today wasn't your fault, Ed. I don't see how it could have worked out any differently no matter who was running things."

"It ain't just about today. You know that. They got to show they in charge. They'll dump the blame on me an' turn the whole thing over to Lanier. That's what they'll do. Makes 'em look in control."

"Maybe you're right, but dammit, go ahead and give them what we've got. The code's been broken, right? Take credit for it. Be my guest. We found where some of them were holding up, didn't we? Okay, somebody got shot and dragged off. We couldn't help that. It happened before we got there, but by the look of it, we were real close. Someone is just one step ahead, and they can't stay that way forever."

Sprague grunted and spurred his horse on ahead. The night was given back to the sound of hooves.

They had almost reached the city limits when a gunshot exploded the stillness. The horses reared.

The shot was Sprague's.

"What the hell!" Ramsey roared, struggling to calm his mount.

"Goddammit, I need more time. I'll tell 'em I fired my gun. I'll tell 'em I wounded one of the wolves but he got away. Ain't no one but Cecil Waugh to say I didn't. An' we just give him a horse an' a real nice rifle, didn't we? He'll back me up if I get word to him. Maybe Whit will see we're gettin' close. It might back him off. A few days maybe. Just might give ol' Ed a chance."

"You're out of your damn mind."

"Maybe I am, and maybe Willis Lanier can do better, but I ain't gonna drop this thing now and go back to huntin' horse thieves and firebugs."

The two men stared at each other in the moonlight.

"Ed, think about it. Just think it through. Whit Anderson won't like hearing you've wounded a man in Sheriff Powell's jurisdiction. Besides, how does that help? I don't see how that makes anyone happy or buys you any time?"

"I'll take my chances. What I want to know is what *you're* gonna do."

Ramsey didn't answer. He spurred his horse and rode on, too tired to think anymore. His body ached, and his head throbbed.

They were almost back on Smoky Row when Sprague reined in his mount. Ramsey did the same.

"So what you gonna tell the judge?"

"First, I'm going to get some sleep."

"Then?"

"Then I have no damn idea."

"Ramsey!"

A fist thundered on the door.

"Ramsey, wake up!"

Ramsey rolled over and struggled to shake the mist from his mind. He forced himself out of bed and pulled on his pants. When he opened the door, Duncan Moore pushed past him into the room, carrying a lantern. He swung the door shut and tumbled into a chair.

"Jesus, Duncan, you'll wake the dead."

"They've found another body!"

"Oh God. Where?"

"Off in the woods near Smoky Row. Mr. Henry came and told the police and then went for the judge. Whitaker sent me to get you."

"Has anybody told Sprague?"

"He's already there with Marshal Anderson. I heard Mr. Henry say his nephew was the one who found the dead man. They hung him, Ramsey! They hung him from a tree!"

"They hung Gideon?"

"Oh for God's sake! He's the one that found the body. It's hanging from a tree, and there's a sign on it."

"A what?"

"A sign. It says MURDERER. Come on!"

Ramsey struggled to the washstand and splashed water on his face. He desperately needed sleep. The mirror showed the bruise on his forehead was now dark and not well hidden. God, what he'd give for coffee. He pulled on the rest of his clothes. His pocket watch read twelve minutes after four o'clock. Grabbing his hat, he rushed out the door with Duncan close behind.

In better circumstances, Ramsey liked the early morning. It was then that the world stood apart from the bustle of men in timeless darkness and abstraction. It was a time when a scout, if he knew his business, could travel unseen in a hostile land. Ramsey drew the chill moist air into his lungs and felt some energy return.

Duncan, clearly past his distaste for corpses, outpaced Ramsey. When they turned toward Decatur Street and Smoky Row, Ramsey looked out into the darkness toward the spot where Bill Tully's body had been found barely a week ago. It hardly seemed possible that he was off once again in the night with Duncan—only now three men were dead.

Ahead, lanterns winked and bobbed among the trees in the darkness. Sometimes the lanterns would come together to form a cluster before dispersing like oversize fireflies. Stars dotted the black moonless sky high above the trees. Ramsey, giving in to the demands of his leg, slowed as he approached the path that led into the wood. "Give me your lantern, Duncan."

"Come on, Ramsey, we're almost—"

"Give me the goddamn lantern!"

The boy handed it over and rushed off toward the lights.

Ramsey walked slowly along the edge of the road and soon came to a place where the passage of a wagon had broken the brush and crushed the grasses. Wheel ruts led toward the clearing. He followed the track. Ahead, in a circle of lanterns, stood Mr. Henry, Gideon, and Ed Sprague. Sprague spoke with Gideon. In another circle of light, Whit Anderson, Judge Whitaker, and three policemen examined the ground. The limbs of an immense chestnut oak spread out above them. A man hung from the tree like a sack, his hands tied behind him. Beneath his head hung a small board with MURDERER scrawled in dried blood.

Sprague stood by. His sagging body, puffy face, and disheveled hair told all. The deputy was having a very bad day even before the sun was up. Ramsey walked by him and looked up at the corpse.

The head canted forward from its broken neck in penitential submission, but the face was contorted in fury. Unblinking eyes glared out at the world. Orville Hackett's miserable life had come to its close at the end of an old rope barely serviceable for the task.

Ramsey examined the ground below the dead man carefully. Many feet had trampled the area, but off to one side remained signs of a horse. The rope that suspended Hackett crossed over a large limb and was tied off to a smaller tree. The noose had been put around his neck while he was on the ground and a horse was used to hoist him into the air.

When the ground could tell him no more, Ramsey looked back at Hackett. His feet were bare. He was dressed in shabby brown pants and a torn blue shirt that was dark with dried blood. Beneath the tattered shirt, a bandage bound his abdomen.

Sprague strolled over. "We gonna cut him down." The deputy gave a nod to two policemen at the far end of the rope. With a jerk and bounce, Hackett returned to the earth.

Sprague squatted beside the corpse and poked at the dead man's abdomen before checking the pockets. They were empty. "Okay, take the body over to Doc Pierce." Sprague rose without further comment and joined Marshal Anderson.

Ramsey took a last look at Hackett. Gut wounds like that were fatal. Whoever had tended to him bought him very little time.

The police loaded Hackett's body onto a wagon. When it left, so did most of them. Sprague, Whitaker, and Duncan joined Ramsey.

"What do you think happened?" Duncan asked.

"Can't you read signs, boy?" snapped Sprague. "I'd say this was the one that killed all them others. I'd say that he got to feelin' so damn bad about it, he put a sign round his neck and hung himself. I'd say this goddamn case is—"

"Enough, Deputy!" Whitaker glared at Sprague. "Duncan meant no harm." He turned and patted the young man on the shoulder. "Why don't you run back to the office, Duncan, and write something about what you've seen. Just stick to the facts and keep it simple."

Duncan nodded and ran off to hitch a ride with the police.

"Supposing the police theory of suicide proves incorrect, Captain Ramsey," Whitaker said, "what is your opinion?"

Sprague threw his hands in the air. "Dammit, Judge, I was—"

"What do you think, Ramsey?" Whitaker repeated, ignoring Sprague.

"Well, we obviously have a lynching. I'm sure the man is Orville Hackett, but you already know that. Yesterday evening, just a few hours ago, Ed and I rode out Decatur Road to check some information we'd received. I believe we found where Hackett was shot. The shooting happened shortly before we arrived, since the blood had just begun to dry. I didn't send you a message when we returned, because it was so late."

"Deputy Sprague has told us about Decatur Road. Do you have any thoughts on why Hackett was killed there and then hanged miles away?"

"No idea." Ramsey turned to the deputy. "Did you report to the marshal last night?"

"What do you think? He's waiting for me back at his office." Sprague had the look of a condemned man. He turned and walked away.

"There's so much at stake right now," Whitaker said. "When you're finished here, please come to my office. Let's say in an hour. I want to discuss this with Steele first."

"Yes, sir."

The judge climbed into his buggy and drove off into the rising dawn.

Ramsey had a last look around before he, too, headed back. He hadn't gone far when a voice behind him said, "Guess I can walk back with you."

It was Sprague.

"I thought you were with the marshal."

"Hell, that shit's been settled. I just didn't want to hear any more from the judge. I am sick and goddamn tired of every son of a bitch who thinks he's somebody in this sack-a-shit town tellin' me I gotta make an arrest. Hell, I'm tryin' ain't I? They just killin' themselves faster than I can find 'em. Why didn't you Yankees set on each other this way during the war? Huh?" Sprague spit angrily. "An' then I go and offer the marshal a little bullshit so's he'll get off my back, and what happens? Goddamn, Ramsey, maybe the judge and the marshal ain't tumbled to it, but this hangin' was done by at least four men. And we only got two of them Yankees left alive. Maybe only one if Turney gets his dead ass delivered somewhere."

"I saw the wagon tracks and the footprints around Hackett," Ramsey agreed. "The members of the gang aren't killing each other off. Someone else is doing the honors, but God only knows who that might be."

They walked on in silence for a time before Ramsey spoke. "If Gideon found the body before dawn, how did he see it in the dark?"

"Yeah, I asked him that. He said he seen a man ridin' out of the woods. Couldn't make out what he looked like. Too dark. But the boy was curious 'bout what a white man was up to around here and went to have a look. Says it scared him half to death seein' a man hanging there, so's he run for Mr. Henry, and Mr. Henry went an' woke up half the goddamn town."

"Just one rider?" Ramsey asked.

"That's all he said. 'Course, we both make out the tracks of at least four, even with that herd of idiots tramplin' around. There was a wagon too. Thank God horses is heavier than men. The Gideon boy is lying, but I don't blame him. If he seen somebody, he sure as hell won't want them to know it. Don't take much for a darkie to get strung up these days, and the boy's bright enough not to want to join Hackett. Something more I guess I should tell ya before somebody else does."

"What's that?"

"You gonna be workin' with Willis Lanier from now on. Marshal's real pissed off about yesterday. Says it weren't right not to bring in Powell. An' I can tell you this too: he don't want you around neither. Him and the judge was havin' words before you got there, and for once, the judge didn't get the best of it."

"I think you'll agree, Captain Ramsey, that things have gotten out of hand."

Whitaker's voice was calm and judicial. The stubble on his chin, the taut skin on his cheekbones, and the fact that the meeting was taking place at 6:15 a.m. betrayed his attempt at normalcy.

"Atlanta has never been a city of choirboys, but we now have three murders—three related murders—and the Army is questioning our ability to manage our affairs. These problems have to be dealt with by us, not them. They must see us as in control. You do understand the importance of that, don't you?"

"Yes, sir."

"You were with Deputy Sprague yesterday?"

"I was."

"We've spoken with the deputy, but perhaps you would be kind enough to tell us what you know?"

Ramsey related the events of the day before: the message from Sanbourne, the search along Decatur Road, the meeting with Cecil Waugh, and the discovery of the bloody room. He shaped the story as best he could. The reasons he gave for not alerting Sheriff Powell were unconvincing, but that couldn't be helped. He stuck close to the truth, though he neglected to mention the horse and rifle left with Waugh. He assumed Sprague had done the same.

John Steele joined them. "I suppose you know," he said, "that Deputy Sprague has been removed from this case. Willis Lanier has taken over."

"Yes, he told me."

"It's for the best," Whitaker said. "New man, fresh ideas—it just makes sense."

"Sprague was doing—"

"Nothing," Steele snapped. "He was running in circles."

"He did everything that could be done," said Ramsey grimly.

"Sprague has been active, quite active," said Whitaker. "We are not here to judge him or you. However, Deputy Sprague has been assigned other duties and Marshal Anderson asked that you stay away from the investigation. I will accommodate his request. Deputy Lanier will contact you for whatever information he needs, but from now on, you will have other duties."

"But—"

"Other duties. I strongly suggest that you attend to them. Henderson will begin covering the story. Maybe you could go out of town and do a special for us. I believe we could manage something like that, don't you, John?"

"Of course."

"Well then, I leave you two gentlemen to plan this project, and I shall go deal with other matters."

Ramsey did not return his employer's smile.

"What's going to happen now?" he asked when the judge was gone.

"Happen to you?"

"Happen with everything."

When Steele spoke, his voice was almost friendly. "That trip out on Decatur Road was a mistake. It wouldn't be a problem if you'd made an arrest. Sheriff Powell might have been upset, but I don't suppose anyone else would care. Instead we have this mess. Think how it looks. Right from the beginning, you and Sprague have been a day late and a dollar short. Then yesterday, by your own admission, you failed to catch two men you were after. Men you knew to be involved in the murders. The rather embarrassing discovery of one of them hanging from a tree in the deputy's backyard was the last nail in his coffin. The events of yesterday and last night don't give the impression we're on top of things, now do they?"

"What else could we have done? Sending for Powell would have taken time, and I doubt things would have turned out differently."

"Look, I know there wasn't much more you and Sprague could have done. Hell, Whit Anderson would probably say the same thing in private, but that doesn't count for much. The usual rules don't apply. The Army is watching to see what we do with our problem. Everyone in the city is second-guessing us. I know you never darken the door of a church, but let me assure you that the clergy are weighing in on the matter along with everyone else."

"So Sprague gets offered as a sacrifice to public opinion."

"Well, I suppose that would be the unvarnished version, but yes."

"He thought it was going to happen, you know. He told me so last night as we rode back to town."

"The deputy's not a stupid man. And don't pretend you're surprised either. These things happen." Steele lit a cigar. "But there's something else you ought to know. I don't want you to spread it around, but Willis Lanier won't be working alone. The Army is assigning a special investigator. It's unofficial, of course. Let's just say that they offered help in a way that caused Mayor Williams to accept. That ends our need to have you as a liaison."

Steele sat back and blew a smoke ring.

"Besides," he continued, "Whit Anderson can't stand you. He doesn't like what you write or where you poke your nose. Anderson's feelings don't trouble the judge, and frankly, I enjoy his discomfort. But under the circumstances, we felt it was in everyone's interests to take you off the story. So there it is—you're out and Henderson is in."

"I'll write up society weddings and Sprague's off to catch chicken thieves. 'God's in his heaven and all's right with the world.'"

"I think that sums it up."

"Will Whit Anderson produce a killer for the Army the way he produced evidence against Rafe Jenkins?"

"If I were you, I'm not sure that's a drum I'd beat. Rafe Jenkins is scum, and justice was done. Maybe not in a way one would want, but it was done. In this town, Ramsey, you don't have many friends, at least ones who count for anything, and you've got more than your share of enemies. A man who goes around saying the wrong thing right now might wind up with all enemies and no friends. That could make life very hard."

"Is that a threat?"

"That is a fact. I'm asking you to take some time off. Work on whatever you like. We'll keep paying you for now. Just lay low and be nice to everyone you see. All this will blow over. But for God's sake, stay out of it."

"It's your call, John. You give the orders."

"Don't give me that good soldier nonsense. You always go your own way. Always have. The trouble with you is you've got larceny in your heart."

"I've got what?"

"Larceny in your heart. My father used to say that about some men. They bend the rules. They act as they see fit and don't give a damn as long as it's all square to them. The problem, Allan, is that your rules aren't the only ones the world cares about."

"Bit much, isn't it, John?"

"Well, why don't you surprise me and do what you're told."

"Rabun, do I have larceny in my heart?"

"*Oui, mon ami.* It is one of your interesting traits. Do not trouble yourself."

Despite his exhaustion, Ramsey needed a drink and a friend when he left the newspaper. As the tavern keeper went about his morning tasks, Ramsey told him about recent events, partly out of sociability and partly to stay awake.

"God, Rabun. The city's going to do whatever it takes to satisfy the Army, the newspaper is trotting along like a trained dog, and Steele says I'm the one with larceny in my heart."

"It is not the same, but I think you do not look for sharp reasoning. Another brandy? Perhaps to soothe your injured scruples?" Rabun filled the glass. "You will enter a monastery and escape the corruption of the world? Perhaps in your time as a journalist you have not noticed the self-interest of politicians?"

"Don't be ridiculous." Ramsey lit his pipe.

"The woman who has the dreams, how is she? You have not spoken of her. Is she the one who beat your head?"

"I haven't seen Mrs. Maynard lately," he said, gently touching his scalp. "This happened when we were out on Decatur Road."

"You fell from your horse?"

"Something like that."

Ramsey puffed his pipe in silence. Rabun counted bottles and made notes with a stub of a pencil.

"Rabun, why would you hang a dying man?"

"I would never do such a thing."

"Okay, but someone did. Why would anyone bother?"

Rabun poured himself some coffee.

"Perhaps death itself was not the point. Perhaps, it was the manner of death. Death is a sentence that hangs over us all. A man dies. So? Good men die. Bad men die. Even I, it is rumored, will one day die. But though our end is certain, we hope for a decent death. We do not long to hang degraded from a tree, laughed at by our enemies. Hate. Hate makes a man hang one who is dying. When one hates, then any trouble is worth the bother."

"If what Johnny Bass says is true, there are quite a few who felt that way about Hackett. I wonder who hated him enough to act on those feelings. Sprague and I saw signs of four men and a wagon, which means a group of some sort. Yet the only members of the original gang that might still be alive are Turney and Mason. It's hard to see them doing it even if they got help. I saw Turney. He didn't look like he'd have the fire in the belly to take on a man like Hackett. We haven't seen Mason so far, but Bass described him as 'muscle that would do what it was told.' That doesn't sound like the makings of an avenging angel."

Ramsey drained his glass and stood to go. "You know, none of this matters now, at least not to me. I'm out of it. It's someone else's problem." He dropped his pipe into his pocket and placed some coins on the bar. "See you later."

"Goodbye, *mon capitaine*. May God watch over you." With his free hand, Rabun made a sign to ward off the Evil One.

The afternoon sun glowed on the wall across the room. Voices, horses, and the huffing of a departing train rose from the street. Perhaps the screech of its whistle had awakened him.

Ramsey rubbed the sleep from his eyes. The stubble on his chin scratched his hand. He swung himself to the edge of the bed, gently touched the bruise along his scalp, and rose to begin what was left of the day. A gulp of water eased his stale mouth. He refilled the glass and drank again, deeply, gratefully. His derelict image looked back from the mirror with puffy red eyes and dirty hair. The bruise was larger now and presented a palette of deepening purples mixed with sickly yellows.

He pulled the rubberized mat from behind the wash basin and unrolled it. Standing in the center of the mat, he sponged away the road dirt and sweat. The cold water was bracing, and his skin glowed as he dried off. The shave that followed considerably improved his appearance. Brushing his teeth with a liberal mound of Dr. Maxwell's World-Renowned Tooth Powder improved matters further, though he wondered how much of the world was aware of the good doctor's product.

He descended the stairs into a quiet house and saw Elijah washing windows, his head making a slight circular motion that mimicked the movement of his hand. In the kitchen, Mrs. Carraway and Katie prepared the evening meal. The landlady stood over a large bowl, kneading dough. The muscles in her forearms rippling with each push.

"Well, well. Good afternoon, Captain Ramsey," she said.

"Good afternoon, Mrs. Carraway. I appear to have missed breakfast."

"By more than a little. You've missed most of your meals lately. You should take better care of yourself. Nothing good can come from running about in the night the way you do."

She frowned. "Wasn't that terrible about the hanging? I don't know what the world is coming to. Murders, hangings, stealing—respectable folks just ... well. .. it's just terrible that's all."

"Times are difficult."

"It makes us wonder what is to happen next."

"I don't suppose I could have something to eat?"

Mrs. Carraway's hands continued their steady rhythm. "There's not much. Help yourself to some bread. Katie, get Captain Ramsey a slice or two of ham from the sideboard. I've made some tea, and you can have a cup if you like. I find I can't get through the afternoon without my tea."

"Thanks."

"Just eat here in the kitchen so the others won't see."

Katie set a plate with ham slices in front of him. He cut some bread, buttered it, and wrapped it around a piece of ham. A cup of tea arrived, and the two women let him eat in silence while they worked.

When he leaned back from his plate, Mrs. Carraway said, "Katie, go see if you can help Elijah finish those windows. That man's going to take till Christmas at the rate he's going. I'll finish up here. Just be back in time to serve at table."

Katie left them.

"What is going on with these murders?" Mrs. Carraway asked.

"I wish I knew."

"Mrs. Alston says they're the beginning of an insurrection."

"What?"

"Oh, not that I believe her. Mrs. Alston is, well, one hates to be uncharitable, but she's sometimes rather excitable."

"I wouldn't worry. As you say, Mrs. Alston is not reliable. Did she tell you where she had heard such things?"

"She told me it was a secret and I shouldn't tell anyone, but the way she gossips, I suppose my promise doesn't count for much. Her husband, Jabez, has been to some night meetings. Jabez told her the freedmen were going to rise up and take away all the property of the white folks and murder us. He said the Army would stand aside and let it happen. They'd protect the colored folk if we tried to fight back."

"Jabez Alston is a foolish man. Did Mrs. Alston say where these meetings take place?"

"She didn't. I don't suppose she knows."

"Well, there are enough angry men to make such meetings possible, but rest assured, Mrs. Carraway, nearly everything that's known about the murders has been printed in the newspaper. The murdered men were nothing more than criminals. We don't know the full story yet, but none of this is part of an insurrection."

"I'm sure you're right. It's just that no one could have imagined all that's happened lately. It seems as if we're being tried by God for our sins."

"The times are difficult, but you have nothing to fear from the freedmen. They are trying to figure out this strange new world just as we are. And I assure you, the Army, which is both well-organized and well-armed, would never stand by while the white population is pillaged."

"But the Negro troops. I doubt they'd restrain their brethren."

"The black units fought effectively in the war and are well-disciplined. They will do precisely as they are ordered, just as all good soldiers do."

The landlady finished with the dough, rolled it into a ball, and slapped it into a bowl. "I hope you're right, Captain, I certainly hope you're right."

Back in his room, Ramsey settled into an armchair. Steele was right. Time for a rest. He should seize this opportunity; Whitaker wouldn't pay him for nothing for very long. Perhaps, now would be a good time to start the book an Army friend had sent him. He found it under some papers and looked at the spine. *Woman in White* by some fellow named Collins. It didn't sound promising. He opened the book. It was almost dark when a knock woke him.

"You in there, Mr. Allan?" said Mr. Henry.

"Just a minute." Ramsey opened the door.

"Evenin', Mr. Allan. Mind if I come in?"

The old man entered and sat primly on the edge of a chair. "I did what you asked, Mr. Allan. Been down with the folks in the Triangle."

"Did they tell you anything?"

The old man shook his head. "Naw. Probably don't know much, and besides, they scared. But they give me this. None of 'em can read, so they ain't got no use for it." He held out a battered dime novel. Ramsey glanced through the pages before tossing it onto his desk.

"Thanks, Mr. Henry. Sorry I wasted your time."

"Weren't no trouble. Gideon's there most days, an' the early vegetable crop ain't in yet. Jist waitin' on that. Was one more thing. That ol' man, Papa Squirrel, is missin'. Been gone since the day they found the first dead man. The one on the tracks."

"Papa Squirrel?"

"You know, that skinny fella, real dark skin, drunk all the time? Got him a little hole in the ground he sleeps in. Passed out on the tracks a while back and got arrested. Real lucky he didn't get himself run down. He's been gone for some while. Folks said he'd been drinking down near the trains. It's kinda strange, though. He left all his junk behind."

"I don't see how that matters to anyone but him."

"Well, I don't neither. But he's never been gone before, an' he's gone now."

"Where is this *hole* of his?"

"It's up on a hill 'bout a half mile from the Triangle. Cain't take you there myself, but I'll send someone to show the way if you want. You jist tell me when. I got to go back to Gideon now."

The old man slipped out the door, and Ramsey thumbed through the dime novel. It was wretchedly written and poorly printed. A dirty, dog-eared, unremarkable little book—except for the word COVINGTON printed in crude letters at the top of page thirty-four.

The clock in the hallway struck the half hour. Ramsey looked up from his writing and checked his pocket watch. After midnight. His back was stiff and his hand ached. He had written himself empty. Yawning, he reached for his pipe, lit it, and then pushed his chair onto its back legs.

His mind turned to the cipher he'd brought to Sanbourne, the one concocted as a test.

For there is nothing either good or bad, but thinking makes it so.

Sanbourne had chosen another quote in his response to Ramsey. Perhaps it was a little joke, or maybe he didn't agree with what the Bard had written.

. . . Thinking makes it so.

Was that true? Granted, many things, and certainly most people, could be judged good or bad depending on circumstances. Georgiana used her influence against Rafe Jenkins. Was that good or bad? The means used were questionable, but the outcome was probably best for everyone except Jenkins. A city will have its vices, and it was best if sensible people like Georgiana administered to them. Still, it wasn't a high-water mark in civic history.

But true evil did exist. Beyond self-interest and cheating; beyond lying, whoring, and stealing; beyond all the sordid things people do day after day, there is true evil. A fetid corruption seeped into the hearts of a few lost souls and perverted all that was in them. Was that true of Tully and Hackett? Was there a point when they went beyond brutish greed and became genuinely evil? Such men did great harm in their time on this earth. How much more might they have done if they had not been killed? O'Bannion was weak and lazy; one could see it on his face even in death. He was a man who would steal what he would not work for. A worthless man but not an evil one. Tully and Hackett were different. They fed on the pain they inflicted, nourishing their twisted spirits with the fear of others. The hand that killed them had been a benefactor to mankind.

He reached for his whiskey and poured the last of it into his glass.

Abigail Maynard? Who was she? What did he really know about her? She'd come to him asking for help, but when he was with her, she hardly seemed to need him at all. Was she telling him the truth about her situation? Perhaps, but she certainly wasn't an open book. She didn't tell him her sister was a twin. Why would she? Why wouldn't she? And what of her claim that he'd sent Mr. Henry to her? He'd forgotten to ask the old man about that. Why did Hackett and Turney run away when they saw her in the newspaper office? Most likely, they had seen her sister at some point and mistaken the two women. But why would that frighten them? What did they know about Susan? Was Abigail Maynard really a Bostonian war widow? Or could she be Susan Knowles pretending to be Abigail Maynard? He sipped his whiskey and tried to clear his mind.

His thoughts turned to the Coldwaters, father and son. Their motives seemed clear enough: they wanted Charlton. They had wanted it for a long time. So what were they prepared to do to get it? Denton denied a friendship with Franklin Knowles, but Sheriff Powell said differently, and Sheriff Powell was the more reliable man. Perhaps Denton killed Franklin Knowles only to have an unforeseen brother show up to take possession of the land. And what better time to get rid of Alfred Knowles and his wife than in the middle of a war? Blame their deaths on the slaves or on the Yankees. It didn't matter. But if the Coldwaters killed Alfred and Susan, they'd leave the bodies to be found. They were many things, but they weren't stupid. No one would connect them with the crime, and the certainty of Knowles's death would make the purchase of Charlton possible. Surely fate would not produce yet another heir who wouldn't sell. As it stood now, precisely nothing could be done.

And what of Munford's tale? Granted, parts were nonsensical. The slaves didn't kill each other at the bottom of the cellar stairs. They had been shot by someone. But by whom? And then there was the question of the Confederate dead. Who killed them? Why were they buried and for what reason? If they'd been ambushed by a Union detachment, they would have been left where they lay. Ramsey had seen many things during the war, but he never saw a cavalry unit so scrupulously tidy it buried the dead as it fought. Had Susan and Alfred done so out of Christian kindness before some unknown fate overtook them too? If so, it must have happened earlier in the day, but Susan had seen Munford that morning. Surely she would have mentioned such a thing. Another question popped into his mind. How had the Coldwaters gotten Abby's name and address? A mistake not to have asked them during the meeting.

A few drops of whiskey puddled in the bottom of the glass. He poured them on his tongue. The taste of liquor and pipe smoke reminded him of nights he'd spent with Grenville Dodge during the war, poring over maps, talking with scouts, and questioning prisoners. They'd gleaned slivers of information from a hundred different sources. They'd spend hours weighing and evaluating these threads until they'd woven a tapestry of probable fact. Ramsey reveled in the moments when the pieces came together, when they pointed the way. He and Dodge would then go to headquarters with what they'd found.

Sherman could be impossible, bombarding them with questions, suppositions, and facts of his own. He would listen in the end, but it was exhausting. Grant would simply sit, his intense blue eyes attentive, waiting as everything unfolded. Finally, he would ask a few questions. Simple questions that lay bare the possibilities in the data. Sherman challenged, demanded. Grant engaged those around him in a mutual search. When everyone had their say, Grant would offer his thanks and turn back to his work. Later, puffing on an ever-present cigar and absentmindedly whittling a stick into nothingness, he would make his decision—alone. In that loneliness he bore the weight of an Army—and in time, the fate of a nation.

Grant stands before him now, his eyes searching the reporter's face. What, he wants to know, is going to be done? Three men are dead, and the present state of affairs is unacceptable. You must act soon, or the situation will get out of hand.

The general isn't given to anger, but Ramsey senses his displeasure.

The enemy holds the advantage, sir. I cannot anticipate him, nor can I see my way clearly through the contradictions and vagaries that surround this matter.

It's true, Grant replies, that things have not gone well thus far, but this fight is a campaign, not a skirmish. One day does not make or break a campaign. Hooker would have been in Richmond before I got to Vicksburg if he'd understood that. The general stops to light the stump of the cigar between his lips. And what of Mrs. Maynard? he asks. You have a responsibility toward the wife of a fellow soldier. I knew John Maynard. He was a good man.

The question hurts Ramsey. I've done what I can. I don't have the resources to do anything more.

Grant takes the cigar from his lips. You must do more! You will never have all the resources you think necessary! You must find a way. Use what you've got. The issue of the day is still in doubt, but there are others who will share the burdens. Use them. Trust them. The general holds something in his hands. You'll need this. I think you were once very fond of it. There is still danger, so I give it to you. A Spencer Carbine.

Ramsey reaches for the gun . . .

Ramsey's pipe clattered on the floor. He sat befuddled, caught between dream and reality, and felt a pang of loss when the carbine wasn't there. He'd carried it through the Atlanta Campaign. It had disappeared when he'd been ambushed.

He bent to recover his pipe, relieved to see it hadn't broken in the fall.

Sprague looked up from his newspaper when Ramsey entered the office.

"What you reckon is gonna happen in Washington?" he asked. "Can Congress actually throw out what the president's done? Folks down here ain't gonna like that." He folded the paper in half and flipped it on the table.

"If the Radical Republicans have the votes in Congress, they can. They'll pass whatever they want, and if President

Johnson can't make his veto stick, then that will be the law of the land."

"Seems like you Yankees was damn hot to win the war. Why didn't nobody think what came next?"

"You didn't ask me here to discuss politics."

"Nope. I hear you're off the case too. Henderson, that asshole, is hangin' around." The deputy shook his head. "Ain't we a sight. Whit Anderson told us we had to go, and *bang*! We went." Sprague made a soaring movement with his hand.

"That's about the size of it."

"You found out any more?" the deputy asked. "I know ya still have your eyes open."

Ramsey took the dime novel out of his coat pocket and pointed to the word COVINGTON.

"Mr. Henry brought it back from the Triangle. It must have belonged to O'Bannion, since it has the code word. You could offer it to Lanier as a gesture of goodwill."

"Mr. Henry come up with anythin' else?"

"He said an old drunk they call Papa Squirrel disappeared the day Tully was killed. He thinks we should check into it."

"Has that ol' darky gone crazy or he just bein' funny. Ain't nobody gonna look for an ol' drunk who's probably dead in a ditch somewheres. I'll take that as a no, you ain't got nothin' else."

Sprague pulled a mahogany box, eight inches long and three inches wide, from his pocket and set it on the table.

"Don't go telling nobody you got it from me, but when they checked out the things we found at Decatur Road, this turned up."

Ramsey carefully examined the exterior before opening the box. Inside were the tools of the lock breaker's trade: picks, tensioning tools, skeleton keys, and tiny files. They were laid out neatly and separated by green felt.

"It must belong to Turney," Ramsey said. "According to Bass, the others called him Turnkey. Guess we know why. What else did you find?"

"Couple a decks of marked cards. And this." He picked up a cloth bundle that lay next to his chair. He unrolled the cloth and a handgun appeared: a battered Colt Navy revolver. "Doesn't mean much. We knew they was armed."

"Does Willis know you're showing me this stuff?"

"What the hell do you think? But you was out there with me, an' I figured I owed you somethin'."

"These things don't tell us any more than O'Bannion's dime novel, but thanks."

"Yeah, we knew they had guns, an' we knew they was thieves."

Sprague spit, hit the spittoon by his desk, and folded his arms across his chest. He looked hard at Ramsey. "Maybe we was too busy chasing down clues to look hard at what's really goin' on. Whit sure thinks that's where we got lost."

"What do you mean?"

"Takes a lot to cause all these murders, am I right? What would cause a man to kill? Huh? Money comes to mind. Some greedy bastards'll do 'bout anything for money. Revenge might too. Maybe them fellas come here to kill somebody and got the worst of it. Thought they'd get him, and he got them. Huh?"

Sprague shook his head in disagreement with his own idea.

"Don't think so, though. One man out for revenge, maybe two, okay, but I can't see everybody in the whole damn gang so pissed off they need to show up in our fair city."

Sprague carefully put away the wooden box. "'Course, it might be a woman. Men fight over women. Always have."

"What?"

"A woman."

Ramsey frowned. "What the hell are you talking about? Ed, there is no woman."

"That ain't what Willis thinks. He talked to Duncan and he hears about Hackett and Turney and how them bastards run off when the Maynard woman walked into the room." Sprague held his hand up to quell Ramsey's protest. "I wasn't there, and I don't know. But Duncan musta told a pretty good tale, 'cause Lanier's got a real bee in his bonnet about the Maynard woman. Says she's what we missed."

"That's idiotic." Ramsey's voice hardened. "I've met her. He hasn't. He's wrong."

"Yeah, well hold on. Why did them fellas run off when they saw her? That's what they done, huh? Was Duncan right or wrong? You ever run from somebody you never seen before?"

"Christ, Ed, something spooked them." Ramsey shrugged. "I guess they did run away after she came down the stairs, but they just sensed something was wrong. You know, we damn near got them that day. If you'd arrived a little quicker, we would have."

Sprague held his hands up. "Don't you go puttin' this on me."

"Okay, okay, but how could Mrs. Maynard be involved? She didn't come to Atlanta until after Tully was dead."

"Yeah, and ya know that—how?" Sprague leaned forward and cocked his head.

"Well, she—"

"She told you, right? That's how ya know. Claims she's a twin and what not, but how much do you know she ain't just told you? You took her tales at face value, even though she pops up just when the murders start. She might be slingin' enough bullshit for a whole pasture."

"You don't believe that nonsense, do you, Ed? Lanier's lost in the case. He's spinning fantasies about the Maynard woman and cooking up theories so everyone will think he's getting somewhere."

"Maybe he's right and maybe he's wrong. But I'll tell you what is true: three men are dead and we're down a shithole." Sprague paused and looked hard at Ramsey. "Can there be a link to that woman, Ramsey?"

"Ed, she's a war widow from Boston. She arrived in Atlanta after the murders started. Whatever caused Tully and the rest to come back to Atlanta happened during the war, and it happened while she was a thousand miles away. She has nothing to do with it. And I believe she does have a twin sister—a twin sister who, with her husband, was running a school. That is absolutely plausible. None of this has anything to do with either woman. Hackett and Turney were edgy before she came down the stairs. On my orders, Duncan wasn't coming back with the newspapers. I was keeping them there, waiting for you. They sensed a trap."

"Lanier and Anderson like the idea about the Maynard woman."

"Lanier and Anderson are idiots. Do you really think one lone woman killed three men—trained soldiers—who for all their many, many faults knew how to defend themselves? And then, just to further impress the world, she found a way to lynch one of them in the middle of the night? It's utterly ridiculous."

"Nobody says she done it alone. Lanier and Anderson think she might be here with a gang of her own."

"What?" Ramsey said in disbelief. "The one she keeps hidden over at Mrs. Hoehling's boarding house?"

"Okay, maybe it don't make a hell of a lotta sense to me neither. But I'm tellin' ya what I know. An' there's more."

"What?" Ramsey said angrily.

"They think you was in Atlanta at the same time as Tully an' them others. The wolf is always just a little bit ahead of the law, right? Like he knows things as soon as we know 'em. They hear about you and her running off to Decatur all sweet an' happy and meetin' with Munford and Denton—can't deny you didn't—and it makes 'em wonder 'bout *both* of you."

"A hundred thousand Yankees came to Atlanta with me. As I remember it, we fought our way in."

"Yeah, but there's only one of them soldiers running around with the Maynard woman. Lanier may wanna check out everyone in Sherman's Army, but he's gonna start with you."

Sprague gathered up the novel and the gun, putting them in his desk next to the cracksman's tools. "If you're listening, Ramsey, what I'm sayin' is Lanier's watchin' you."

"He's barking mad!"

"Could be. Maybe there's nothin' to any of it. But if you're listenin' to me, what I'm sayin' is don't get stupid. Maybe she's playing you for a fool, boy. You ever hear of a woman lying?"

Ramsey walked angrily back to his room.

Was Sprague told to deliver the message that if all else failed, the city's leaders were willing to go far afield to "solve" the case? So how did things stand in light of this warning? Ramsey still had confidence in Sprague, but the deputy had slipped far down the greased pole of civic trust. Whitaker and Steele would only protect him to a point, and that point wasn't far off. Anderson and Lanier were openly hostile. Who knew where the Army stood in the matter. Ramsey was an outsider— a useful tool, but nothing more. Tools can be disposed of.

Yet, why would Lanier go down such a crazy path? Wasn't there a more obvious way? Turney must be around somewhere. Maybe Mason was too. If Lanier could lay his hands on them, the murders would be declared solved. Evidence could be found, a jury convinced. They were friendless men with criminal pasts. The case might be implausible—clearly more than one or two must be involved—but that wouldn't matter. This mess would be put to rest. At the end of the day, that was all any of them wanted.

Raindrops ticked softly against the window. The meandering rivulets traced erratic paths down the pane. Some lingered, some raced ahead. Some stopped moving until another raindrop joined and swelled it. Sometimes a drop would follow one of its predecessors for a time before it ran off on a tangent of its own as differences in wind strength or surface tension came into play. Was there a pattern in this apparent randomness? Maybe the drops, like people, became individuals with age, refined by the forces of the world.

Ramsey withdrew *Peterson's Sermons and Meditations* from the shelf. Whatever solace the reverend's book offered him lay in the $87 hidden in the hollowed center. He withdrew $20 and put it in his wallet. Perhaps he might try his luck in a poker game.

He lit his pipe and pulled a chair over to the window. Below in the street, two men, their hats pulled low, strode through the storm. Their boots left tracks in the mud that the rain erased. A buggy splashed by. Across the street, a man in a dark coat leaned idly against a building. Strange. Even sheltered by the eave, he couldn't be comfortable. A wagon loaded with barrels lumbered by. The driver cracked his whip, forcing his team up the muddy street. When the wagon passed, the dark-coated figure was gone.

Ramsey resumed work on an article for *The Atlantic*. An hour passed, perhaps two, before there was a knock on his inside door.

"Yes."

Elijah placed an envelope on the table. "Message, Cap'n Ramsey."

He opened it.

> *Dear Allan,*
>
> *I want to thank you once again for your friendship and for all you have done to aid me in my search for my sister. I will be leaving Atlanta soon and would like to see you before I go. Perhaps we could have lunch tomorrow at the Atlanta Hotel? If this is not convenient, please name another time and place that is satisfactory.*
>
> *With warmest regards,*
> *Abby*

So she was leaving Atlanta. When they'd met, he'd urged her to return to Boston; now that she might do so, he did not want her to go. She was making the right decision, of course, so why did it matter to him? He thought back on the little time they'd spent together. She was so strong during the interviews, first with Sheriff Powell and then with the Coldwaters. What had prompted her to leave now? Had something toppled her hopes?

Susan Knowles. She was a high-spirited woman who knew her own mind. That was clear enough. She'd won the respect of her neighbors, though they disliked her beliefs. Even Munford Coldwater said as much. Such a person would not simply run off. Her silence must mean she was dead. Susan and Alfred must both be dead. But if they'd died that day at Charlton, wouldn't they have been left where they fell, just as the slaves had been?

The rain stopped. Ramsey's watch read half past two. He scribbled a quick note to Abby, requesting she postpone their luncheon. She knew nothing of Lanier's bizarre thinking or

Sprague's warning, but under the circumstances, a meeting was a very bad idea.

He slipped the note into an envelope and went downstairs in search of the latest copy of the *Intelligencer*. He found one laying on the hall table.

He was relieved by what he read—a largely accurate description of the discovery of the hanged man. The writing was straightforward, even restrained; matters were sensational enough on their own. It was Steele's work. The deft touch was beyond the scope of Henderson's hand. The public was informed Deputy Marshal Willis Lanier now headed the investigation. Glowing praise was bestowed on Deputy Marshal Ed Sprague for his previous efforts—efforts that produced, the city was assured, considerable progress. The Army's interest in the case met with the writer's approval. Quotes from Mayor Williams and Marshal Anderson offered a promise of vigorous action. No mention was made of the events on Decatur Road.

Ramsey sipped whiskey in The Isle of Capri while thumbing idly through a copy of *Leslie's Illustrated*. Chatsworth White slid a chair back from the table and sat down.

"I just thought you should know, your lady friend, Mrs. Palmerstan, took the train south this morning."

"Thanks, Whitey. Any problems?"

"No. Everything went smooth as can be." Whitey hesitated a second and then said, "Ramsey, I thought you should know, she paid my sister twice over what we agreed. That money's gonna save them. When my sister opened the envelope Mrs. Palmerstan left for her, she just sat down and cried. Your friend is a saint, Ramsey, a woman with Jesus in her heart."

"I've not heard that said before, but she does often surprise. I'm glad she is safely on her way."

Jasper Dunlap came over. "No chess game this evening?"

"I begged off," Ramsey said. "Just wasn't up for it."

"Not a wise move, my boy. You lose a game and then refuse to play. It suggests you fear your opponent. Rabun's ego is likely to explode and engulf us all."

"You're not with General Gordon tonight. No falling out, I hope."

"Sadly," Jasper said, "things are no longer on a good footing. The general's gone to Savannah and won't be back for at least a week. And I am compelled to add that we have severed our connection. Jed Varger nosed in and provided something I was unable to."

Ramsey smiled. "Like a well-healed backer for the sawmill venture?"

"Precisely."

"Well, Jasper, you'll always have poker."

The pudgy gambler smiled. "Poker—an unchanging verity in an unstable world."

"I thought that was chess."

"Don't be silly, my boy."

Jasper held up his glass. "Rabun! Another round if you please!"

Rabun Perdido strolled over with a bottle. Carefully filling Jasper's glass, he looked questioningly at Whitey's empty one. Whitey shook his head no. Rabun ignored Ramsey.

"I'd reconsider the chess, Allan," said Jasper.

"Do you have a card game tonight?" Ramsey asked.

"Just a frolic to pay the bills. There's a chair open if you want it."

"Thanks, Jasper, not tonight. Good luck." Despite his earlier thoughts of playing, he couldn't summon the will.

Jasper raised his glass. "Same to you, my boy."

Rabun's deafening silence gave him little reason to stay, so Ramsey left early. Dusk had just turned into night. Lamps glowed in the windows, and those people still out and about were hurrying home. Someone he didn't recognize waved to him. He returned the gesture. A slight movement in the alley across the street caught his eye. Ramsey watched for a few moments but saw nothing more. He stepped off onto the damp ground and checked his footing. It would be solid enough if he stayed close to the building.

"Hands up!" a voice growled in his ear. He felt a gun barrel ram into his back. An unseen hand dragged him into an alley. He tried to turn toward his attacker, but the gun jammed harder against his spine.

"Don't try it!"

A hand patted his sides. It found no weapon. The pressure of the gun at his back eased slightly. Would it be a beating? Probably. If the attacker wanted to kill him, he'd be dead.

The assailant slammed Ramsey against a building wall and pinned him with his weight. Peeling paint crumbled against Ramsey's cheek as his head was forced sideways. The toe of a muddy boot appeared next to his foot. The gun barrel was now cold and hard behind his ear.

"Stay away from the Maynard woman. You got it! Next time I have to tell you, I ain't gonna be so friendly. Understand?"

Ramsey gasped. "I understand."

"Louder, you son of a bitch!"

"I'll leave her alone!"

"You do that. And you remember me. I'll be watching."

The gun pulled away from Ramsey's neck. The man turned to run. Ramsey slammed his heel down hard on the toe of the man's boot. The attacker fell heavily to the ground.

If the man had been a professional, he would have rolled and come up firing. Instead he tried to push himself up where he had fallen. Ramsey's kick caught him squarely in the face. With a cry, the man grabbed his nose. His gun fell to the ground. Ramsey seized his attacker's coat and slammed him backward into the wall on the other side of the alley. His head hit the bricks with a dull thud. His knees went slack. Ramsey shoved his derringer under the dazed man's chin, forcing his head back.

"Isn't much of a gun, but I can't miss from here, now can I?"

The man's eyes bulged wild with fear. His Adam's apple bobbed convulsively. Blood from his broken nose streamed down his lips and chin.

"Please, mister, I got a family," he panted.

"Congratulations."

"Please . . ."

Ramsey knew such men—weak, brutal, and ineffectual. He drew back the hammer on the derringer. A metallic click rang out. A flatulent rumble preceded a rising stench. The man went limp and began to sob.

"Who sent you?" Ramsey's voice was flat and controlled.

The sobbing continued.

"If you're not going to talk, you're going to die."

"Coldwater. Denton Coldwater. Please—"

"What did he tell you to do? Kill me?"

"No!"

Blood flew from the man's lips and spattered on Ramsey's face. He remembered the movement in the alley when he'd left The Isle of Capri.

"Are you working with someone?"

"No."

"How did you know where to wait for me?"

"Followed you. Knew which way you went. Knew you'd come by."

"Why doesn't Denton want me around the Maynard woman?"

"I don't know. Please, mister—"

"I'll mention you to Denton. Now it's time we said goodbye."

Ramsey pressed the derringer hard against the man's chin. The man stiffened against the shot he knew would kill him. Ramsey snapped the gun back and fired into the air an inch from his attacker's head. The man dropped in a dead faint.

Ramsey picked up his assailant's handgun and walked out to the street. In the distance, the silhouette of two men appeared. One pointed in his direction. He took out his handkerchief, wiped the assailant's blood off his face, and walked back to his room. It didn't matter who found the man in the alley. The fool would have nothing to say.

Ramsey wearily opened the door and lit the lamp. The mirror told him the encounter with Denton's thug was messier than he'd thought. His coat would clean up, but his shirt was likely to stain. Ramsey washed himself carefully, scrubbing long after any trace of the man in the alley was gone. He put the bloody shirt in the cold water to soak, then pulled on a fresh one and poured himself a whiskey. He examined his attacker's gun, a standard-issue Army Colt .44. Like its former owner, it was a battered, pathetic thing. Part of the handle was broken, and it badly needed cleaning.

Thousands of such guns were around. Like the men who once carried them, they had been released from the war without ceremony. And his attacker? Some ex-soldier without prospects, most likely. A fool who thought he could make a way for himself with a gun. Ramsey checked the cylinder. Only two chambers were loaded, and they were on the wrong side of the hammer. The man was incompetent in every way possible. Perhaps when he returned to consciousness, covered in his own blood and excrement, he'd consider a new line of work.

"Well," said Al Bates, "look what the cat dragged in."

"That will be enough, Bates," snapped Willis Lanier. "Wait outside."

Bates shuffled out of the marshal's office.

"Good evening, Captain." Willis Lanier gave a deferential nod to Ramsey. "Glad you could come by." He just missed being civil.

"What do you want, Willis?"

"Ah well, I suppose it saves time to dispense with pleasantries. I asked you here so I wouldn't embarrass Mrs. Carraway with a police visit."

Ramsey said nothing.

"You needn't thank me."

"We have nothing to say to each other," Ramsey said. "Ed has told you everything I know."

"Deputy Sprague has been helpful—that's true—but no one remembers every odd detail. I'd just like us to have a little chat."

"I don't have anything to add."

"I'll be the judge of that," Lanier said. "What is the nature of your relationship with Mrs. Maynard?"

"That's no concern of yours."

"Are you working for her?" Lanier cocked a quizzical eye at Ramsey.

"No. She wanted me to help her find her sister and brother-in-law, which I declined to do."

"And yet you escort her rather frequently."

"No, Willis," Ramsey said, exasperation rising in his voice. "We've met twice, not 'frequently.' I escorted her to Decatur to see Sheriff Powell. Later she asked me to accompany her to a meeting with Munford and Denton Coldwater. Both times concerned the whereabouts of her sister, Susan Knowles."

"But the two of you are on good terms."

"I hope so."

"Well, since you're her friend," Willis Lanier smiled, "I want you to give her some friendly advice. Would you do that for me? Ask her to stay in town for a few more days. She intends to leave, and I'd prefer that she didn't."

"I think that's your job. I'm not your errand boy. Mrs. Maynard can do as she pleases. She has no—"

"Stop! You're going to tell me she's guilty of no crime. Then you're going to tell me I have no right to keep her if she wants to go. You'd be right about the last part. I have no legal footing at present. I am merely asking that you pass on my request—and that's all it is."

"Then ask her yourself."

"I have, but I'm not sure she was listening to me any more than you are. Look, Ramsey, we have a complicated situation, and it would be wise—very wise—if the police got as much help as possible from everyone involved."

"She has nothing to do with the murders."

"Perhaps not," Lanier agreed. "But we think she might be able to illuminate a dark corner or two. We have some questions, but now isn't the time to ask them. We're waiting on further information, so I want her to stay in Atlanta."

"Willis, she is looking for her sister. You're wasting your time with her."

"I'll be the judge of how to spend my time. I want the Maynard woman to stay in Atlanta a little longer. I want you to ask her to do so because she might listen to you. Is that so difficult?"

"Willis, this is—"

"Just do it!" Lanier snapped.

An awkward silence followed as Lanier fought for composure.

"Are we finished," Ramsey asked.

"No. I ask you one last time. Do you know anything about these murders that you haven't told Deputy Sprague or Mr. Steele?"

"Well, maybe there is one thing."

"Yes?"

"Mr. Henry told me an old drunk named Papa Squirrel disappeared the same night Tully was killed. I didn't have time to look into it. I suppose you'll have to."

"Damn you! Don't mock me!" Lanier took a deep breath to calm himself. "Ramsey, help me keep the Maynard woman in town. That's all I'm asking. And just to show you how nice I can be, I'll give you a little news."

"What?"

"Mrs. Maynard's room was burgled."

"Is she all right?"

"It seems so. Earlier today she left her lodgings. While she was away, letters and jewelry were taken. I've interviewed her and will do all I can but . . ." Lanier shrugged.

"I heard you were robbed." Ramsey said when Abby came down from her room to meet him.

"I was a fool. This morning I received a note asking me to meet you at your boarding house. The note seemed genuine and gave your address, so I went. You weren't there, but Mrs. Carraway was very kind to me while I waited. I stayed for a while and then came back here. It was obvious that someone had rifled through my belongings while I was away." Her voice broke, "my letters from Susan were gone."

"I am so sorry."

She forced back her tears. "I sent for the police. A man named Lanier tried to pacify me. He gave me some meaningless assurances and asked me to stay in Atlanta while they searched for the letters. When I didn't agree to do so, he changed his story and said my presence was necessary in a matter that he wasn't at liberty to discuss. What is he talking about?"

"Lanier summoned me to his office a short while ago and wanted me to convince you to stay. He has some questions to put to you about the recent murders and wants you to remain in Atlanta until that can be arranged."

"That's ridiculous! None of that has anything to do with me."

"Of course not, but remember the day you visited me at the newspaper? There were two men looking for a back issue. They ran out the door when you came down the stairs. One of those men was the latest victim. Someone at the newspaper told the police the men recognized you when you entered the room. Lanier thinks you might be the reason they ran away and therefore that you are somehow involved."

"That's foolish beyond imagining."

"On their better days, the police would probably agree, but unfortunately they aren't having many good days lately. They're grasping at straws."

She frowned. "Have they been watching me?"

Ramsey raised his eyebrows. "Why would you think that?"

"Oh, I've seen odd things. Nothing much out of the ordinary, but sometimes there's a man outside. He seems to be watching the house. It could just be my imagination, but I think not. I've caught just a glimpse of him a time or two. Could it be the police?"

"I doubt it. The last time I spoke with Deputy Sprague, he didn't mention surveillance."

She thought for a moment. "Do you think the police took my letters?"

"No, they wouldn't resort to a break-in; they could easily get a warrant."

"Then who would want them?"

"Perhaps the Coldwaters?" he wondered.

"Why do you think that?" She seemed more curious than surprised.

"I was attacked in the street yesterday evening by someone Denton hired. I was warned to stay away from you."

"My God, Allan! Are you all right?"

"The other man had the worst of it."

"I'm so sorry. Why would Denton do such a thing?"

"Well," said Ramsey, "aside from his dislike of me, he wants your sister's land. We shouldn't jump to conclusions, but not long after our meeting with him and his father, I was accosted. Then you were robbed. My guess is that he wants to isolate and intimidate you. If Denton doubts that Susan is alive, he'd assume he'll be dealing with you for the land. Maybe he thought the letters would reveal something useful to him."

"I hardly think so. Susan and Alfred had no wish to sell. They were struggling, but they planned to reopen the school. Franklin left an inheritance that was enough to see them through."

"What about the jewelry that was taken?"

"Just pieces of no consequence. The ones that are important to me I wear each day." She held out her hand to show a ring and gestured toward a pendant.

"Well, I hate agreeing with Lanier, but if the Coldwaters are up to something, it might be best if you stayed in Atlanta a little longer. Perhaps we can find out what that something is."

"I don't know, Allan . . ." Abby shook her head as she spoke.

"If there are answers to be found concerning your sister," Ramsey continued, "they will be found in the events of two years ago. Munford Coldwater's story seemed to be straightforward, but you have to wonder what was left out. Some of what he said did not add up. Perhaps you could ask for another meeting. Say you're planning to leave town but would like to work out a preliminary understanding about the land."

"What is to be gained by that?"

"It's been my experience that people who hold secrets are influenced by the knowledge they withhold. When pressed they sometimes slip, revealing things related to what they conceal. Sometimes what they hide can be deduced. For instance, keep asking for details about the day Charlton burned. Look for inconsistencies. Abruptly present information—the theft of your letters—and gauge their reaction. Try to put them off balance and listen carefully. When a complex lie covers the truth, mistakes are inevitable."

Abby listened with her chin lowered, looking away from Ramsey. When he finished she stood thinking a moment longer, then nodded. "I'll do it. If there must be a second meeting, then so be it."

"Very good. I'll leave it to you to arrange things."

She gave a second nod of consent.

"And there's one other matter to consider," Ramsey continued. "Willis Lanier's desire to talk with you is, of course, pointless. Still, it would be a good idea if we aren't seen together, at least until the powers that be go sniffing in another direction. Should I need to meet with you in person, I'll find a way that doesn't attract attention. I'll communicate by courier. There's a boy I've come to rely on, and you may entrust your replies to him."

"If we must."

Before leaving, Ramsey looked at her carefully. She was strangely composed for a woman who had been robbed and told she was involved in a murder investigation.

"The Western and Atlantic, that's the worst of 'em. Then I guess the Georgia, though it's not nearly so bad. The other railroads are basically sound." The man from Biloxi stabbed the air with his fork to emphasize his point. "The track repairs are well underway. The problem is the condition of the rolling stock. It's poor on all the railroads. That's where the trouble is, but we'll fix things. In another year everything will be in tip-top shape." He looked earnestly across the table at Ramsey and lowered his voice. "Fact is, sir, a man can make a lot of money in railroads. Invest with care, mind you, but it's railroads where fortunes will be made. Used to be cotton, but that's over now. You need to own railroad stocks."

Ramsey's noncommittal grunt went unnoticed.

The man poured himself more coffee and swabbed his plate with a bit of biscuit. "I've got a little money in the game," he confided while chewing. "I put it in the Central of Georgia. I figure cotton will have to pass over those tracks if it's to be shipped out through the port of Savannah. The Central's got to turn a good profit. Don't see how it can go any other way."

Ramsey agreed that profitability was a marvelous thing and rose from the table. His fellow diner smiled happily, thinking of the wealth that would one day be his.

Coffee in hand, the previous day's *Intelligencer* under his arm, Ramsey climbed the stairs to his room. He glanced at *Peterson's Sermons*. He would not be investing in railroads in the immediate future.

He looked at the papers on his desk—the article for *The Atlantic* that was almost finished. Its title, at least for the moment, was IN SHERMAN'S WAKE. It chronicled the recovery of Atlanta and the problems of postwar life. With the war over, readers in the north had considerable interest in their former enemy.

Elijah entered with an envelope. "This just come, sir."

Ramsey opened it.

> *Allan,*
>
> *Denton Coldwater is in Savannah and will remain so for at least another day. I have made arrangements through his partner to meet him and his father upon his return.*
>
> *Abby*

So Denton preferred Savannah to Atlanta these days. Had he'd learned the fate of his henchman?

Ramsey picked up the newspaper. Nestled among the ads he saw: WALL COLLAPSES! TWO WORKMEN INJURED!

A work crew repairing a damaged building tried to use part of the existing structure. A masonry wall, weakened by fire and weather, collapsed. One man escaped with cuts and bruises but the other broke his leg.

NEW SMALLPOX CASES FEWEST IN THREE MONTHS.

The epidemic was slackening.

Reprinted stories from other newspapers around the nation followed. He ignored them. Then his eye caught THIEVES ATTEMPT BREAK-IN AT COTTON FACTOR'S OFFICE.

> *The offices of Howell & Coldwater were broken into last night. Mr. William Howell confirmed that the would-be thieves secured entrance into the building through the back door by defeating the lock. Whether*

anything of significance was taken cannot be determined, Mr. Howell tells us, until Mr. Denton Coldwater, his partner in the enterprise, returns from a business trip to Savannah.

What the hell was going on? He had been attacked, Abby's room had been robbed, and now apparently Denton Coldwater's offices had been rifled. That made little sense. Denton had arranged an attack on Ramsey. Maybe he'd had Abby's letters stolen. But he certainly wouldn't have robbed himself as well.

Ramsey checked the byline. Willie Isaacs had written the piece on the break-in.

Isaacs looked suspiciously at Ramsey through small gold spectacles that seemed an afterthought on his large round face.

"Yes, I wrote about the robbery at Howell and Coldwater," he said. "Is there a problem?" He readjusted his glasses as if to see Ramsey's reply.

"No, Willie. I was just curious about a few things."

"If you read my story, Allan, it told you all I know."

"Yes, but I have a few questions. You talked to Howell, right?"

"That is correct."

"Did Howell want to talk to you?"

"Can't say as he did. A little bird told me the police had been called to Howell and Coldwater. That same little bird said that someone got in through the back door. I went round to see about it. Howell admitted that the report was true, but he didn't know what the thieves were after. He said there wasn't any money taken."

"You wrote, 'defeated the lock,' so I assume the door wasn't broken in."

Willie Isaacs leaned back in his chair and made a little tent with his fingers.

"Allan, I know you go your own way around here. Can't say as I blame you. Henderson hasn't exactly been a friend, and some of the others don't like having a Yankee around. As for me, well, we're not best of friends but you know I've never crossed you. So before I answer any more questions, I'd appreciate you telling me what is going on?"

"Simple curiosity, Willie. I—"

"Nothing is simple about you, Allan. What's more, it's common knowledge you're in some kind of trouble. Since Henderson started working with Lanier, he's been putting it around that you're one step ahead of being arrested—or in his words, 'The police have you in their sights and a finger on the trigger.' He won't say what for, but he's close to Lanier, so there might be something in it."

"Willie, it's—"

Isaacs held up a hand. "We all know that Jack can stretch a point. Let's go back to my question. Why are you interested in this break-in?"

"You know I've written about the cotton factors and their dealings. Howell and Coldwater are cotton factors. I'm just curious, like I said."

"Ramsey, my mama didn't raise no stupid children. You're wasting my time. Besides, Steele said we weren't to talk to you. That's something I bet you didn't know. And what else you don't know is that he wants to be told if you come around asking questions."

"Willie, if you don't want to talk to me, that's fine. Go tell Steele you were a good little soldier and sent me packing."

"Hold on, don't get all tetchy. I said that's what Steele *told* us to do. I'll make up my own mind about what I'm *going* to do."

He folded his arms across his fleshy chest and looked squarely at Ramsey. "Maybe I'll tell you more about what happened at Howell and Coldwater and maybe I won't. We could cooperate. As reporters we might choose to share information."

Ramsey hesitated.

Isaacs picked up his hat. "Perhaps we should take a walk," he said. "Fresh air always stimulates the mind. Besides, I expect Steele back any minute."

They were on the street before Isaacs spoke again. "I'll give you this much right up front. There was something strange going on at Howell and Coldwater. And I'll tell you something else. William Howell didn't report the break-in to the police."

"Who did?"

"Day's started getting warm." Isaacs removed his hat and wiped his brow. "What's your interest in the matter? Why do you care what happens with these fine gentlemen?"

"Willie, I don't mean to play shy on you. I've had some dealings with Denton lately, and I was curious. There are others involved, so I need to be circumspect."

"Ah, the Maynard woman. She's not Atlanta's best-kept secret. Does Coldwater have anything to do with her or the murders?"

"You're making some awfully big jumps, Willie. Denton Coldwater just wants to buy some land from Mrs. Maynard."

Isaacs cocked his head. "That's it, is it?"

"That's it."

A skeptical frown passed over Isaacs's broad face. "Not helpful, Allan. You know something more or we wouldn't be talking."

The two men walked on in silence.

Finally, Ramsey said, "If I tell you something, will you keep this under your hat for a while?"

"I'll be the judge of what goes under my hat. I won't cause trouble if I don't have to."

"There was another break-in, only it didn't make the papers. Willis Lanier kept it quiet."

"What happened?" Isaacs betrayed only modest curiosity.

"Mrs. Maynard was lured from her room at the Hoehling boarding house. Some jewelry and letters were taken."

"How does that lead you to Howell and Coldwater?"

"Like I said, Denton Coldwater is trying to buy some land from Mrs. Maynard. The land is owned by her sister and brother-in-law, Alfred Knowles. They both disappeared back in '64. He seems to think Mrs. Maynard will have a legal claim on the land if they aren't found. I escorted her to a meeting with Denton and his father where all this was discussed."

"Why would Denton's desire to buy land have anything to do with a break-in at the boarding house or at Howell and Coldwater?" Isaacs asked.

"I don't know. There may be nothing in it, but two break-ins raise questions."

Willie Isaacs wiped his brow. "Might it just be thieves looking for valuables?" he asked. "Robbery is all too common these days, though Mrs. Hoehling's establishment is respectable."

"It could be lots of things, but now it's your turn. What else do you know about the break-in at Howell and Coldwater?"

"Well, like I said, I got word there had been a break-in, so I went over there and checked it out."

"If Howell didn't report it, who did?" Ramsey asked. "And how did you find out?"

"One of the clerks did, and the rest is my business. I can tell you Howell wasn't happy about the police getting involved.

He was even less happy when the press showed up. He tried to shoo me away. The intruders came in through the back door, the one in the alley. And just like I wrote, the lock was defeated—I think the current phrase is 'picked.' The clerk found the door ajar when he arrived for work. He'd checked it the evening before as part of his duties. Only he and the owners had keys. That entrance was rarely used. Howell told the police that nothing was taken, but when I asked him how he was so sure, he backed off and said that he wouldn't know until Denton got back. I can tell you something more. Howell was nervous and just pretending he wasn't worried."

"So you think something really was taken?"

Isaacs shrugged. "Who knows? Denton, Munford, William—there's something a bit queer about all of them. We'll never know half of what they get up to. They're tight-lipped and it all stays in the family."

"Howell is family? I thought he was just a partner."

"He's Denton's cousin, Munford's sister's boy. William handles the day-to-day business, and Denton makes the deals. Munford is involved too, more than he likes people to think. All that jabber about being a simple farmer yearning for peace in his golden years is pure hogwash."

"I gathered as much during the meeting with Mrs. Maynard."

Isaacs looked up at the sky. "Doesn't make much sense to me unless one of them had something the other wanted—or they both had something that someone else wanted." Isaacs laughed and looked at Ramsey. "Did that sound as foolish as I think it did?"

"I get your meaning."

"I'll find out from Hendricks if the police are interested in the Coldwaters. Don't worry, I won't tip your hand. Jack isn't as smart as he thinks he is, not by a longshot."

"Thanks, Willie."

Isaacs turned to walk back to the newspaper. "Let me know if anything else crops up. What with us being friends and sharing information. You'll do that, won't you?"

◇◇◇

Rabun Perdido sat at the end of the bar, lost in concentration. He held a small book in his large hands.

"Good book?" Ramsey asked.

"Benedict Spinoza. Like yourself, he exalted the reason, and like yourself, he was not a chess player. *Ethica Ordine Geometrico Demonstrata*."

"My Latin isn't up to the task."

"Pity. His writings could not fail to improve you."

"Many things could improve me, but in lieu of philosophy, I'd settle for a drink and a game."

A hand clapped him on the back.

"Allan Ramsey!" There was no ignoring Jed Varger's presence.

"Evening, Jed."

"Gonna play chess tonight?"

"Can't avoid it."

"Well, you're drinking whiskey and Rabun's drinking coffee. I think I'll bet on the saloonkeeper!" A hearty laugh followed.

"Did you know either of the men who were hurt when that wall collapsed the other day?" asked Ramsey.

"No, can't say as I did. Lots of new fellas are building these days. Besides, I don't do much commercial work. It's mainly homebuilding for me. We're working up on Ivy Street, on John Bellows's new house. You know him? No? Fine man, John."

Ramsey signaled Mr. Winks for a drink.

"It's easy to see how the accident happened," Varger continued. "The wall looked sturdy, but nobody tested it. Fire can weaken a masonry wall. You need to check them very carefully, but that often gets forgotten. Greed takes over. If you use existing walls, you finish the job faster. The quicker a job gets done, the quicker the landlord starts making money, not to mention the bonus the builder gets when a project is done early. Things get rushed and people get hurt. Sometimes money talks so loud, a man can't hear anything else."

Varger spied someone at the door. "Excuse me, Allan. It's my next house." He gave a wave and pointed at an empty table.

Rabun set up the chessboard on the bar. "I find I have time for a game, *mon ami*. You will play the black—it suits you." Rabun pushed his king pawn forward.

Ramsey looked down at the familiar pieces—the knight with its nose cracked off, the chipped rook, the bishop with its paint worn thin—and considered what to do.

Chatsworth White walked over and he, too, looked quizzically at the board.

"Well?" said Rabun impatiently. "Surely this is a moment that offers few problems."

Ramsey pushed the queen's bishop pawn.

"What the devil was that?" said Whitey.

Rabun looked with surprise at Ramsey. "You have not played the Sicilian before."

"I have now."

Rabun moved his queen knight and Ramsey did the same.

Whitey frowned. "Will somebody tell me what's going on?" Joe Frank looked around as if someone would.

Rabun moved his king knight out. Ramsey countered with the king knight's pawn and moved it one space forward.

Four soldiers ambled over and joined the group that had gathered to watch. The oldest of them, a major, took particular interest. The game began to move quickly. Ramsey took

Rabun's queen pawn. Rabun retook with his knight. Ramsey brought the king bishop forward. On the seventh move, Rabun moved his king rook pawn forward.

The major shook his head as if to change the move with the force of will. A few moves later, the major again frowned in dissent. Ramsey looked up, and the two men exchanged glances.

Seeing this exchange, Whitey asked, "What was wrong with that? Rabun's going to attack. Captain Ramsey had better watch himself."

"It's always good to watch oneself," said the major quietly.

"Rabun's clever," said Whitey, in vague defense of moves he failed to understand.

The major studied the board. "Black will win somewhere between the twenty-seventh and thirtieth moves unless he blunders."

Whitey laughed at what he thought was a joke and went off for a drink. The major did not laugh and took advantage of Whitey's departure to move closer to the game.

Ramsey won in thirty-five moves. The game might have ended sooner, but Rabun hung on, hoping for a mistake that never came.

The major shook Ramsey's hand. "I congratulate you, sir. You played a fine game."

"Thank you, Major . . ."

"McGrath. Ben McGrath." He turned and rejoined his companions.

"Hold on a minute." Ed Sprague ducked through the door of Dobson's Dry Goods and reappeared with a twist of tobacco. "You was sayin'?"

"I was saying that Denton Coldwater sent a man to attack me," Ramsey said. "He warned me at gunpoint to stay away from Mrs. Maynard."

"Well, it weren't done right, but Denton ain't givin' you bad advice."

"That's all you can say?"

"You're still in good health, ain't ya? What happened to that other fella?"

Ramsey sighed. "I may have roughed him up a bit, but that's not the point. The point is—"

The deputy waved a stubby finger at Ramsey. "The point is that Denton Coldwater ain't in town. You told me that yourself. So what do you expect me to do? Where's that fella with the gun? You wanna tell me that? He waitin' around to testify against Denton? Maybe you think Denton's gonna have a religious conversion and own up to the nasty stuff he's done his whole rotten life? If you're just saying he's a bastard, I already know that. Where we goin' with this?"

"I just thought you should know about it," Ramsey said.

"Well, now I do. You want to come with me today? I gotta pick up Rufus Parker. He threw the Baskin boy into the counter over at Wilson's Dry Goods. Broke a glass cabinet. Seems young Baskin's been payin' too much attention to Sadie Tompkins." Sprague readjusted his hat and spit. "Old man Wilson just wants his case fixed, but Parker told him to go to hell. When the law shows up, he'll see reason."

"I'm sure he will," said Ramsey. "I'd go with you for the company, but I have something else to take care of. Remember when I told you Mr. Henry said that old drunk they call Papa Squirrel disappeared the night that Tully got shot?"

"Yeah, I seem to remember you ravin' along those lines."

"Well," said Ramsey, "I told Lanier about it, but he just got mad. Thought I was insulting his investigation."

Sprague whooped with laughter. "You're more fun than a carnival sideshow! First you have a late-night dust up, and now you're off searchin' for Papa Squirrel!"

"It won't hurt to check it out," replied Ramsey defensively.

"Well you have yourself some fun squirrel huntin'. Lanier ain't gonna concern himself with that broke-down old man."

"So who *is* Willis Lanier concerned with these days?" Ramsey asked.

"You still worried about the Maynard woman? Or just scared for your own sorry ass?"

"Come on, Ed. If you've got something, let's have it."

"Well, I don't know much, seeing as how I ain't so popular these days, but I hear Lanier sent wires to Boston 'bout the Maynard woman. An' he's havin' her watched, but I don't care 'bout none of that. No concern of mine."

Sprague stopped at the corner of North Calhoun Street. "If you ain't coming, I guess this is it."

The ground on the hillside was slippery from the recent rain, but the young woman moved along the muddy trail quickly. Ramsey struggled to keep the pace. She held in her arms a sleeping baby wrapped in rags. Mr. Henry had said Papa's "hole" was hard to find, and she was the guide he provided. Maybe she was kin to Papa Squirrel. Not many except family would know or care where a derelict lived. Mr. Henry told Ramsey to give her a dollar for her efforts. He was firm about that. "It's more than you should pay, but she needs it, Mr. Allan, she really does."

The girl didn't look at him or speak. At length, they came to a high point along the trail. She indicated his destination with a movement of her hand. Only then did she meet his gaze.

He saw fear that he would betray her and give her nothing. A deep scar ran vertically down her broad black face, giving it a shrunken appearance. The eye above the scar was unfocused, blind.

Ramsey reached into his pocket and pressed a $5 gold piece into her hand. She took it and wordlessly turned away. The baby awakened and cried as she retraced her steps on her muddy return.

She'd pointed to a rubbish heap at the bottom of a ravine. A path snaked its way down to its center. What insane logic underlay the effort to accumulate what others cast off? A broken picture frame lay tottering on a wooden box. The parched bones of what had once been a deer lay scattered on the ground next to a small mound of sodden clothing and a pile of rusty cans.

Ramsey doubted Papa Squirrel's disappearance had much to do with Tully's murder. Perhaps the old man had seen or found something that worried others. Maybe that caused him to flee. Maybe it had gotten him killed. As Ramsey looked around, he found it impossible to discern anything in the clutter. During a search, one looked for something out of place, something that did not look quite right. Here, everything was out of place and nothing looked right.

He approached a pile of books and picked one up. Moisture had fused the pages. He grabbed a bent fireplace poker and used it to probe places he couldn't easily reach. With it, he forced open a battered cabinet. Inside were piles of mildewed sheet music. A broken wheel lay on the ground next to a wagon body nestled in the weeds. Perhaps Papa Squirrel, a slave who had owned nothing, came to see the possession of objects as an end in itself.

Ramsey found a small shelter of boards, bricks, and rocks near the center of the rubbish. It was barely large enough for a man to crawl into and stank of urine. Inside, a matted pile of dry grass served as a bed. Three empty whiskey bottles lay near a battered hat. He used the poker to retrieve the hat. Spidery white sweat lines radiated from its brim.

Maybe if he could see the clutter in its totality, he thought, an anomaly among the anomalies might emerge.

The idea was probably foolish, but it would make an appropriate end to a fool's errand. He climbed up the slope to get a wider view.

Movement on the hill caught his eye.

He crouched and scanned the ground above him. All was still. The afternoon sun cast its long shadows across the knoll. He had the unmistakable feeling someone was watching, but there was no hope of running up the hill to surprise this person. Even with two good legs, the muddy incline would make him far too slow. Was he in danger? Not likely. He'd been a target since he'd arrived.

Could it be Papa Squirrel?

Ramsey pulled some coins from his pocket, stood, and let them drop from one hand to the other, hoping the tinkling sound might attract the old man.

"Papa Squirrel! Mr. Henry sent money for you! Money, Papa Squirrel!"

Nothing.

He began climbing. Weeds springing up from the slippery red earth and new growth rising from stumps made the way difficult. Near the top, he stopped and listened but heard only the sound of his own panting. He crested the hill and called again for Papa Squirrel. If he did manage to spot the old man, could he win a foot race with the ancient drunk? Ramsey looked down on the clutter below. The accumulation was as insane in total as it was in detail.

Fallen branches crackled to his left.

Ramsey spun around just in time to see a figure disappearing down a ravine. A white man.

When Ramsey returned to the Carraway house, he was far too late for dinner once again. He wearily climbed the outside stairs to his room, his mind turning to Sprague. The deputy would have a good laugh over today—it had produced no answers, only another question. Who was the white man? Who in God's name would follow him out there? It didn't matter. He was too tired to think. A whiskey and some rest were in order. He unlocked the door and lit a lamp.

Someone had been there. Without knowing quite why, he could feel it. Alert now, Ramsey scanned the room. Nothing appeared disturbed. He pulled open a drawer. His guns were accounted for. He checked *Peterson's Sermons*. His money was there.

He flopped into his desk chair and looked at his workspace. The pigeonholes had been searched. A slight reordering told him the papers had been carefully removed and replaced. He reached down to pull out a drawer. On top of crumpled wads of paper in the wastebasket lay the note from Abby. It was carefully smoothed and positioned in the center.

Someone wanted him to know they had been there. Was it just to tell him his room had been searched? Or was the carefully positioned note meant to tell him something more? A subtle message from—whom? Not from Denton. He'd sent a gunman. Not Lanier. He'd crash in waving a warrant. The Army? But why?

Ramsey examined the room more closely. Stacked next to his desk were neatly tied bundles of paper. They were the notes, papers, and reports he'd kept from the war. They documented a time and a life he no longer wished to write about. Nothing was amiss. He was sure. There was a special order to how they were placed. That order was intact.

Whoever had searched his room had come and gone. What was done was done. He poured himself a whiskey. A second followed the first. Some crackers from a tin and a bit of cheese restored his spirits. A third whiskey did more. He pulled off his boots and placed them at the foot of the bed. At the wash basin, he sponged away the grime of the day.

He looked in the mirror and saw the face of a tired man. Tired of war widows and tired of murdered thugs. A face tired of newspapers and tired of policemen. Tired of the Army and tired of Munford and Denton Coldwater. He sat down in his desk chair and closed his eyes, not opening them even as he finished his whiskey.

He'd nearly dozed off when it came to him. Perhaps a woman did link things together.

He rose, splashed some water on his face, and tried to shake some clarity into his foggy mind. Taking a deep breath, he bent and found the bundles that were marked '1864.' Setting aside the ones prior to the battle for Atlanta, he found the ones dealing with July and August.

The reports and dispatches were arranged in chronological order. Quickly scanning and carefully setting aside a third of the first stack, he stopped when he arrived at papers marked GARRARD'S RAID, JULY '64—a cavalry action meant to cut the railroads east of Atlanta and restrict the Confederate supply line. He set a hand-drawn map made at the time to one side and read.

Garrard with his 2nd and 3rd Brigades leaves Decatur on the evening of July 21st. Camps that night at Rockbridge on the Yellow River around midnight. The 1st Brigade catches up just before dawn.

He flipped through a series of supply requests and duty rosters.

Two companies of the 98th Mounted Infantry dispatched to the southeast soon after the column began its march.

Tully, O'Bannion, and Hackett were all in the 98th Illinois. He narrowed his focus now, following that unit's trail.

98th Mounted sent to destroy the Georgia Railroad trestle spanning the Yellow River east of Conyers. 98th reaches Conyers midmorning, captures and destroys a train and railroad depot, taking 16 prisoners. Rides east to the river. Weak local resistance at trestle. One Confederate killed—trestle, wagon bridge, and flour mill burned. 98th continues two miles past Covington, meets 1st Brigade, which provides cover while 98th destroys the track back to Covington. 98th burns warehouse filled with furniture, a cotton warehouse, water tank, and the Confederate commissary. Blaze reaches 100 feet high. Along with the 1st Brigade they capture the hospital which is left unharmed.

Such mercy wouldn't have been Tully's decision, but the 98th was proving quite a plague upon the land.

Garrard's column retires through Oxford. Colonel Abe Miller and the 98th remain as rearguard and burn another cotton warehouse containing several hundred bales. They find a warehouse containing 8,000 pairs of shoes and 100 boxes of tobacco. Foraging as much as they can carry, they burn the rest.

It must have been a carnival for Tully and Hackett.

Garrard calls a halt the night of 22nd at Sardis Church. A high-ranking prisoner, Colonel Hamilton, escapes. Garrard believes the guard was bought off. No disciplinary measures taken.

Garrard really was a slack son of a bitch.

Four hundred more bales of cotton burned at Loganville and a large stock of rice scattered and destroyed.

No mention of the 98th.

Garrard divides his command. The 1st Brigade goes to Lawrenceville, and the 2nd and 3rd Brigades turn southwest along Stone Mountain Road toward Decatur.

Ramsey thought for a moment. Abe Miller was in command of the 3rd Brigade, so that meant the 98th was traveling toward Decatur with Garrard.

The 3rd brigade reaches Decatur approx. noon. Shots exchanged with Confederate rearguard. The Union baggage train in Decatur attacked and destroyed by Wheeler's cavalry.

While the cat's away the mice do play.

Stragglers and foraging parties continue to trickle in throughout the afternoon of the 24th.

Garrard's Raid, 98th Mounted Infantry, Covington Road, Covington Hospital, Charlton, stragglers trickling in during the afternoon of July 24. Munford Coldwater had said, "It was the end of July and Yankee's were everywhere." The 98th—containing Tully, Hackett, and company—had been right in the thick of it. Had they seen Susan Knowles at the Covington Hospital? Munford said she worked there. Why would a woman that resembled her have surprised them? Were they surprised because they never expected to see her again? Had they run from a woman they'd thought was dead?

If they'd killed Susan Knowles during the battles for Atlanta, what did that mean? God only knew how many innocents had been robbed, raped, and murdered during the war. Why did they *keep* coming back to Atlanta? It must have something to do with Garrard's raid. They hadn't ever been near Atlanta prior to that. But what was it? And whatever it was, it must still be present. After two years, they came back to Atlanta for something, something they must have known was still there. But suddenly things went very wrong. Tully was shot, then O'Bannion. Hackett was shot and hanged. That accounted for three of them. Giles didn't die in Atlanta, because he'd managed to do it somewhere else. That made four. Turney was hiding and possibly on the run. Mason was missing. The casualty rate was worthy of a full-on battle.

But maybe Turney and Mason weren't on the run. The break-ins suggested the presence of Turney's lock-breaking skills. Could Mason be with him? And what about Abby saying she was being watched? Who was the figure she'd seen in the street? Was it someone sinister or simply a trick played by bad nerves? Was it the man running away at Papa Squirrel's?

Ramsey had done his share of surveillance during the war. Running an intelligence operation meant watching your prey, understanding him, finding his strengths, seeking his weaknesses. It is a great mistake to strike in ignorance. If someone was out there, he seemed content to remain in the shadows. But was that still true? For some reason he had now made his presence known. If that person was about to strike, he had a powerful advantage. Those who wait choose the time and place for confrontation. It is they who control the game. The defender must lose, because a reactive defense is a losing defense. An effective defense must always have counterattack in its heart.

So there it was. His path was clear.

He must become the attacker.

But first he must become the watcher.

Surveillance is simplest in broad daylight. Then the watcher need only trick the subject's rational mind into not seeing him. The watcher blends into his surroundings. If surveillance must last more than a day, he changes appearance. On a crowded street, he can use the help of a second person to good effect. The watcher will appear to chat while he observes the subject over the other person's shoulder. All the methods boil down to one basic principle—allow the subject's conscious mind to see what it expects to see.

Night is another matter entirely. The animal mind now stands guard. It is less easily fooled. The smallest things reveal the watcher's presence. The eye is designed to catch movement, so he must remain stationary. Stare too long at a subject, and they will sense it. The slightest out-of-place sounds set off alarms. The curiosity of a passing dog can be disastrous. The watcher must use his peripheral vision and the senses of sound and smell. Extraordinary patience is required.

On his first night, Ramsey nestled behind some shrubs across from the Hoehling house, hidden in darkness. He was not alone. Al Bates relieved a colleague who'd watched during the day. They chatted a bit before Bates took up a poorly disguised position. Soon he lit a cigar. At times he could be heard humming to himself. Considering it was Bates, none of these things surprised Ramsey. However, when Dennett Wilson arrived and did little more to conceal himself, the police showed their hand. They wanted to be seen.

This sideshow didn't concern Ramsey. He waited for another to reveal himself.

The first night, no one did.

The second night, Ramsey did not go to the Hoehling house. Instead, he watched his own rooms. It was a poor call. No one showed. Not even the police were present to break the monotony. With daylight, he climbed the stairs and went to bed.

While Ramsey spent sleepless nights watching, the police spent their days in a flurry of activity. They went over the ground Ramsey and Sprague had covered earlier, but they made a grand show of it. The people in the Triangle were rounded up and questioned. Crime scenes were reinvestigated. Witness statements were taken from people with only the slightest possible involvement. Much was made of the "discovery" that O'Bannion's body had been thrown from the trestle above the Triangle. The press in general, and the *Intelligencer* in particular, trumpeted each effort no matter how trivial. Lanier was going nowhere, but he was going there in style.

Ramsey sat in the disorder of his room, carefully wiping excess oil from his recently cleaned Colt .44. Next to it was the Adams .32, awaiting similar treatment. Later that night he would again take up a position watching the Hoehling house, but for now he had time to relax.

A tap preceded Elijah's entry through the door.

"Cap'n Ramsey. Someone here for ya."

"I'd rather not see anyone just now, Elijah." Ramsey spun the cylinder on the Colt and listened to the smooth rhythm of its clicks.

"He's Army."

"Ah." Ramsey sighed. "In that case, send him up." He removed the cylinder and began to carefully load the cap-and-ball handgun.

Major Ben McGrath appeared. "Good afternoon, Captain Ramsey."

McGrath was shorter than Ramsey, but well-built and muscular. His uniform was neat without showing undue care, and his boots were polished but worn. Their eyes met. Ramsey remained at his work, allowing the lingering silence to force his visitor to speak.

"You played a fine game of chess the other night," McGrath said. "I watched much of it. The Sicilian Defense."

"Yes."

"Based on the reaction of the gentlemen standing near me, I don't believe you play it often."

"I've played it in the past but not recently. If you know that opening, you must have seen many mistakes."

"You made a few, but nothing of importance."

McGrath moved about, examining the room's contents.

"You didn't come here to critique my play," Ramsey said.

"No."

"Then I suppose you have questions about the murders of Tully, O'Bannion, and Hackett. Are you the Army liaison? What would you like to know?"

McGrath smiled. "Should I bother you with questions about the investigation? Is there anything new you wish to tell me?"

"No."

"I thought not."

McGrath completed his examination of Ramsey's bookshelf. "I am not the liaison with the police. Someone junior to me carries that burden. I simply came by because I wanted to meet you in person. Until the night of the chess game, I knew of you only by reputation." He looked squarely at Ramsey. "Your presence in Atlanta has suggested some possibilities."

"The Army and I are not on the best of terms, as I'm sure you're aware. I very much doubt I could be of use to you. If that's why you're here, it's a waste of time. Time is in short supply for me at present."

McGrath strolled to the window and looked out at the street. "Do you keep up with your old colleagues? Dodge had high regard for your section."

"We exchange the occasional letter. Gunter Hahn might win a seat on the Cincinnati City Council."

"Ah, Gunter. Your forger and counterfeiter. I hope that goes well."

McGrath sat down in one of the stuffed chairs. "From what I hear, Freddie Ross is in the Savannah jail—a legal entanglement with some cotton factors. The matter is ambiguous, but the plaintiffs are powerful men. He finds himself in a tight spot."

"I'm sorry to hear that," Ramsey said.

"I wouldn't be overly concerned. Freddie still has friends. His fortunes are about to take a turn for the better. He doesn't know it yet, but he will be leaving Savannah soon for Raleigh, North Carolina. The Savannah cotton factors are about to realize their mistake and drop their action against him. They will have the realization it was all a misunderstanding."

"I applaud Freddie's good luck."

"Yes, good fortune is always pleasant," McGrath agreed. "Have you heard from Sam Frazier?"

"Not lately. Some say she went out west, but who knows. Sam writes infrequently and often changes plans. Nat Brewster headed to Texas. I received a letter from him postmarked San Antonio two weeks ago. He plans on raising cattle."

"I imagine Nat will do well. From what Dodge told me, the open spaces of Texas suit him. On the other hand, Sam will not be found west of the Mississippi. I have reason to believe she never got farther than Memphis. It's always difficult to know about her. She sows a screen of rumor to obscure her activities. A trick she learned from you, I believe."

"There was very little I could teach Sam."

"Well, I mention Memphis because the police there are looking for a widow named Dilys Lambert. Apparently, the charming widow's marriage into a prominent family has been abruptly called off. Sad to say, some valuables have gone missing along with the would-be bride. Dilys Lambert is one of Samantha Frazier's aliases, if I'm not mistaken."

Ramsey could not resist a smile. "Nothing Sam gets up to would be a surprise. But knowing Sam, she'll have her payday. The family won't press charges if they get the jewelry back. Fear of scandal is a powerful thing. And, of course, they won't get all of it back, or if they do there will be a cash settlement. I suspect there are letters in her possession that her former fiancé now regrets sending."

"I doubt that's far from the mark." McGrath laughed. "Quite a crew you assembled. Colorful characters all. They face the challenges of peace in their unique ways."

"Not all," Ramsey said.

"No, not all."

"Have you had any word about Vera Conover?" Ramsey asked.

"Perhaps we should speak of something else." McGrath said quietly.

"I see no need for us to discuss anything." Ramsey's voice had a harder edge. "My former colleagues aren't saints, but saints weren't fit for the work we did. And they were damn good. They made a difference, and the nation owes them thanks they will never get. I know it and you know it."

"Quite true. I imagine your current network struggles to live up to their standards."

"What?" Ramsey said, surprised. "I don't have a network."

"I suspect you do. Men like you create them like beavers build dams."

"Major, I have much to do. You have a busy life as well. I must ask you to leave."

"Of course you're right. The past is best left to itself. It's the present that weighs upon us. And in my case, I must divine the future as well."

"We all have difficult lives," Ramsey said.

"Your services, Captain, could be helpful to both myself and your government."

"My services?" Ramsey laughed. "There's nothing further I owe you or my government. And there's nothing I can do for either of you. Around Atlanta, my reputation is very much in decline."

"If you're referring to Havermeyer and Stevenson, you're right. They both despise you, though neither man counts for much. Havermeyer is a paper shuffler and Stevenson gives him the papers to shuffle."

"It would be hard to argue with that."

"Captain, I'll be frank with you. I'm not interested in how this drama with your local murders plays out. The overdue deaths of some criminal ex-soldiers holds little concern for me.

While I keep myself abreast of events, I do not see their murders are of any consequence. The Atlanta police can have a free hand."

"Then what do you want? Why are you here?"

"These are uncertain times. Only a fool would speculate on how matters will stand in Atlanta six months or a year from now. My mission is to ensure that order is maintained. Atlanta will not descend into violence like Memphis or Mobile. It's a difficult task, and I possess few resources with which to shape events. Putting soldiers on the streets is useless unless we want another war. Indeed, some would like us to take those very measures to spark a violent reaction. Other means must be found. I must find them."

"That is not my concern."

"Perhaps, not. But whether you want it or not, I imagine at some point I will ask for your help. You know this city and its people better than anyone on my staff. You are a man who has kept secrets and indeed keeps them still. You've shown you can be trusted. I know your reasons for refusal—at least some of them—still I thought it best to reach out to you before my back was against the wall. You may choose to help me, or you may not, but from one officer to another, that is about as plain as I can make it."

McGrath gestured toward the guns on the table. "You know, when a man cleans his guns as carefully as you are doing, he's either very fastidious, which"—he indicated the room with a wave of his hand—"you are not, or he may have some use for my help as well."

Ramsey liked McGrath. He suspected McGrath's powers were considerable and his orders loosely specified. Better to have such a man with you rather than against you.

"I'm listening, Major."

McGrath laid out his concern about Atlanta's witches' brew of angry ex-Confederates, chronic crime, vigilantes, racial fears, citizens of uncertain loyalty, the freedmen, and a City Hall with little means of managing it all.

When he finished, he asked, "Would you agree with my summation?"

"Yes, all you say is true. However, there's a bit of detail I can add. City Hall's desire to maintain control aligns with the goals of the Army. However, the city authorities mustn't be seen as overly reliant on the government or the locals will turn against them. With few exceptions, the citizens of Atlanta were staunch Confederates during the war. Now most accept the outcome and wish to move forward, but that acceptance is shallow. The police are ex-Rebel soldiers enforcing the policies of the mayor and his circle. Their loyalty is uncertain at best. Ed Sprague is by far the most able man on the force, but he has little standing with the powers above him. They need him, but they don't want him. Judge Whitaker is a former mayor and was a local Confederate leader. That, combined with the fact that he publishes a newspaper, gives him considerable sway in civic affairs. He's pragmatic by nature and won't do anything foolish, but keep an eye on him. If you start losing his cooperation, I'd worry. And there are more radical people in this city who also have influence. Former Mayor Luther Glenn comes to mind. Counterbalancing that faction Richard Peters and George Adair who, like Whitaker, want peace at any reasonable price. I have reason to believe the power of the vigilante societies is growing—the attack on Otis Timmons may have been the work of such a group. It might also have been a few angry drunks beating up an obnoxious Yankee. The two aren't mutually exclusive. There is a person of considerable character and resolution that—"

"His name?" McGrath asked.

"A person who has expressed concern about such organizations. If trouble comes, I imagine it will first come from that direction."

McGrath nodded and stood up. "Thank you, Captain Ramsey. I've taken too much of your time and will leave you now. I appreciate all you've told me. We may have a reason to speak again in the future."

"Major, before you go, I have a question. I assume the Maynard woman has been investigated by the Army or the police. What was discovered about her?"

"She is exactly who she says she is. John Maynard and the Maynard family are well known. Sadly, he died this past winter. At the request of the police, I made discrete inquiries into her past. She was born Abigail St. Clair, and she has a sister, Susan, who is her only sibling. Their mother died in childbirth. Her father was some sort of literary man and a person of irregular habits. The two girls lived with him in Europe until he returned to New York shortly before his death. The Maynard family was unhappy with their son's marriage and cut him off financially. They considered his wife below them socially. Since his death, the family has washed its hands of Abigail Maynard."

"Did you have her room searched? Are you watching her?"

"No, of course not. Whit Anderson asked us to find out about her past, so we did. Our involvement stopped there."

"The police seem to think she is somehow involved."

"Don't give much credence to anything you hear from them. I wouldn't be surprised to discover that Marshal Anderson is a frustrated dime novelist. There isn't much clear thinking going on in those parts. I'm aware he has men watching her, but I can't imagine why. I know nothing about her room being searched."

"One other thing. Can you get Johnny Bass transferred out of Atlanta?"

McGrath's face fell. "Stevenson won't sign any orders for Bass that don't involve a court-martial."

"Bass was once a good soldier. He needs a chance. I think his commanding officers during the war would back me up.

Use my name if you think it would help; the further you go from Atlanta the better my reputation gets."

McGrath offered his hand. "If you will work with me, I will work with you."

Ramsey shook McGrath's hand.

Ramsey could think of only three reasons someone would be watching Abby Maynard. The first was to know if she stayed put or left the city. The second was to monitor any clandestine activity she might be engaged in. The third was to threaten her. Whatever the reason might be, at some point his adversary would move in for a closer look. Ramsey was counting on that.

On the third night Ramsey returned to the Hoehling house. Once again, only the police and the wild night creatures kept him company.

When evening slipped into darkness on the fourth day, he approached the Hoehling house from the rear. Reversing his position placed him opposite to the police as well as to anyone watching from their side of the street. The need to avoid being spotted by Bates, who was across the street, made the going slow, but he worked his way along the side of the house and hid in some bushes near the front.

Time passed. Dennett Wilson replaced Bates. A half-moon rising in a cloudless night sky lit the street. Ramsey made himself as comfortable as possible. With only the moonlight, bright as it might be, he knew he couldn't identify anyone— that would be asking too much. But he only needed to know for certain *that* such a person was there and watching.

He wished he could team up with Wilson. The young man was clearly intelligent and would be a great asset in such work. Too bad he was being wasted on a fool's errand across the street. Ramsey's mind went back to the day at the hotel. The boy paid attention to detail. He—

Ramsey cut his eyes to the movement of tree limbs across the street. A cat? A raccoon?

The silhouette of a man moved between the shadows and paused. Ramsey quickly scrambled back along the side of the house, around the back to the other side. The figure was gone.

It didn't matter. He had seen the third watcher.

The fortunes of young Cassius were thriving. Captain Ramsey sent messages and required errands several times a day. Aware of his usefulness, Cassius doubled his price to a dime a trip. Ramsey paid without protest. Cassius was considering a further increase as he puffed his way into the front hallway of the Hoehling boarding house. Mrs. Hoehling took the envelope and sent him to the kitchen to wait.

Abigail Maynard sliced open the envelope.

> *Abby,*
> *I trust that this note finds you well. Could you meet me*
> *at Hutchinson's Millinery Shop tomorrow morning at*
> *ten o'clock? It is a matter of some importance.*
> *Allan*
>
> *PS: You need not concern yourself with Munford and*
> *Denton Coldwater at present.*

A few minutes later Cassius raced through the street to deliver his next message, her reply safely in his pocket.

An orderly saluted and handed Ben McGrath the note a small
black boy had brought minutes earlier. It was from Ramsey and
came directly to the point.

How did Simon Giles die?
He already knew the answer. When he'd spoken with
Ramsey, he stressed his distance from the investigation, but
there were inquiries he hadn't mentioned.

Below Ramsey's question he scribbled:

Simon Giles died along with two other prisoners in a fire.

He thought about what other information Ramsey might
want and added:

Bodies were identified by prison doctor using written records.

He folded the note and handed it to the orderly.
"How did this message arrive?"
"A boy brought it, sir."
"Return it to him immediately."
"Yes, sir."

"So let me see if I understand what you say." Rabun poured
coffee for himself and Ramsey. "First you appear in the dreams
of *la belle femme*, and now a dead man murders the villains of
our city. Perhaps you have a bit of the poet in you? Your
thoughts are of more interest than usual."

"No, Rabun, I said that the events surrounding the recent murders become clearer if we suppose that Simon Giles is not dead. I have no way of knowing if that's the case; it's only a supposition. But the records say he died in a fire. Fires make identification difficult. Furthermore, the body was identified by a prison doctor who didn't give a damn. Three prisoners were absent from roll call. He had three burned bodies. He had three names to attach to them. His job was done. Giles was cunning enough to have navigated his way through a lot of shady business. Is it too much to suppose his death was a setup? Is it possible none of those bodies was his? A clever man passing out bribes to underpaid guards could arrange it."

"Such things are possible."

"And who else is in the picture?" Ramsey asked. "Turney, a lock breaker? Mason, a bit of muscle? If my guess is right, Giles is the only one who could manage putting Tully, O'Bannion, and Hackett in their graves, especially if he had the help of others."

"Perhaps that is true. Or perhaps your imagination just wishes it so."

"Well, there is more. The police are watching Mrs. Maynard, but now I know someone else is too. I caught a glimpse of him. I didn't see much, but he was there. It's not anyone from the Army. I asked McGrath, and he said they had no interest. As for the Coldwaters, considering the fool sent to warn me off, I doubt someone working for them would be difficult to spot. That leaves us with either Turney or Mason or someone we haven't considered: Giles."

"So, I give you your dead villain, but I ask you this. Why does he run about killing men who might be useful to him? Why not use them? One by one they meet their fate. Why does he do such a thing?"

"I don't know. Perhaps they betrayed him."

"You make many suppositions. The house you build is shaky, *n'est-ce pas?* Logic is in your blood, but such thinking is not the flower of reason."

"I'll grant that it's based on educated guesses," Ramsey admitted.

"But there is more, is there not? You care for the woman with the dreams, but there are doubts about her too."

"I don't doubt her. McGrath says she's on the level. It's just that I find something unsettling about her."

Rabun looked earnestly at his friend. "Does your heart say this lady from Boston is evil? Does it say she will betray you? Does it tell you these things?"

"No, my heart does not tell me that."

"Well, *mon ami*, that is a good thing."

Rabun leaned back and sipped his coffee. "I think there is something else you have not talked about. You do not say what you intend to do."

"You're right. Something must be done. Whoever has been watching Mrs. Maynard—whether it's Giles or not—let her see him more than once. That means it was intentional. He must believe his presence means something to her. I suspect he may be growing impatient and is using subtle means to force the issue."

"So what course will you take?"

"I think we should give him what he wants. He expects her to do something, so we'll arrange a sudden dash out of town. Perhaps we can surprise him and draw him out. If we get him to follow us, we might isolate him and get the odds in our favor."

"Why not guard the lady here? Your man must come from the shadows in time."

"And when he does, he'll strike at a place and at a time of his choosing when we're most vulnerable. The best course is to take that advantage away from him. My plan is to get Mrs.

Maynard out of Atlanta and lodged in a safe place. Giles, or whoever it is, will be forced to react to me. With a bit of luck, I will control the time and place."

"And if he does nothing?"

"At least Mrs. Maynard will be safe. I'll try something else."

Rabun poured them some mineral water. "Take it. It is good for the liver."

Ramsey looked at the glass in silence. Moments passed before he spoke again. "Sometimes during the war, Rabun, we'd reach an impasse. We had all the information we were likely to get. The possibilities had been considered and reconsidered. Still, the correct course of action remained unclear. If at those times we could do something that made the enemy respond to us—something that would upset his planning and force him to respond in ways he'd never intended—the balance often shifted in our favor. I believe this is one of those times."

"As in war, so in chess." Rabun arched an eyebrow. "You play these things the same, *mon ami*."

There was a hard knock on the outer door.

"Who is it?"

"Sprague."

The deputy entered the room.

"Ain't seen much of you lately," Sprague said.

"The judge was clear about what I wasn't to do and who I wasn't to see."

The deputy smiled. "Yeah, Anderson and Lanier been real happy 'bout how good you been. Makes life easy for 'em." The deputy took out a large stained handkerchief and blew his nose. "Damn horses," he muttered. His hound-dog eyes returned to

Ramsey. "Ya know, I been a good boy too. Chicken coop gets robbed and ol' Ed comes right over. Horse gets stole and ol' Ed's out lookin' for a horse. We both good fellas, you and me." Sprague nodded in agreement with himself.

"Of course," he went on, "I been wondering what you *have* been up to, since I been hearin' some strange things."

Ramsey said nothing.

"You remember Wilson? The young fella who was with us at Tully's room?"

Silence.

"Thought ya did. Wilson's a bright boy. We get along real good. He's gonna do okay at police work if he sticks at it. Anyways, he's been watchin' the Maynard woman at night. Young fella like him stays awake better than us ol' folks. Wilson says it's mostly quiet over there. He don't see much. There ain't much for him to do. But he does notice things. Sees this or that." The deputy paused. "He seen *you* last night." Sprague chuckled to himself. "How'd he make a mistake like that? I mean, he's so clever and has such good eyes and all? How'd he make that mistake?"

"There isn't much light on the street at night, Ed."

"No, there ain't much light. But the fella he seen runnin' alongside the Hoehling house wasn't exactly runnin'. He was doin' that jump and hop thing you do when you *try* to run. Maybe Wilson was dreaming or drunk, but that's what he says he seen."

"Moonlight and shadows can play tricks on the best of us."

Sprague looked hard at Ramsey.

"Yeah, that's what I told him. He don't think that's what happened, but that's what I told him. I also told him not to say nothin' to nobody about his little mistake, 'cause he ain't gonna ever make it again. Did I tell him right? I hate to mislead a nice young fella like Wilson."

"I don't think Wilson will make that mistake again."

"Good. Then everybody's happy."

"Happiness is a wonderful thing, Ed."

"Yup, happiness is what we need. See ya 'round. Time I got home."

Gideon tied up the horse and mounted the stairs to Ramsey's door. "From Mr. Heflin, suh," he said, and handed an envelope to Ramsey.

"Thank you, Gideon. You've been a big help. Please give my best to Mr. Henry. You'll return the horse to the livery stable?"

"Yessuh."

Ramsey watched Gideon ride back up the street. The cost of the horse strained his dwindling resources, but it was the safest way to get a message to Heflin Sanbourne.

The reply was satisfactory.

The rear of Hutchinson's Millinery Shop served as a work room and a storage space. Buttons and cloth ribbons cluttered a bench amid partially finished hats that awaited the heads of Atlanta's fashionable ladies. Pattern books, newly arrived from New York and Boston, lay open nearby.

In the far corner of the room, Allan Ramsey dozed in a chair. He'd arrived early, and the gentle murmur of voices at the front counter proved soporific. The morning sun fell across his body and lighted him as a scientist might light a specimen.

When Abigail Maynard entered, she was struck by the quiet vulnerability of the sleeping man. Her gaze was sympathetic, which was fortunate. The room was warm. Sweat glistened on his forehead, where wisps of his graying dark hair stuck to his skin. The care-worn face needed a shave.

Her mind turned to John and the countless hours she'd spent watching her husband sleep. John had been a good man. He had firm ideals. His principles remained pure when he died. The death mask his family ordered had no lines of uncertainty etched upon it. John and Allan could not have been more than a few years apart in age, but John, even in illness, seemed the younger man.

Ramsey stirred, eyes fluttering slightly before he slipped back into sleep.

His worn countenance suits him, she thought.

They were much alike, she and Ramsey. They walked the world on an uncertain path. She glanced at his boots and smiled at the prosaic association. Scuffed and muddy, they showed evidence of an attempt to clean them. His hat lay loosely in his lap.

"Allan," she said softly. Clearing her throat, she repeated his name louder. "Allan."

He shook himself awake and stood up. "Terribly sorry," he said, trying to clear his head. "It's kind of you to meet me." He rubbed his reddened eyes and took a deep breath. "I'm sorry about having to meet this way, but we must avoid being seen together. Mrs. Hutchinson is Mrs. Carraway's sister."

"If you're worried about the police, they haven't bothered me further. Indeed, I think they're guarding me. There's one of them outside most of the time."

"I know. That's not why I asked you here. You told me you thought someone else—someone who was not the police—was watching you?"

"Yes, but I'm no longer sure that was the case."

"You were right. I've spent five nights watching your boarding house. I saw that person. The police are there, of course. They make no effort to conceal themselves. But I've seen someone else."

"Who is it?"

"I don't know for sure. I have only conjecture. But think, Abby. Since that first time you thought you saw someone, has it happened again? Maybe someone who seemed out of place? Someone you've noticed more than once?"

"No—well, maybe," she said slowly. "Two days ago I was standing at the parlor window looking out on the street. A man was standing there. He looked directly at me. He just stood there and didn't take his eyes off me until he finished lighting a small cigar. Then he strolled off. The next day much the same thing happened."

"Did you recognize him?"

"No," she said.

"What did he look like?"

"A dark gray coat and hat. There wasn't much to see. Why do you ask?"

"I think I caught a glimpse of the man you describe," Ramsey said.

"Have you told the police?"

"No. There's little point. They wouldn't believe me. Abby, is there anything you haven't told me? Something about yourself perhaps? Something about Susan?"

"There's nothing to tell. None of this has anything to do with me. Or her."

"And you have no idea of the identity of this man you saw?"

"I do not." Her voice was on the edge of anger.

"I believe he expected you to recognize him."

"What? No. That's nonsense."

"Maybe it is nonsense. But I believe you're being confused with your sister. I've worked things out as carefully as possible. That's the only way it makes sense."

Abby stood shaking her head. Words would not come.

"Do you remember," Ramsey continued, "the day you came to see me at the newspaper? Do you remember how those two men—we now know their names are Turney and Hackett—rushed away when you came down the stairs?"

"Yes," she said with hesitation.

"Hackett was the one who was hanged."

"But how could I or Susan be involved?"

"The murdered men served in the same unit during the war—the 98th Mounted Infantry. The 98th was sent to destroy Confederate communications east of Atlanta. There is no question they were in the vicinity of Covington, and it's likely they were near Charlton when your sister and Alfred Knowles disappeared."

Abby's face grew pale.

"Something may have happened between them and your sister. Seeing you, they thought they saw Susan."

"So this other man, Turney, is he the murderer?" Abby asked uncertainly.

"I doubt it. He might have searched your room. Maybe he broke into Coldwater's office. But you saw him. A man like that couldn't kill three battle hardened thugs."

"What about the police?" she asked. "Aren't they looking for him?"

"Of course. but even if the police find Turney, it doesn't solve anything. Think about what you and I have seen. The man you saw in the street wasn't Turney. Someone else is involved. And the man you saw watching you from the street wanted you to see him. Perhaps he believes the sight of him will frighten you. Maybe he intends to do more but the police—clumsy as they are—have prevented him. I don't know. But I think he will act soon. We must get you out of Atlanta."

"The police have told me to stay."

"They can only *ask* you to stay. They can't keep you here."

She searched his eyes. "Do you have a plan?"

"First, we get you to a safe place. Then an associate and I will go to Charlton and thoroughly search. No one has done that. With luck we'll find answers. We might even draw out this man and deal with him."

"Allan, it all sounds so bizarre."

"I won't deny that. In honesty, I can't give you certain proof that what I say is true. But consider this. Acting as I suggest might not help us, but it won't harm us. And if I'm right, doing nothing is the greater risk. If you stay where you are, you wait to be a victim. Someone has killed three men. If he has revealed himself to you, you must be of importance. If he could ignore you and accomplish his ends, he would, wouldn't he?"

"But all he would need to do is ask a few questions. He'd soon find out I'm not Susan."

"He might not have known your sister's name. Besides, the use of an alias is more likely than having a twin sister." Ramsey's voice grew soft. "Abby, I can't offer you certainties. I just ask you to trust me."

Knaves, she thought, hide behind false assurance and confidence. Foolish men ignore uncertainty and risk. Allan Ramsey was neither a knave nor a fool.

"Tell me what you wish me to do," she said at length.

"For the present, be very careful. Stay in your room as much as possible. Go nowhere outside this house. Don't open your door to anyone you don't know. My plans are nearing completion. You won't remain locked away long."

He pulled the derringer from his pocket. "I suggest you keep this with you. It only has two shots, and it doesn't do much beyond make a loud noise. Still, it might startle an attacker and give you time to run away. Do you want me to show you how to use it?"

She examined the small weapon and slipped it in her purse. "I have seen such things before."

"Munford Coldwater said your sister was riding bareback when he last saw her. Are you as good a rider?"

"Better."

III

The parlor clock read 7:40 p.m. when Abigail Maynard and Allan Ramsey walked out the front door of the Hoehling house. Abby wore Chatsworth White's linen suit and carried the carpetbag he brought when he'd arrived with Ramsey a half hour before. By the time they reached the street, Whitey was making a less formal departure down a drainpipe at the back of the house.

They walked down the street in what appeared to be easy conversation. Abby had pulled Whitey's hat low over her face and tucked her hair beneath it. She forced herself to keep Ramsey's pace. The sun's afterglow still lit places on the street not covered by shadows of buildings. They stayed in those shadows as best they could until they turned a corner and escaped the eyes of the police.

Ramsey abruptly pulled Abby into a side street. Two horses awaited, watched over by Joe Frank.

"That's not Whitey," Joe Frank said in confusion.

"He'll be along very soon, Joe Frank. Don't worry," Ramsey assured him.

They mounted quickly and headed up the darkened street, then turned on to another. Ramsey kept the pace at a slow trot and Abby rode slightly behind, letting him dictate their way. It wasn't direct. After a series of turns, they rode into a dark alley and drew up, watching to see if anyone was following. No one was.

Lights glowed in the houses. Businesses were shuttered. They continued on their meandering way until a final turn brought them to the back of a building. There stood an elegant open carriage pulled by a handsome black horse. They dismounted. Ramsey went to the back door and tapped. Abby strolled over to look at the carriage.

"A barouche," she said. "It's beautiful. I hardly expected to see such a thing in Atlanta." A large muscular man standing in the shadows mumbled, "Yes ma'am." He gave Abby an unsmiling nod and looked away.

Ramsey joined her. "We'll be using it later," he said, "but right now we'd best get off the street."

The back door opened and a dim light filtered out.

"We shouldn't be long, Jake," Ramsey said to the man in the shadows, "and Whitey will be along shortly."

Abby followed Ramsey through the door. He led them through a room piled with crates. A staircase waited at the other end. Climbing, they came to another door, which Ramsey opened without knocking. They emerged into a comfortable sitting room. A tall dark-haired man turned up a lamp. The room filled with light, revealing finely made furniture and a piano.

"Abby, let me introduce Mr. Rabun Perdido. Rabun, Mrs. Abigail Maynard."

Rabun Perdido bowed. "*Enchanté, Madame.*"

"*Enchantée de faire votre connaissance, monsieur. Je suis bien reconnaissante de votre assistance ce soir,*" she replied.

"*Je vous en prie, Madame.*"

"Did you notice anyone following?" Rabun asked.

"No."

"Will we be using the carriage?" Abby asked.

"*Oui, Madame.*"

She smiled. "So we are to travel in style."

"Yes," said Ramsey, "but, aside from comfort, it affords us certain advantages. Rabun will drive. He can see what's ahead. I will sit in the seat directly behind and be ready if anyone tries to overtake us. An open carriage allows us to see all around us."

"Is the carriage yours, Mr. Perdido?"

"*Non madame*, it is owned by one who helps in this matter. I am privileged to drive it."

"We'll leave soon," Ramsey said. "The moon is only now rising. Its light will be necessary for the trip. We're also waiting for Whitey. I want to talk to him before we go."

"So he accompanies us on our journey?" asked Rabun. "Surely he is not needed."

"No, he won't be coming."

"So why do we wait for him?"

"Walking out the way we did probably fooled the police, but a clever man could catch the switch. It's an old trick. Our route here was meant to confuse anyone who followed us and make their pursuit more obvious. I also had some people posted along our way to see if we were followed. Whitey is checking with them."

Rabun walked to a sideboard filled with bottles and glasses. "Perhaps some refreshment while we wait, *Madame*? And I have an excellent Madeira."

"Thank you. Madeira would be wonderful."

She accepted the glass and idly strolled around the room. Ramsey declined a brandy. Rabun poured a large measure for himself, sat at the piano, and played.

"That's very nice," Ramsey said.

"Chopin's E Minor Nocturne," said Abby. "You play it quite well, Mr. Perdido."

"*Merci, Madame.*" He looked over his shoulder at her. "It is very fine, but not played as often as the others."

"Will we spend the night in Decatur?" Abby asked.

"Yes," said Ramsey, "arrangements have been made."

Rabun's hands moved deftly over the keys. "We shall lodge with *Monsieur* Heflin Sanbourne."

"Really?"

"*Oui, Madame.*"

Abby watched Rabun's hands move gracefully over the keys and then turned to examine his bookshelf. "You have a great many of my father's works, Mr. Perdido."

The music stopped.

"You are Arnaud St. Clair's daughter?"

"Yes, I am. Did you know my father?"

Rabun threw his hands ecstatically in the air. "*Madame* Maynard, *votre père, c'est un des dieux de la poésie! C'est le meilleur explorateur de l'âme!* I met him only once, but I shall never forget. *Incroyable!* I—"

A knock.

Ramsey pulled his revolver and unbolted the door. Chatsworth White stood in the hallway.

"Did anyone follow?" Ramsey asked.

Whitey stepped into the room. "No. I think you're okay."

"Well then, we'd better get going. If the police spotted something, we don't want to meet them on our way out of town."

"Are we square now, Ramsey?"

"Yeah, we're square, Whitey."

Chatsworth White paused at the door. "When will I get my suit back, ma'am?"

"Believe me, Mr. White, I will not wear your clothes a moment longer than absolutely necessary."

"Yes, ma'am," he said and closed the door.

"What did Mr. White mean by being square?" Abby asked.

"Some men fight for honor, *madame*," said Rabun rising to his feet, "and others for money. I believe there was a debt involved."

Rabun bowed and offered her his arm. She took it, and he led her out the door.

Rabun mounted the driver's seat at the front. Ramsey and Abby took seats in the carriage.

"Thanks for keeping watch, Jake," Ramsey said to the man in the shadows. "We'll return the carriage tomorrow. Do you want to pick it up here?"

"Yes. Mind you take proper care with it." Abby's ear caught the soft Irish lilt of Jake's voice.

They made their way down Decatur Street. Rabun set a brisk pace. His belt held a revolver, and he kept the whip ready in his right hand. Behind him, on the seat across from Abby who sat in the back, Ramsey lay unseen under a blanket, cradling a shotgun. To the casual observer, there appeared to be but two in the carriage—a man and his driver.

They soon came to Smoky Row, busy with its raucous trade. Music poured from half a dozen establishments and clashed in the street. People stopped to watch them pass, perhaps surprised that such an elegant carriage was out and about at night. Once they left the city behind, Ramsey sat up, folded the blanket on the seat beside him, and settled himself.

The moon, bright and rising, lit their path. Suddenly, a horseman galloped up from behind. Ramsey tensed and raised the shotgun. The rider sped by.

"Did you recognize him?" Rabun called over his shoulder.

"No."

Rabun kept the fastest pace he dared on the rutted road, but the half-light made steering between the ruts mere guesswork. With each pothole came muttered curses from the driver.

"Things seem to be going well so far," Abby said.

"True, but this is dangerous country at night."

The carriage rocked badly. Abby caught herself and pushed back into the seat. Whitey's clothes fit her tolerably well. In the poor light, one might easily think her a man.

Ramsey took a revolver from his coat. "Would you feel better holding this?"

"I would," she said, reaching for the Adams .32.

"My father won a set of dueling pistols in a card game. One summer in Italy, Susan and I entertained ourselves by shooting fruit as targets. When our skills improved, we moved on to shooting the weathervane to make it spin. We got rather good at it."

"Well, it's no dueling pistol but it might prove useful."

She held the gun in her lap, her body rocking with the movement of the carriage.

"Rabun seems to think very highly of your father," Ramsey said.

"My father was, in his way, a remarkable man. He was a writer, poet, artist, sometimes a revolutionary—the sort of person who crams several lifetimes into one."

"You must have had an exciting childhood."

"It wasn't a typical one, but not as glamorous as you might think. When we weren't running from the authorities, we were running from our creditors. What I remember most was the loneliness. Mother died giving birth. Father was kind but selfish in his way. He shut himself up for days when he wrote. We had times of prosperity, but they were rare. I don't think we stayed in any one place for so much as a year. A bohemian life is better read about than lived. With John, I thought I'd found stability. I thought my life would be settled and secure. Now here I am, riding through the night with a revolver in my lap. It makes me wonder if there's a family curse."

"I think you've done the right thing, if that helps."

"Well, I'd made up my mind to leave Atlanta even before we met at the millinery shop. It was my plan to go to Charlton to search for information about Susan. Getting to Decatur is what mattered to me. I've no interest in the fantasies of the police or this murder case."

The carriage stopped.

"*Regarde,*" Rabun whispered and pointed to the road ahead. Ramsey pulled himself up for a better look.

Sandwiched between saplings and scrub brush, the moonlit road was clear until it made a leftward turn into a grove of trees. There it disappeared into darkness.

"The light is difficult, but I felt someone move in the trees as we crested the hill."

"*Felt?* Did you actually *see* anything?"

"That is uncertain. I do not think those trees are a good place for us."

"Drive on. When the time comes, I'll drop off. If no one bothers you, wait for me on the other side. If you're ambushed, I should be able to provide a diversion. I'll meet you once you're clear."

Rabun flicked the reins, and Ramsey slid back into his seat.

"Abby," he said, "if someone is waiting in that grove, they're thieves, not murderers. It's our valuables they'll want. Do what they ask and stay out of the way. Trust in Rabun's good driving and judgment. Only use the gun if it's absolutely necessary."

Ramsey crouched on the floorboards. They were forty yards from the grove when he whispered goodbye, tumbled out, and was gone.

A few moments later, Rabun's baritone split the night.

Va pensiero, sull' ali dorate,
Va, ti posa sui clivi, sui colli
Ove olezzano tepide e moli
L'aure dolci del suolo natal!

The horse shivered nervously as Rabun's voice rang across the landscape.

Del Giordano le rive saluta
Di sionne le torri atterrated

Rabun's performance did not slacken as they entered the darkness of the trees. His tone grew better, and his whip hand gestured with the words. The horse, now used to this eccentricity, trotted on.

Oh mia patria si bella e perduta
Oh membranza si carra e fatal!

A man with a handgun jumped into the road ahead of them.

"Cut the racket and get down!" he demanded.

"Verdi is not racket!" Rabun shouted. "Who are you to tell me anything!"

"He's the man who's going to make your wife a widow and your children orphans," said a second voice from the trees. A tall thin man stepped to the edge of the road. A spasm of coughing seized him. Another man slipped up behind the carriage.

"There's someone behind us," Abby whispered. Rabun did not acknowledge her.

"Now," said the thin man, regaining his breath, "I believe we have you outnumbered, sir. Please drop your gun at your feet. We are gentlemen and wish no harm to you or your passenger. However, I must ask you to surrender your valuables."

"Music is my most valuable possession, *monsieur*," Rabun said as he set his pistol on the floorboard.

"Then you understand what true riches are. We shall allow you to keep your music, but I must insist on baubles like your wallet and pocket watch."

"*Monsieur*, you have the advantage." Rabun gave a slight nod of his head.

"Fred, collect the weapons and valuables from these gentlemen."

As the man in front of the carriage stepped forward, a rock about the size of a hand landed at his feet. All three ambushers spun to see where it came from. A shotgun thundered. The three men fled from the road.

Rabun shouted and cracked his whip, sending the carriage bolting. Abby fell to the floor. A shot rang out. The shotgun boomed again.

When they found themselves back in the moonlight, Rabun reined in. He jumped to the ground, gun in hand.

"*Madame*, are you well?" he asked anxiously.

"What about Allan?"

Rabun scanned the land behind them for movement.

"Our friend is in the hand of God," he muttered.

A dark figure emerged from the trees.

"And it seems God has returned him."

A few minutes later, Ramsey climbed into the carriage.

"Thank God you're safe, Allan," Abby said.

"They were just thieves. Sorry you had to endure that."

"Did you . . . did you kill them?"

"Oh no, I just cleared them out of our way. I shot high to scare them."

The road now crossed through the defensive works they'd seen from the train. The devastated land was ghostly in the moonlight, a place of tragedy where the spirits of the dead danced.

Ramsey took shells from his pocket and reloaded the shotgun. "Actually, those men back there aren't thieves. They are men reduced to thieving. Did you hear the one who gave the orders? His was an educated voice. He still possessed a remnant of dignity. I doubt he ever saw himself living as a common highway robber. His world is destroyed, and consumption is tearing at his lungs—a doubly cruel fate. Before long he'll die of his disease or be shot along the road. I want no part in the destruction of such a man."

"I know that cough. John died gasping for breath."

"I'm sorry."

Far away on the barren field, a campfire glowed in the dark until it faded from view.

"John was a good man. He had dreams and ideals. I found it exciting just to be near him. All that is good in me would rise up when we were together." A tear traveled down her cheek. She did not wipe it away. "We received word he was in an Army hospital. Then one day he left and came home. Perhaps it was an act of desertion in a legal sense, but the war was nearly over. I don't think anyone cared. He was of no use to them. At first I believed all would be well. I would nurse him. I would somehow fix him and make him whole. I made him endure the doctors, looking for one who would tell us the others were wrong. It was a foolish thing to do. Nothing could change what was to come. In the end I realized what he'd known all along. He'd come home to die." Tears stained both cheeks now.

Ramsey handed her his handkerchief.

"He hated dying. I think he came to hate me for living. I suppose I came to hate him for wasting away before my eyes. We would sit through the night as the coal glowed in the grate. A mantle clock ticked his life away. Once, while he slept, I stopped it. I couldn't bear to have our remaining time measured that way. I told him it broke while he slept. He knew I was lying, but he wouldn't let anyone start it back.

"During the day, his family was with him, but at night it was just the two of us. I suppose that was fitting. We'd chosen each other in life, not realizing we'd chosen each other in death. Dying is such a selfish act. It's terrible to say that, but it's true. The dying strip everything from the living. They leave nothing but a vast emptiness."

She paused and again wiped her eyes.

"The night John died, he appeared to rally. For a short time he seemed so much stronger. It was as if pain and despair had tried to rob him and failed. He begged me not to remember him as he was then. I said I wouldn't, but that's not possible."

They left the battle-scarred land behind. In the moonlight, the trees once again threw their shadows across the road. Sometimes Rabun would rein in, waiting and watching the road ahead, only to drive on without comment. The moon slipped lower in the sky.

Abby stared out into the darkness in silence.

They entered the outskirts of Decatur and wound their way to Heflin Sanbourne's house.

When the carriage rolled to a stop, Cassie stepped out with a lamp. She led them down a hallway to the back of the house and opened a door.

"They here, Mr. Heflin."

Sanbourne was reading. He set down his book and stood up.

"Thank you, Cassie. I'm afraid Jeremiah is indisposed, so I must also ask you to care for the horse."

"Yes, suh." She left them.

"Good evening, Captain Ramsey. I hope your journey was not troublesome."

"It had its moments, but we are well. May I present Mrs. Abigail Maynard and Mr. Rabun Perdido."

Sanbourne bowed slightly in acknowledgment.

"Mrs. Maynard, it is a pleasure to meet you. I understand you were recently here with Captain Ramsey. I see how foolish I was not to make your acquaintance." Sanbourne undermined his attempt at gallantry by avoiding her eyes.

"And Mr. Perdido, I bid you welcome to my home." Heflin Sanbourne stood six feet tall, but his frail body and delicacy of gesture exaggerated the disparity between the two men. Rabun shook Sanbourne's hand, holding it as if it were fine china. "A pleasure, *monsieur.*"

"Well, then . . . ah yes, your bags. Yes. We shall see to those when Cassie returns. I, ah, have taken the liberty of having something prepared for us. I know it is late, but perhaps after your trip . . ."

"That would be splendid, Mr. Sanbourne," Abby said.

Relief came over his face. He led them to a set of double doors that opened into a beautifully appointed room. In the center stood a highly polished mahogany table. Four chairs covered in rich burgundy brocade surrounded it. Landscape paintings flanked a cabinet with glass doors revealing fine crystal within. On the table were various breads, meats, and relishes. Wine had been decanted. The scent of coffee hung in the air. Ramsey looked about in some surprise—it was not the lair of a recluse.

Heflin Sanbourne said to no one in particular, "I do not entertain at present, but there was a time when my house was not without guests."

Cassie appeared in the doorway.

"Ah, Cassie," said Sanbourne, "perhaps you could show our friends to their rooms. I imagine they might want to freshen up after their travels." He stole a questioning glance at Abby's coat and trousers.

Cassie, lamp in hand, led them silently back through the dark house and up a staircase. At the top she lit a wall lamp and took them to their rooms in turn.

Coming to her door, Abby reached into Whitey's coat and handed the Adams revolver back to Ramsey. "Thank God the need for this is over," she whispered.

They arrived at Ramsey's room last.

"Where is Jeremiah?" he asked Cassie. "I expected to see him."

"He's sick."

"But he's here, isn't he?"

She looked sharply at Ramsey.

"He ain't here. He's off drinkin'."

She left the room, leaving her contradiction hanging in the air.

Abby had changed into the traveling dress she'd stuffed into Chatsworth's bag and fixed what she could of her hair.

"You are a picture of loveliness, Mrs. Maynard," Sanbourne said, when she rejoined the men. "Mr. Perdido has been telling of your adventures on the road tonight. He also informs me that you are the daughter of the writer Arnaud St. Clair. I'm sorry to say I never met your father, but he was a correspondent of mine."

Sanbourne gestured to the table. Rabun pulled out a chair for Abby. Sanbourne filled her request for a glass of claret. Rabun chose the same. Sanbourne had coffee. Ramsey asked for water.

"I'm a bit surprised, Mr. Sanbourne," Abby said, "my father was not a friend to science."

"No, he was not. I received a letter from him in '53 that made his feelings clear. I did not take offense. I wish my colleagues wrote with as much originality. His understanding surprised me, and I thought him correct in some of what he said. He was at all times provocative and thoughtful."

"*Tout à fait!*" exclaimed Rabun raising his wine.

"I think my reply surprised him as much as his letter surprised me. We were soon writing at regular intervals. We began to discuss nearly everything—philosophy, music and art, sometimes world affairs. He certainly had original thoughts concerning religion and God. We also shared a great interest in gardening. Two avid gardeners can never be adversaries for long."

Abby smiled. "Father was a determined gardener, but not a talented one. It is pleasant to hear of your friendship."

"Captain Ramsey," Sanbourne said, "I believe you have some pressing matters. Perhaps I should leave you."

"That isn't necessary. I thank you for your willingness to help us. And please, call me Allan. My days as Captain Ramsey are over. I wish to lock them in the past."

Heflin looked fully and frankly at Ramsey. "As do we all."

"There really isn't very much to discuss at this point," Ramsey continued. "It is dangerous for Mrs. Maynard to remain in Atlanta. Tomorrow she will remain here under your care. Presumably, Jeremiah and Cassie will aid in that. Mr. Perdido and I will ride to Charlton."

Their conversation and dining continued for a little over an hour before Ramsey and Rabun excused themselves, pleading an early start in the morning.

Ramsey stopped Rabun in the hallway. "It would be foolish not to post a guard tonight." He checked his watch. "Rabun, will you go first? I'll relieve you later."

"You think of sleep, *mon ami? C'est impossible.*"

"Perhaps, but some rest would be welcome. Be alert. If we've been followed, someone may be watching. If it's the man I saw outside Abby's boarding house, he will not make himself obvious."

Ramsey lay on the bed and closed his eyes.

Heflin Sanbourne and Abby Maynard also found sleep impossible and remained at the table.

"How long did you correspond with my father?"

"Oh, right up until the war stopped the mail north. I now know he passed in '62, but I didn't hear about it until later. You have my condolences." He paused. "Would you like to read his letters? I could have copies made and give you the originals if you wish."

"If it is not too much trouble," said Abby, "I would be grateful. I'm sure that somewhere in his papers are your own letters to him. Would you wish me to have them sent to you?"

"You needn't bother. I've always saved my drafts and sent out fair copies. The drafts may not be pretty, but they contain all I need. Your father mentioned you often—you and your sister. Susan wasn't as interested in gardening as you, I believe. Arnaud wrote that you experience the world through your hands and senses. Susan, he said, experienced it through her mind."

"Susan always had her nose in a book. Throughout our life with father, rushing from place to place, she carried an ever-growing pile of books she kept in a steamer trunk. I'm sure porters still tremble at the thought. Father used to call it 'the anchor.' When we'd reached a place where he intended to settle for a while, he would tell her to 'let go the anchor,' meaning she could unpack her books."

"Arnaud said you could grow anything, that plants bloomed in your hands."

She laughed. "Father could exaggerate."

"And your photography? Does that still interest you? I believe you were quite taken with the process."

"The times haven't been kind to that part of my life. My equipment is in storage at present. I tried to set myself up as a portrait photographer in New York before the war, but clients were few. It wasn't considered a proper occupation for a woman. Yet some good came of it. That was how I met my husband. He was one of my customers."

"Is there anything else I might get you? No? Well then, perhaps we too should retire."

"Yes, of course. It's quite late. I've enjoyed the evening, Mr. Sanbourne." Abby did not rise to go. After a moment of hesitation, she said, "I watched the way you and Allan spoke with each other. I hope you don't think I'm prying, but how do you know each other?"

"You are as quick as your father. Yes, we have met before, and it is the war that weighs on us. Captain Ramsey, for I think I should call him that for the moment, gathered information and used it in various ways that would benefit his army and confuse ours. He was a reporter before the hostilities, and one of his weapons was words. He became essential to General Grenville Dodge, a man who caused our Confederacy no end of trouble. Though Captain Ramsey was very good at what he did, such a life takes its toll. Men lived or died based on information the captain provided. Sometimes that information was wrong. He is an intelligent man, but no one is always right. The terrible consequences of error rest easier on some shoulders than others. Captain Ramsey did not take his duties lightly."

Sanbourne looked past her to a place only he could see and continued.

"We met in our own battle once. He did his duty just as I did mine. He thinks he did me a terrible wrong, but that is incorrect. What happened was our fate. If my commander had been wise, rather than petty and vindictive, Captain Ramsey would not have succeeded. General Bragg wanted, for his own reasons, to believe false dispatches. I grant you, they were artfully done. I was slow to catch the deceit myself, but in time I did see it. I warned Bragg. He wouldn't listen. He ordered Longstreet's Corps to Knoxville so he would not have to look at a better man." Heflin's voice dropped so low, Abby had to lean forward to hear him. "It is Captain Ramsey's curse to be ruthless enough to do what is necessary, but too moral to be at ease with his actions. You see, he, too, carries demons from the war. He, too, was broken."

"Broken?"

"He was ambushed as Sherman was leaving Atlanta. Shot down by those too weak to stand and fight like soldiers. He was in a very bad way for quite some time. Surely not all the scars are on his body. The worst ones never are."

Sanbourne looked into Abby's eyes. "You think I am his enemy. You believe it is strange he has come to me in a time of danger. You wonder why."

"Yes."

"I believe he has come for the sake of his soul. He must find the means to forgive himself. He would never tell you that—he may not realize it himself—but he wishes to heal the past, and that is only forgiveness by another name."

"And you? What of you?"

"For me? For me it is no longer a question of friend and enemy. We are frail creatures who must do the best we can for one another."

Rabun Perdido watched. An owl hooted. Another called back. Dogs barked and fell silent. The moist night air was rich with the smell of recently turned earth. Rabun shifted his weight slightly to ease the strain on his legs. He peered again through the leaves of a shrub.

Shortly before, he had sensed another presence. He now searched the darkness for the slightest movement, listened for the smallest sound. He focused all his energy on his senses. The presence was not far away; it was only unseen.

The moon was below the horizon and darkness nearly complete. A slight breeze rustled the branches above him. An animal scratched on a tree trunk—a possum? A whiff of mint touched his nostrils. Something larger than a possum had crushed the plants. He searched his memory for a damp place he might have seen when the light was better—a place conducive to the herb's growth. He fixed his eyes just off-line, hoping his peripheral vision would pick up movement. He waited in expectation of what he must see, waited for what might present itself now that he was ready to receive it.

The enemy was behind the second of five bushes near the fence.

A stone landed quietly in the grass near his feet. He understood its message and moved around the corner of the house and slipped through the door.

"We need to talk," Ramsey whispered as Rabun entered.

"Someone hides himself out there. I could not see, but I know."

"Really?"

Rabun nodded. "*Certainement.*"

"Did he see you?"

"*Oui.* Such a one, he is no fool."

"Only one?"

"The one is certain, and he is enough."

"Then we have to change plans. Sanbourne came to my room to say that Jeremiah is gone. Apparently he disappears without explanation now and then, only to reappear as if nothing happened. He picked a damn fine time to run off. Without him, Sanbourne and Cassie can't protect Abby, and there is no guarantee whoever is out there will follow us when we leave. You must remain." Ramsey pulled the Adams revolver from his coat pocket. "Take this. I believe Abby can use it if necessary. Give it to her when she wakes. You have your pistol, and I will leave you the shotgun."

"*Non!* You must not ride alone! We must send for help and then go together."

"The time to do this is now. Only one of us can go, and you should be with Abby. If he could make the choice, Arnaud St. Clair would want you to guard his daughter."

"*Non* . . . ah . . . *oui.* But *mon ami,* you must consider there may be more than one against you."

"True. But if my leaving divides our forces, it also splits our opponent between two objectives. He must think Abby is useful or he wouldn't be here tonight. I may not even be followed if she is his main objective. However, events suggest that Charlton has something to do with all this. I'll be on my guard. Do you mind taking guard duty again? Perhaps I can get a bit more rest before I go."

"There is little to watch. It is enough for them to know we are not sleeping like fools. I shall resume my post with one of *Monsieur* Sanbourne's cigars and a brandy."

Ramsey planned to leave just before daybreak. If those watching left before he was on the road, they could set an ambush. That assumed they knew where he was going. If Charlton wasn't part of their equation, his adversaries might set up in the wrong place and their paths would never cross. If they anticipated his move toward Charlton, things could get sticky. On the other hand, they might watch him ride away and attack Sanbourne's house, attempting to take Abby Maynard by force. That would need more than one man and it would have to be done quickly. Sanbourne lived in a town, and the fighting would be noticed. A third possibility came to mind. They might ignore his departure and continue waiting, or perhaps discreetly follow him. Patience itself is often a potent weapon.

What if they did attack the house? Sanbourne would be useless in a fight. Cassie had spirit if she chose to help. Abby knew how to use a gun, but could she shoot a man? Firing at a weathervane is a long way from putting a bullet in a person. Rabun. He would be enough with even minimal help. The shotgun was a formidable weapon, and Rabun would put it to good use. Ramsey was comforted to have him there.

Having given away the Adams and the shotgun, Ramsey had only his Colt for the trip to Charlton. That was enough. There would be no stand-up fight. If trouble found him, he would only use the Colt to buy time and run.

What were the police doing? Had they discovered Abby's disappearance, or were they watching an empty room? Probably the latter.

He struck a match and looked at his watch. Time to go. He splashed water on his face, slipped on his coat, and examined the Colt one last time.

Rabun, empty glass in hand, slipped through the back door.

"*Bonne chance, mon ami,*" he said.

On the sideboard, Ramsey found, along with a canteen, bread and cheese for his breakfast and a parcel containing food for the trip. Sanbourne was a thoughtful host.

Ramsey moved quickly down the path to the stable. Once inside, three curious equine heads peered at him from the stalls. The gray whinnied. Rabun's horse nodded and snorted. A large bay filly mutely stared at him. He saddled the bay.

Who did the riding? Certainly not Sanbourne—Jeremiah? Cassie?

He cinched the saddle, checked it, then led the bay to the stable door and peered out. The house and yard were still. Opening the stable door enough for the bay to slip through, he again surveyed his surroundings. Only the sounds of the morning birds met his ear. He mounted and trotted onto the street. The bushes along the fence gave no evidence of anyone's presence.

The road was dusty, and the morning dew did little to settle it. He turned and rode south toward the junction with Covington Road, his horse's hooves loud in the still air. After what seemed an eternity, he slowed and looked behind him. All was still.

He set a faster pace now and didn't break his speed until the next turn. A dense grove of trees ahead remained in darkness. He reined in and thought of the thieves from the night before. His Colt in hand, he gently spurred the bay onward, leaning forward to make a smaller target. The horse's mane touched his cheek as they trotted through the shadows. A bird, startled by the bay's hooves, exploded from a thicket. Ramsey spurred lightly. The bay responded and carried them into the light. He stopped and looked back. The bay snorted and pawed. He patted the horse. "Well done, girl. Well done."

Beyond the trees the land opened its arms to receive him. Fields waiting for cotton to break the ground ran on both sides. He slowed his pace to a walk. Despite the rising sun, the morning air was cool against his skin. A haze not yet burned off by the rising sun hung over the rolling fields. He reached into his coat pocket and pulled out some cheese and bread. Now that the danger was less, the calls from his stomach grew louder. He reached forward and offered the last bit to the bay.

The fields ended and gave way to scrub pine. Neither the fields nor the low thin pine offered cover for a would-be attacker. Ramsey reined in again and drank from the canteen. The sun was higher in the sky. He checked his pocket watch. He'd been on the road for almost two hours. He sipped again from the canteen and tried to ignore his fatigue and gritty eyes.

The respite from danger ended at the crest of the next hill. Ramsey stopped to consider the problem that lay ahead. The road dropped into a heavy mist that clung to one of the creeks lacing the countryside. The mist was heavy and lay across the road and spread out into the fields. It would burn away with the sun, but fed by the cool air and moisture from the creek, that might take an hour. He hadn't time for the sun to do its work. Sensing his uncertainty, the bay grew restless. He patted her flank.

If he rushed through at a gallop, he would be past an assailant before that person could react. That would work with a sandy ford. If it were a stony ford, the horse might lose her footing. And worse, he might miss a bridge if one existed. Dismounting and walking the bay through was safest but would leave him vulnerable.

"What's it going to be, girl? Any thoughts?"

The bay snorted and bobbed her head nervously. "I don't like it either," muttered Ramsey. "I don't like it one damn bit."

He spurned to a trot and drew up at the edge of the mist, listening with all his might. No point in trying to see someone waiting in ambush. Even a fool could stay hidden in that blanket, but sound might give him away.

The raucous call of crows came from the distance.

Ramsey drew a deep breath. His heels gently tapped the horse's flanks.

"Okay, girl. Let's go."

It occurred to him that he didn't know the horse's name. It seemed wrong to ride into the danger not knowing the name of his ally.

"Steady now, girl."

They entered the misty world ahead. He bent low, keeping his eyes on the bit of road he could see. The bay's hooves thundered, the sound distorted by the mist. Ramsey rode at a bare walk—watching, listening, scarcely breathing. Water roared ahead. The creek.

Well, if I can't see, they can't see, he thought, and dismounted.

He held the reins and led the horse forward. The bay skittishly trailed. A dark form loomed ahead. Ramsey crouched and pointed the gun. The horse whinnied and shied. Ramsey edged forward. The silhouette of a tree darkened the white of the mist. Ahead, the rushing water grew louder.

Ramsey's boots touched wood. A bridge. The bay's hooves crossing resembled artillery fire.

Once over, he remounted and spurred forward in a trot. The white shroud grew thinner as the ground rose away from the creek. Large trees came into focus. Soon the view was clear, and he slowed again to a walk. His horse abruptly stopped. Ramsey snapped up the Colt and looked around. A cascade of urine relieved the horse's needs. Ramsey shoved the Colt back into his belt.

As good a place as any for a rest; he gratefully drank from his canteen.

"Let's hope we don't have too many more of those to cross, old girl.'" He tapped the horse's flanks, and they resumed their way.

From behind came an unmistakable sound. Hooves rumbled on the bridge. Just one horse. The slow rhythm of the hoof beats meant the rider was walking his horse over—no fool, he. The pursuer must have ridden hard until he came to the mist on the creek. Ramsey had seen no one following earlier. The rumble stopped. The pursuer was across the bridge.

Fifty yards ahead, a copse of poplar and pine stood off to the left. Ramsey spurred his mount to the grove, dismounted, and tied the horse out of sight.

The rider came into view. A small man. Turney, most likely.

Ramsey pulled his pistol, but hoped surprise would carry the day. He wanted a prisoner.

The rider rode hard and was nearly abreast. Ramsey leaped into the road, his gun held high, waving his hat, and yelling. The horse, edgy from its trip through the mist, reared wildly. The rider fell. The horse bolted back down the road toward the creek.

The man lay face down on the ground, stunned. Ramsey cocked the Colt and aimed it at the man's back. He listened for other riders. Nothing. Even the frightened horse, now lost to the mist at the creek, was silent. The figure groaned and stirred.

"Turn over slowly!" Ramsey barked.

The fallen rider did as ordered.

"Abby?"

She struggled to a sitting position. Whitey's suit was covered with road dust.

"What the hell are you doing here?"

She said nothing.

Ramsey went to his horse and brought her his canteen. "Are you all right?"

She poured water in her hand and splashed her face. "I think so—no thanks to you."

He helped her to her feet and led her back to where his horse was tied. She was steadier now and seated herself on a fallen tree. She checked her arm and the leg she'd landed on. "I don't think anything is broken."

"For God's sake, Abby, what possessed you to—"

"I want to see Charlton for myself."

"You're a damn fool!" Nervous energy and fear exploded from him.

Abby stood unsteadily. "Get out of my way!" The once white suit was torn at the knee. Ramsey grabbed her arms, and she slumped back down on the tree trunk.

"You aren't fit to go anywhere," he said.

"Find my horse."

"You don't need your horse."

"Find it!"

"You're in no shape—"

"Get my horse!"

"Abby, just—"

"Now!"

"We're going back to Decatur. This is madness."

He untied his mount and rode back toward the creek. Her horse wouldn't have gone far once it had reached the mist.

For a second time, he entered the still whiteness. His search was deliberately slow, relying more on sound than sight. He worried that if he approached her horse too quickly, it would bolt again. Slowly he made his way forward, his thoughts racing to form a plan. She'd utterly wrecked everything—damn her. The only thing left was to start over. She'd want to ride on to

Charlton, but he had to make her return. He'd manage it by force if necessary. He searched in the mist for some sign of the creature, though finding it could be a mistake. Putting her on the back of his own horse guaranteed they'd both return to Decatur.

Twigs cracked to his left.

Ramsey drew the Colt and eased his horse toward the sound.

He heard it again. Something moved by the trees. He edged closer. The dark form resolved into a horse munching grass.

It was tied to a sapling.

"Lose your horse, mister?" a nasal voice sounded behind him.

Ramsey spun in the saddle. A revolver pointed at him.

"Throw down your gun and get off your horse!" The man stepped closer and moved where Ramsey could see him. "Throw down the gun first. Gently."

Ramsey tossed the Colt between his horse and his assailant. The man bent to pick it up. Ramsey spurred the bay into him, knocking him sprawling on the ground. The assailant struggled to stand, but Ramsey rode him down again. A third pass was unnecessary. The man lay stunned and bleeding. Ramsey dismounted, reached down, and threw his assailant's gun into the bushes. The man held his right arm and moaned in pain.

Ramsey trained his gun at the man's head. "Are you Lewis Turney?"

The man looked up and nodded, his eyes glued to Ramsey's gun.

"Are you alone?"

The man nodded again.

"Where's your horse?"

Turney indicated the horse tied to the sapling. "There."

"Try again, Turney. If I don't like your answer, you're dead." Ramsey cocked the Colt. "Where is your horse?"

"Back there," Turney said, indicating Abby's direction.

"I came that way. There was no horse." Ramsey raised his gun.

"Wait!" Turney shrieked. "Tied in the woods. I can show you!"

Ramsey lowered the gun slightly. "How come I didn't see it or you?"

"It's off the road aways. I saw the other fella's horse run off. Since you two was arguing, I just thought I'd get it. It's worth something. That's all I did. Honest. We—I—"

Ramsey swung the butt of the Colt with all his strength into the side of Turney's head and dropped to a crouch.

We. A second man.

Turney lay on the ground unconscious. Ramsey waited and listened. The horse returned to munching grass. Nothing else moved. Ramsey mounted and spurred back toward Abby.

She was sitting on the tree trunk, just as he'd left her.

"Abby!" he called as he dismounted.

"Allan, run!"

A figure rose from behind Abby and placed a gun against her head.

"That would be unwise, Captain. Stay where you are and raise your hands, or this woman dies." The words were precise and spoken with a distinct English accent.

Ramsey paused, the Colt revolver in his hand.

"You have far more to lose than I do," said the Englishman. "You really do."

Ramsey dropped his gun to the ground.

"Thank you, Captain. I've been anxious to meet you. It would be a shame if things went wrong for us."

They sat on the ground tied back-to-back. A horse fly buzzed around their heads. A rock dug into Abby's leg. They were alone; their captor had gone to look for Turney when his calls went unanswered. His search wouldn't be difficult—the sun was up, the mist was lifting, and Turney wasn't moving.

"He was on me so fast, Allan. It was over before I knew what happened."

"Does anyone know you followed me?"

"No, I slipped out shortly after I heard you leave. Rabun locked the door to my room, but there was a key on the nightstand. I let myself back out. What happened to the other man?"

"He's where I left him."

"Is he—"

"Dead? I hit him pretty hard, but I don't think so."

Their captor returned, leading Ramsey's and Abby's horses. Abby's had Turney lying across it.

"I see you've made Lewis's acquaintance, Captain Ramsey. I doubt he gave you much of a fight. His gifts lie elsewhere."

The man who spoke was of medium height and wore a neatly trimmed beard that did credit to his regular features. His light brown hair was cut short.

"You're Simon Giles, aren't you?" Ramsey said.

"Why yes. I thought you knew that."

"Mr. Giles, we have—"

"Much to discuss. But not now. I have things to take care of. I shan't be long."

Giles tied the two horses then mounted his own and rode off.

"What do you think will happen to us?" Abby asked.

"I don't know, but things could hardly be worse. We must keep our heads, play for time, and look for a chance to get the upper hand. If I can jump him, I'll do it. Chances are you'll need to help me. Do you understand?"

"Yes," she said softly.

A wagon harness jingled. Giles returned, driving a wagon drawn by two horses, with his horse tied to its rear. He hopped down from the wagon, pulled Turney from the back of Abby's horse and hoisted him into the wagon. Then untying Abby and Ramsey's horses, he shouted and shooed them toward the creek. As they ran way he fired a shot in the air, sending them off at a gallop. He cut Abby loose and ordered her into the wagon, where he tied her wrists to Turney's arm.

Giles walked over and squatted where Ramsey still sat tied on the ground. "This isn't how I'd hoped to meet you, Captain, but you must believe me when I say that I consider it an honor." He cut the binding on Ramsey's ankles and replaced it with a hobble, then stood and held his gun on Ramsey.

"Get up and go to the wagon. You'll need to drive."

"I can't stand up from this position. I'll need help. My leg."

Giles hesitated and considered the matter. "Get on your knees."

Ramsey shifted and, with effort, got to his knees. Giles went behind him and pulled him to his feet.

"Go to the back of the wagon. You should be able to get in from there."

Ramsey shuffled to the wagon. He managed to work his way past Abby and get to the driver's seat. Giles tossed Ramsey the reins, then hopped into the bed across from Abby and Turney, placing himself directly behind Ramsey.

"We find ourselves in awkward circumstances," he said. "I think a few simple rules are in order. Captain, if you try any foolishness, I'll shoot her first. Then I'll shoot you. You will do exactly as I say or there will be consequences. I hope we all understand each other."

"There'll be no trouble."

"Good."

"What do you want with us?" Abby snapped. "We've done nothing to you!"

"That's rather disingenuous, considering you've killed three of my men and rather damaged poor Turney."

"We've killed no one," said Ramsey.

"Well, the facts point in another direction."

Abby shifted her body to face Giles. "We don't know anything. We haven't done anything. Just let us go. You've made a terrible mistake."

"Just let you go? It's far too soon for us to be waving goodbye. I'm going to ask you some questions and I'd like truthful answers. I'm not the interrogator you are, Captain, but I shall do my best."

Ramsey turned around far enough in the driver's seat to see Giles but said nothing.

"So, this is, I believe, where matters stand," Giles began. "You two are clearly working together. You have killed three of my men. After—"

"We didn't murder your men." Ramsey said firmly.

"After becoming aware of my presence, you've made a bolt from Atlanta. My compliments, Captain. It was a rather bold getaway that I only narrowly caught. I found myself unable to follow you, but I was rather certain you'd head this way—lo and behold, here you are. Now I want to know exactly where you're headed and why. What is your plan?"

"You're mad. We've done nothing to you!" Abby snapped.

"I see. And yet here I find you"—he indicated Abby with the barrel of his gun—"riding through the countryside dressed as a man. I think that alone raises questions about what your game is."

"You've got it all wrong about us," Ramsey said. "This woman's name is Abigail Maynard. She's looking for her sister. Her sister Susan once lived not far from here. We are not murderers. I'm working with the police to apprehend the killer. Someone else killed your men."

Giles laughed. "If that's your notion of an explanation, you insult me. Tully and O'Bannion were dead when I arrived. Hackett soon followed. And for God's sake, it doesn't make an ounce of difference to me if you're working with the police. I'd expect you to be playing both sides."

"We've killed no one and you're spinning fantasies," Ramsey said.

"Perhaps I am, but we can't just sit here and argue. Besides, what we really need to discuss is whether you're working on your own or whether you're working for someone else."

"What?"

"I shouldn't have expected this to be easy," sighed Giles. "You know, Captain Ramsey, I followed your career. It was rather difficult. A hint here, a rumor there—rather like chasing a shadow, but that, of course, was what intrigued me. When Grant and Sherman sent you to find things out, find them out you did. You might say I was one of the few in the audience for some of your greatest performances. Grant's campaign against Vicksburg was a masterpiece made possible by you. And what did you get? Nothing. You won't even be an afterthought in the history books."

"The glory belongs to Grant. There's a long way between knowing the possibilities and having the strength to act."

"As you wish, but don't think I find your modesty becoming. I need information and you're the one who will tell me. I will again pose my question. The lady's fate will be determined by what you choose to say." Giles pointed his pistol at the side of Abby's head. "Are you working with Munford Coldwater?"

"Good God, no!"

"Does he have my gold or do you?"

"Gold? I—"

"Tell me!"

Giles cocked the revolver. Abby began to sob.

Ramsey's mind raced, trying to find a way forward. "The gold is where you put it!"

Simon Giles's eyes darted from Ramsey to Abby and back. He lowered the pistol slightly and shook his head. "You're selling, Captain, but I'm not buying. I know you've met with Munford Coldwater. Turney said he and Hackett followed you there the day after they saw you at the newspaper. And this woman—whatever she calls herself now is immaterial—was there when we hid the gold shipment. She couldn't have seen where it was hidden, but if she survived that day, then maybe one of the slaves did too."

He stroked Abby's cheek with his pistol. "Is that how you found out?"

Unable to speak, she shook her head no.

"Okay, let's try this differently." Giles placed the gun barrel against Ramsey's head and looked hard at Abby. "If you don't want him to die, I suggest you tell me."

"She doesn't know any more than I do," Ramsey said.

"Let her speak for herself!"

"I . . . I . . ."

"Giles, she doesn't know!" Ramsey insisted. "The woman you saw was her twin sister, Susan. Mrs. Maynard came to Atlanta looking for her. Susan was the woman you saw. You're confusing the two. Mrs. Maynard arrived in Atlanta when you did. She has done nothing." His voice grew calmer. "I assume you were the one who broke into my room. You must have figured out I don't have any gold. And if it was you who broke into her room and stole her letters, you'd know about her sister."

Giles sat for a time lost in thought, then slowly lowered the revolver.

"Are you telling me that Munford Coldwater got his gold after all?"

"What's any of this got to do with him?"

"It's *his* gold, for Christ's sake," Giles said. "We were the ones who nicked it."

In the silence that followed, Ramsey's mind raced. If he couldn't give Giles anything more, he and Abby would die.

"Where was the gold hidden?"

"At that plantation. Charleston or something," Giles said doubtfully.

"If it's near Coldwater's place, the name is Charlton," Ramsey said. "If it were me, I'd start looking there. It's more than likely still where you put it. If it's gone, that's where the trail begins, and you move on to Munford. You lose little by seeing for yourself."

Giles said nothing.

"So what do you want to do?" Ramsey prodded.

Giles gave a little shrug of his shoulders. "Your suggestion is reasonable. I suppose we must go to Charlton. But I warn you, if it's a trap, the two of you will be the first to die. Turn the wagon, Captain, and drive."

Ramsey set the wagon in motion.

The road ahead was empty of travelers. Sunlight glinted through the canopy of trees, mixing light and shadow on the ground. Two deer watched them pass before bolting off into the brush. Birds chirped in counterpoint to the tinkling of the harness and the rhythm of the horses' hooves.

When they reached a track that forked to the left, Giles ordered Ramsey onto the smaller road. Once they were off the main road, Giles relaxed.

"Was it you or Coldwater who killed my men?"

"I had no hand in any killings and no dealings with Coldwater. But he isn't the only one who stood to gain from the murders. There's a good case against you. You're the one who benefits. With the others dead, it's down to a two-way split with Turney, and he's lying at your feet unconscious. Maybe it's now a one-way split."

"While that may seem logical, it's utterly wrong. From the moment I arrived in Atlanta, I've been forced to improvise. I expected to find Tully, O'Bannion, Turney, and Hackett here and useful. Instead I found two of them murdered. Before I could locate Hackett and Turney, Hackett turned up dead too. I managed to find Turney, purely by luck. The little bastard was too greedy to run and too scared to do anything useful. He was waiting for Mason to show up. It would have been a long wait. Mason won the favor of another man's wife. Jealous husbands can act rashly. I imagine Mason's chasing wives in a celestial realm now. You know, I quite frightened Turney when I found him."

"Because you died in a prison fire."

Simon Giles chuckled. "You've been checking around I see. Yes, that's how my death certificate reads, but I assure you, I have no personal experience of the afterlife. When Bill Tully got out of prison, it forced my hand. I had to get out of prison and stop the greedy bastard from taking everything for himself. A simple breakout wouldn't do, because I'd have the police after me. To avoid that, I had been content to serve my sentence and become, if not an honest man, one on whom the law had no claim. Bill's release meant I could wait no longer. After considering matters, I decided it made sense to die. A fire suggested itself. Charred corpses are so hard to identify. If I'd realized how easy it was to arrange, I'd have done it earlier and gotten ahead of Bill. A little money goes a long way with prison staff."

"Then you came to Atlanta, caught up with Tully, and settled the matter."

"Again, it sounds logical, but that's not the case. Only two people knew where the gold was—Bill and myself. We sent the others away before it was hidden. If they wanted their cut, they needed one of us. But you're quite right, I was planning to have a reckoning with Bill. Unfortunately, the disloyal bastard was dead when I got here. But whatever I might have intended, I needed the others alive." Giles gestured toward Abby. "Of course, your lady friend was there that day. Don't think I'm swallowing that nonsense about a twin sister. Orville was supposed to kill her, but I guess he got sloppy. That wasn't his way. Still, even a man who enjoyed killing as much as he did can make a mistake. I thought all the darkies were dead too, but I suppose not."

Abby began to sob, quietly at first, and then uncontrollably.

"For God's sake woman! Sit and be quiet!" Giles poked her with the barrel of his gun.

"It must have been a shock," Ramsey said over Abby's crying, "when Turney and Hackett saw her at the newspaper."

Giles poked Abby again. "Quiet down!"

Abby pressed her face into her hands, muffling her sobs.

"God, yes," Giles laughed. "It was all Turney could talk about when I found him. She scared the daylights out of both of them. Hackett thought she'd come back from the grave. Turney, coward that he is, at least knew better. He thought she had survived being gunned down."

"Was it you or Turney who paid my room a visit?"

"Me. I left you a little hint. I assume you noticed."

"I did. When you found Turney, why didn't the two of you just go get the gold?"

"Come now, Captain, you of all people should understand. I arrived to find several of my associates dead. Naturally, my thoughts turned to Munford Coldwater. One thing I learned from dealing with that old man is that it pays to be very, very careful. He isn't the kind to forgive and forget. When I found Turney he told me the woman Orville shot was alive, and she had gone with you to meet Coldwater. I had to ask myself, what did the old man know? Whether or not he'd found his gold, he'd want revenge. It looked to me as if he was waiting for us to come sniffing around and, with your help, was picking us off one by one. A trip to Charlton seemed like an ambush waiting to happen. No, it would not have done for me to run around with a shovel and high hopes."

"Why not just focus on Coldwater?"

"It's quite likely you and the woman are Coldwater's eyes and ears, if not his executioners. It made sense to unravel this Gordian knot by beginning with you two."

Giles called a halt and studied the map.

"May I have some water?" Ramsey asked. "The lady might want some too."

"I think we're all thirsty," said Giles. He jumped from the wagon and returned with a canteen. He took a long drink and walked back.

He offered the canteen to Abby. She looked away in disgust, the canteen suspended in Giles's hand. "Suit yourself," he said.

He climbed back onto the wagon and handed the canteen to Ramsey.

Abby closed her eyes, her head bowed dejectedly.

"Drive on, Captain," Giles said.

They emerged from the wood and traveled along a newly plowed field. The sun was still bright, but storm clouds gathered in the west. Abby caught sight of the charred remnants of a large house in the distance.

Despite fire and exposure to the elements, the magnificent wreck still stood. Though the rear of the house had collapsed, the front with its pillars and balcony nobly greeted the world. Two chimneys protruded through the charred remnants of the roof and two others rose from rubble at the back. The curves of twin stairways swept up to the emptiness of a missing door. Four immense oaks grew along the front drive. Several outbuildings stood around the main building like the retainers of a dead queen.

Tears welled in Abby's eyes. Throughout a childhood spent with a father who wandered restlessly, Susan had longed for a home—a place of family, of roots, of stability. The shattered mansion was what remained of her dream.

"Drive around back, over there where it's fallen down."

Ramsey drove across a yard covered with tall grass and weeds. When they reached the rear of the building, Giles ordered Ramsey out of the wagon and tied him to a charred beam.

He returned to the wagon and prodded Turney, then felt his neck. "It seems you've been tethered to a corpse," he said to Abby.

He loosened the knot that bound her to Turney's arm and pulled her from the wagon onto cramped and aching legs. She, too, was bound to the beam.

"I will go have a look. If the gold is still there, I'll know."

Giles walked briskly around the side of the ruin.

"Abby, are you all right?" asked Ramsey.

She said nothing, her head bent, staring at the ground. Susan was dead.

Simon Giles returned, smiling.

"There's an excellent chance you aren't lying. The gold appears to be where we buried it."

He cocked his pistol. "Unfortunately, we must part company now, Captain. I have the gold, I have the wagon, and I bloody well don't need you two. Sorry it has to end this way. Goodbye."

He raised his gun.

"Shoot us and you're a fool!" Ramsey shouted. He locked eyes with Giles. "You've got the gold, but it's not in the wagon, is it? It's still in the ground. You can use us to dig it up, or you can do it alone. Your choice. But digging alone will take twice as long—time spent in Coldwater's backyard. And the shots will be heard. Why announce your presence? There's no knowing Coldwater's whereabouts; he could be anywhere."

The gun stayed trained on Ramsey, but a shade of doubt passed over Giles's face.

"When we finish," Ramsey continued more calmly, "you can tie us up and leave us here. It could be days before we're found. You'll be long gone."

"You are in no position to negotiate."

"I'm stating the obvious."

Giles lowered his gun slightly, then raised it again.

Abby braced for the shot. Allan would die and then she would die.

Silence—eternity bound up in silence.

Giles lowered his pistol a second time. "You make some sense, Captain."

He pulled two shovels from the wagon and ran back to the house in a graceful trot.

"I thought he was going to kill us," Abby said, her face red and swollen from tears.

"So did I. Now it looks like we're going to dig. That will only buy us a little more time. He'll kill us once he has his gold."

"Surely he'll tie us up and leave us here as you said."

"No, Abby, he won't. Munford Coldwater lives nearby, and he can't risk our getting away. We're only alive until he gets the gold."

Giles pushed Ramsey through what was once a doorframe and into a large musty basement cut from the earth. Charred beams strained to support what remained of the structure rising over their heads. Light filtering through holes in the planking above created a dim malevolent dreamworld.

He cut the rope that hobbled Ramsey's legs to allow him to climb past joists, beams, and flooring that had fallen during the fire. Ramsey's hands remained tied.

Across the room, Abby was tied to a pillar that supported a massive joist. Behind her, the ground rose quickly to a point where it nearly reached the floor above. Across from her, two stone exterior walls came together to form a corner. One wall possessed three small windows, the glass long since shattered and gone. The other showed a door against which charred beams had fallen.

"You must first clear the debris from the door," said Giles.

"I can't manage it alone."

Giles surveyed the situation. "Then the woman will have to help. When you finish, I'll tell you where to dig."

He looked around him at the earthen floor covered with charred detritus. "An inspired idea, don't you think? Once we buried the gold, we set the house on fire. It should have burned to the ground, but sadly, a storm blew in before its work was done."

"And the people who were here—what happened to them?" Abby said.

"There are always casualties."

"Those people died because of *you!*" Her voice was angry, empty.

"Maybe you don't understand what war is." Giles's tone was dismissive. "War means killing. It's just organized murder. For God's sake, what does death count for in war? What occurred was just happenstance. The people here were in the wrong place at the wrong time. It couldn't be helped."

Abby tried to speak but sobs came instead of words.

Ramsey stepped closer to Giles. "So Coldwater lost and you won," he said. "What about Kilpatrick? Did he lose out too?"

"I'm not sure about Kilpatrick. If he was in it, he kept his hand hidden. But you're right, the thing went pretty high up the chain of command." Giles stepped back and leaned against a stone pillar. "There's no harm telling about how events unfolded. Indeed, I'd value your opinion. You and I are alike in our ways. It's nice to have a knowledgeable audience."

Ramsey waited and said nothing.

"I suppose," Giles said, "it all goes back to Billy Sherman. His penchant for destruction and his hatred of the cotton black market set the conditions. It was Coldwater who came up with a plan to take advantage of that. As Sherman's army drew closer to Atlanta in the spring of '64, the local planters were convinced Sherman would burn all the cotton they had in storage. Those fears weren't far off the mark. Coldwater said he had connections that could save the cotton and get them the money they needed. Since they believed their cotton was inevitably lost if they didn't consign it to him, he had no trouble getting them to do so. He amassed a large number of bales, for which he never paid a penny. His story about how he was going to get the cotton out and get them paid had the advantage of being true. Well, almost true. Once the cotton was paid for, the money wasn't going to go beyond Munford Coldwater. He sold the cotton to a syndicate of northern businessmen. Money greased enough palms to get it out by rail to northern mills and through the port of Savannah to Europe."

"And you were the man who arranged it all."

"That's our destiny, isn't it Captain? When the powerful need things done efficiently—but, let us say, off the books—they turn to men like us. Money had to change hands and cotton had to be moved in a way that kept some rather high-ranking officers from getting dirt on their uniforms. I was known in certain circles as a man who could arrange that sort of thing. Indeed, I'd worked with some of those involved in the past—they would cut the deals and I would take care of the details. It was perfectly natural that they'd come to me."

"But why gold? Bulky and inconvenient, isn't it?"

"That goes back to Munford. He demanded gold as payment. He was adamant. No script. No bearer bonds. He said he'd burn every damn bale unless he got gold. I really have no idea why. Maybe he was going to leave the country. Gold works anywhere. I'm sure he had something cooked up. The northern businessmen grumbled, but in the end they did as asked."

"So the deal was done," Ramsey said, "and you had the headache of moving cotton and gold."

"Headache is right. You can't imagine even half the trouble. On top of everything else, since Munford's trust is always in short supply, he insisted that not one, but two, shipments be arranged. A small one to test the arrangements, followed by the main one. So I had to set up two cotton shipments and two payments in the middle of a goddamn war!"

Giles looked over at Abby. She sat staring at nothing, lost in her thoughts.

He turned back to the more attentive Ramsey. "Coldwater released the small shipment, and all went fine. As we prepared to move the big one, the old bastard cut me out! He'd seen how it was done, knew my contacts, and tossed me away like an old rag."

"That comes as no surprise from what I've heard."

"I suppose not, though at the time I didn't see it coming. But I can tell you this, Munford Coldwater crossed the wrong man. I knew way too much. He should have killed me or kept me. You see, the system to move the cotton and gold was complicated, and with complications come opportunities. Sherman was all but in Atlanta, and time was running out. I knew they would be hard pressed to deviate from my plan. There wasn't time."

"Why didn't your army friends just send troopers to grab the cotton from Munford?"

"An obvious move, but more easily said than done. He was hiding it, and there was the likelihood he'd destroy it if he felt pressured. No one knew what that bastard might do. He'd paid nothing for the cotton, so he had nothing to lose. Part of me was pleased that, despite the turmoil around Atlanta, my pipeline functioned well the second time. The cotton left as planned and Munford was sent his gold."

"But you were still present as an interested party."

"A very interested party. You see, even though the cotton and the payment had exchanged hands, Munford still had a problem on his hands. His gold had been turned over to a relative in Savannah. Since Savannah is several hundred miles away from Atlanta, the gold had to be moved overland if he was to get possession of it. To complicate matters, no one knew what Sherman would do next. Munford wanted possession of the gold sooner rather than later. His solution was to dress up trusted men as soldiers to escort it. They mostly wore Confederate uniforms, but if necessary, could dress as Feds. Backhanders were paid where needed so they could pass unmolested."

"But you had an ambush in mind."

"Could it go any other way? On one side we have the gold moving with a small escort, just waiting to be taken. On the other side was me, the man who'd made it all possible and then been shown the door."

"But if you were no longer part of the things," Ramsey said, "how did you know where to strike?"

"Well, like you, finding weak points is something I'm quite good at. I either fix them or exploit them, depending. In this case, it was impossible to know the exact route the gold would take. That old bastard arranged decoy wagons to create confusion. His plan was clever but there was one inescapable weak point, and there wasn't much he could do about it. I'm sure you see it. The gold was coming to *him,* and I knew where *he* would be. All the roads led to Rome, or in this case, Munford. Once the shipment was close, he thought it was safe and dispensed with the decoys. It's always foolish to think of proximity as security. We struck when it arrived in the old man's backyard." Giles chuckled and shook his head. "I find that just delicious, don't you?"

An unwanted feeling of admiration came over Ramsey. Stealing and hiding the gold under Coldwater's very nose had a mad brilliance. "So you had the gold, and Coldwater was left hunting the thieves. Well done."

"Yes. I'm sure he doubted everyone—the other planters, the army, God knows who—but no trails led to me. It was Sam Potter and Black Jack Logan who threw sand in the gears. Thanks to their meddling, Bill and I wound up in prison just when we should have been enjoying the fruits of our labor."

"It must have been maddening to sit in prison knowing Coldwater could find the gold at any time."

"It certainly doesn't do to underestimate that old man. He really is quite clever. You may, if you wish, consider that friendly advice. He obviously has doubts about you. I was in the audience for that pathetic attempt in the alley. Coldwater needs a better class of gunman."

"If you saw I was attacked, why bother further with Mrs. Maynard and myself. The attack should have told you we weren't working with Coldwater."

"Munford will turn on anyone. I should know."

Ramsey eyed the pistol in Giles's hand, calculating the chances of seizing it. He took another step forward. "You say we're alike, Giles, but I served my country, not myself."

"Spare me your sentiment. I've lived through two wars and have no illusions about the dignity of man or service to a higher cause. In the Crimea we were sent by Her Majesty to fight a poorly planned and worse executed campaign. Crooked contractors sold the army shoddy goods and tainted meat. As winter set in, we were dying of exposure and disease, not Russian bullets. My friends died and my innocence perished with them. The difference between us, Captain, is that for all your talents, you don't see the world as it is. There are only those who take and those who suffer. If you don't understand that basic truth, you'll always be the tool of those who do. If a man steals a loaf of bread, they crush him; if he steals the bakery, he becomes one of them. It's said that behind every great fortune is a great crime. I accept the truth of that. I see the world as it is."

Giles pointed the Colt at Ramsey's chest. "We're wasting time." He gave a little shrug. "Vanity. It's my besetting sin."

He kept the gun trained on Ramsey while he walked to where Abby was tied and cut her free.

"Why did you ever come here?" she asked. "Why did you destroy this place?"

"Because it was useful. I'd never heard of it before, and I never want to hear of it again. Now get to work."

The better part of an hour passed before they'd removed the fallen timber and stone around the door. Only one large beam remained.

"I'll need your help, Giles," Ramsey said. "The woman isn't strong enough." He coughed on the dust in the air. "And how about some water."

"Later."

Giles aimed his pistol at Abby. "Lie belly down on the ground. Spread your arms and legs. Don't make a move. Do you understand?"

Abby nodded and lay in the dirt.

Her father was dead. John was dead. Susan was dead. Nothing mattered now. She would do what he wanted until he snuffed out her life.

"Let's move this thing," Giles said. He shoved his pistol in his belt.

Ramsey nodded.

As they lifted the beam, Ramsey twisted and let it go. Giles stumbled and righted himself with miraculous speed.

"Sorry. It slipped."

"Be careful, Captain. Be very careful."

Abby lay immobile, desolate, her hair clinging haphazardly to her filthy face. Here in this dim place, a tomb in all but name, they would die. Rabun, when he came searching for them, would find their lifeless bodies.

"Shall we try again, Captain?"

Ramsey bent down, and the two men heaved the beam out of the way.

"Warm work," Giles said. He slipped off his coat. "I think we've cleared enough." He drank from a canteen and walked to where two shovels lay on the ground.

"Time to dig," he said and threw a shovel at Ramsey's feet.

"You too." He heaved a shovel toward Abby, who groaned as it thudded into her back. She picked it up and walked listlessly to where Ramsey stood.

Giles came toward them pointing his pistol. "Dig right here." He scraped the ground with his boot to make a rectangle on the dirt floor. "You'll have to go down a ways, six feet or so, but the digging won't be too bad. The darkies broke the ground for you. There's nothing like darkies for moving dirt."

A storm was gathering. Above them the house creaked and groaned in the wind, though little fresh air reached them in the bowels of the dilapidated mansion. A shutter squeaked and banged, then banged again.

Ramsey's thoughts turned to Rabun. He imagined a sequence of events. Rabun would discover Abby was gone. When the morning grew late, he would open the door to her room. He would search, then raise the alarm. He'd realize where he could find her and would ride to Charlton. Then he would . . .

A fool's dream. Giles would ambush him. Nothing would be gained. All calculations ended at the same point. They would dig a hole and die.

And the hole was growing. They were down almost a foot. Abby's shovel struck something hard. Giles rushed up to look. A rock. She struggled to remove the obstacle. Unwilling to rush fate, Ramsey slowly dug elsewhere and did not help.

More dirt left the hole.

Abby coughed hard and gasped for breath.

"Give us some water!" said Ramsey. He sat down on the edge of the hole.

Giles threw a canteen at Abby's feet. She drank and offered it to Ramsey. The tepid metallic water soothed his throat. He drank a second time, then wet his handkerchief and tied it around his face to keep some of the dust out of his nose.

"Why don't you do the same, Abby. There's probably one in the coat."

She dipped her hand into the right pocket, removed a handkerchief, and wet it.

Ramsey helped her tie it on.

They resumed digging.

The hole grew deeper. Giles grew restless with anticipation, repeatedly trotting up to peer at their progress. After one of these inspections, Ramsey stopped digging and lifted the handkerchief from his face. "We need a break."

"A short break."

Abby threw herself down in exhaustion.

"She can't go on, Giles. You'll have to take her place."

"Very amusing. I'm not fool enough to get into a pit with you holding a shovel. She'll have to go on or you'll dig alone."

"I'll try, Allan." Abby picked up her shovel, put her foot on it and cut into the earth.

Time crept onward toward Giles's fortune and their death.

Despite the slackened pace, the hole was almost three feet deep. Ramsey's back ached. His hands were blistered. Abby was in pain and utterly played out.

"We have to have more water, Giles."

"I suggest you dig more and drink less."

Ramsey threw down his shovel.

"Water! Now!"

Abby stopped digging and looked at Giles.

A canteen landed at Ramsey's feet. Giles backed away, his gun ready.

Ramsey drank and handed it to Abby.

Abby shook the canteen. "It's almost empty," she said.

"You can have the rest."

She lifted the canteen and drained it.

Giles came to the edge. "Back to work."

Abby stepped forward to toss the canteen away, lost her footing in the loose dirt, and fell. She moaned and closed her eyes.

Ramsey reached his hand out to help her up. "Come on, Abby, just do what you can."

She took his hand and pulled herself to her feet. Her shovel again cut the earth. With a grunt, she tossed the dirt to her side.

How long did they have? An hour. Ramsey looked at Abby. She was filthy. Red clay smears covered Whitey's suit. Varying shades of pink and red ran down the right side of the coat. His eye caught a darker spot among the lighter smears. There was a bulge in her left pocket.

She still had the derringer.

The realization exploded in his mind. They had a chance. The little gun appearing out of nowhere would surprise Giles, maybe force a mistake. The derringer had two barrels. The second shot might find its mark. But how could he get it from Abby's pocket? Perhaps he could push her down and grab the gun. After a first shot, he'd rush Giles. At closer range perhaps—

Impossible. If it all went perfectly, if pushing Abby out of the way didn't throw him off balance, if the gun came out of her pocket easily, if the shot was fairly close to Giles, then— then Ramsey would die before he ever got out of the hole.

Maybe he could demand more water. When they stood close together, he could get the derringer. His digging slowed as he considered.

"Get on with it!" Giles shouted.

Ramsey cut his eyes to Abby. Her face was smeared with dirt, sweat, and tears. She didn't look back at him as she had done before. She was in a world apart, staring at Giles. Her digging became more regular. The difference was slight, but he noticed. Her shovel cut the earth in a slow steady rhythm. She dug, and she did not look away from Giles.

Then he knew.

He watched her silent concentration, and he knew. He knew more certainly than if she'd turned and told him. She was aware of the derringer. He knew what she would do. He knew what she would have to do.

Still she waited. It wasn't from fear. Ramsey had seen fear in others and had known it himself. Fear bored into the soul. It made good men cowards. In battle it could make a man too stupid to live. It numbed the mind and turned the will to nothing.

But at the house on Decatur Road, Ramsey learned something more. There was a place on the other side of fear. It was a place of calm and clarity. A place where, in the absence of hope, the future counted for nothing. In the alchemy of her soul, Abby had found that place.

He was now irrelevant to her. He knew that. She would do what she must do. She would kill the man who'd murdered her sister—or she would die. The outcome made no difference. She'd kept her head when she realized she had the gun. Now she waited. At some point, when Giles came forward to assess their progress, she would act in a cold fury. She would strike with no illusion of survival. That would be her strength.

Ramsey looked at Giles and calculated the possibilities. Somehow he'd have to get out of the hole and across the mound of dirt that surrounded it with her first shot. It wouldn't be easy, not with his leg. He began to dig on the side of the hole nearest Giles. When Giles looked away Ramsey chipped a toehold into the wall of dirt. A moment later he swept away the dirt on the edge of the hole—anything to shorten the hopeless odds.

Abby dug on. Ramsey worked his way around to face her. Having done what he could to prepare his move, he too must wait. He would watch her as she watched Giles. All his trust must be with her. The first instant her hand slipped toward the derringer, he would make his lunge.

Abby watched Giles with the unblinking patience of a hawk.

Barring a miracle, he reasoned, she would miss with her first shot. The little gun was no threat to Giles. But he wouldn't be ready for a simultaneous attack. If Ramsey timed his leap correctly, the surprise would throw Giles off balance. Ramsey could only pray the toehold would give his leap enough range. And whatever happened, Abby would have a second shot. They would make the hopeless gamble together.

A crunch of footsteps brought Giles toward them. Abby's grip loosened on the shovel. Ramsey's muscles tensed for the spring. Giles retreated. Abby threw her weight on the shovel. More dirt left the hole.

The wind outside grew stronger. The derelict building moaned with an agonized voice that said it, too, wished only to die. The minutes turned to hours. Ramsey was careful not to dig near the place from which he would jump. That was deep enough.

Giles drank the remaining water in the canteen. Outside, the sound of a horse's whinny overcame the rush of the wind. Giles looked toward the door.

Check the damn horse! Ramsey willed.

Giles came forward toward the hole and opened his mouth to speak.

Abby's hands slackened on the shovel.

Ramsey spun to make his leap.

Thrusting his foot into the toehold, he used the shovel to push up and forward. Another step and he was flying blindly toward Giles. Giles leveled his gun at Ramsey's oncoming body. The derringer fired. Giles recoiled and fired wide.

With desperate effort, Ramsey hit Giles low and grabbed his waist. The two men tumbled to the ground. Ramsey's face rammed into the dusty floor. His mouth filled with the metallic taste of earth. Giles slammed his gun butt into Ramsey's back. Ramsey groaned in pain. Giles slammed the gun down again. Ramsey twisted violently away.

Abby scrambled to the top of the mounded dirt. She fired her second shot.

Giles grabbed his face and raised his gun.

Ramsey dove into Giles before he fired. Twisting and wrestling, the men struggled, each attempting to control the gun. Giles had the better of it. His finger reached the trigger, but Ramsey was too close. When Giles squeezed, Ramsey pushed the gun away. The shot did nothing but sting his hands.

A red slash from Abby's second shot cut across Giles's cheek. Again the two men grappled, falling and twisting in the dust. Ramsey smashed Giles's hand against a rock, and the pistol tumbled away. Both men scrambled after it.

The agile Giles attacked Ramsey from better and more telling angles. The fight was slipping away. Giles's forearm hit Ramsey's face, and he went down.

Giles leaped and grabbed the gun. He raised it to fire, but Abby crashed into his back. The shot went wild.

Ramsey struggled for footing. Giles threw Abby off his back. She spun away and leaped back at him. Giles whipped the pistol across her face, dropping her half-conscious into the dust.

Ramsey closed again with Giles. He swung hard, his fist falling heavily against Giles's chest. The man fell, rolled, and pulled himself to his knees. Ramsey dove forward. His bad leg crumpled. He landed helpless on the ground.

Gasping, Giles raised his gun. The hammer clicked. Giles's face was stained with dirt and sweat. For what might have been seconds, minutes, or hours the two men faced each other—filthy, bruised, and panting. Dust was thick in the air, creating a swirling dark mist worthy of a circle of hell.

Ramsey accepted his fate. Nothing more could be done. Death had stalked him once; it had found him now. The debt had only been deferred.

"Goodbye, Captain Ramsey, I'm sorry it had to be this way." Giles's voice was almost apologetic. It betrayed no anger. He leveled the pistol at Ramsey's chest.

A shot exploded in the dusty air.

Giles held his pistol, his eyes wide. A red blotch grew on his chest.

He pitched forward into the dirt.

A silhouette appeared in a patch of dim light.

"Rabun!" Ramsey called. "Come quick. Abby's hurt."

He crawled to where Abby lay in the dirt. "Have you been shot?"

"No. It's my face."

He gently drew her hand away. A large bruise ran from above her nose across her left cheekbone.

The figure advanced from the shadows.

"Rabun! Quickly!"

The figure walked nearer.

"I'm not Mr. Perdido."

A young black man stood with a rifle in his hands.

"Gideon?"

"Yes sir, it's Gideon. You'd best get Miss Abby out of here."

Ramsey helped Abby to her feet and led her toward the door. Outside, the sky was dark with the coming storm. The oak leaves thrashed manically in the wind, the larger branches swaying and whipping with its force.

"That house is going to fall before long," said Gideon. "If not today, then sometime very soon." His eyes were soft and sad.

He held the rifle in one hand and helped Ramsey get Abby onto the back of the wagon. The team was skittish in the rising wind. Ramsey went to calm them.

"Do you need to lie down, Miss Abby?" Gideon asked.

"No," she said weakly. "Some water perhaps."

Gideon brought a canteen from his horse. Abby drank deeply, coughed, and wretched. Gideon held her shoulders. "You've had a hard time," he said. His words were barely audible in the wind.

Ramsey looked at Gideon. He wasn't the obliging boy who'd trotted beside Mr. Henry. Even as he comforted Abby, he never let go of the rifle.

"Why are you here, Gideon?" Ramsey asked.

Abby wiped her mouth with the sleeve of her coat. She turned to Gideon in the silence that followed, her eyes asking the same question.

"Miss Susan brought me here," Gideon said at length. "I suppose she brought us all here." He looked at Abby. "'There are conjunctions in the universe we do not understand. They are the rhythm of a music we cannot hear.'"

"My father wrote that in *The Destiny of Prometheus*," Abby said.

"Yes, ma'am, I know."

"You knew Susan, didn't you Gideon?"

"Yes, ma'am."

"Please, Gideon, is she alive?" The words were desperate. Hopeless.

"No, ma'am. They killed her. There wasn't a thing I could do. I saw it all, but I was helpless."

Loss and exhaustion swept over her. Abby wept.

"But it didn't end that day," Ramsey said.

"No sir, it didn't. We waited. We knew what they buried, and we waited. They came back just like we knew they would. And we killed them," he gestured with his head toward Turney, "all but the one dead in the wagon. We killed them all. It's finished now."

"We? Who killed them?" Ramsey asked.

Gideon ignored him.

"Would you like to see her grave, Miss Abby? I buried her and Mr. Alfred up on that hill yonder. I have to go soon, but I reckon I can show you, if you want."

Gideon led them to the top of a low hill. Hidden behind bushes was a clear bit of earth covered with fallen leaves. The view looked across to the remains of Charlton and on to Snapfinger Creek.

"She loved this spot," Gideon said. "We would come here when she was teaching me to read. If I couldn't find her around the house, I would come here to look. It was her secret place, she said. Of course, Mr. Alfred knew all about it, but he was a gentle sort of man and let her keep it for her own."

"What happened that day, Gideon?" Abby asked.

Lightning flashed in the sky above them, and a roar of thunder followed. Dust and leaves swirled in the wind.

"I'm sorry, Miss Abby. I've taken too much time as it is. I've got to go before anyone comes." He turned and started down the hill.

"Gideon! Please!" Abby's cry soared over the wind. A massive lightning bolt lit the sky. A deafening crash of thunder followed. "Please!" she screamed.

The young man halted, hesitated, and came back. His soft brown eyes searched her intense blue ones.

"Let's get off this hill," he said. "Walk with me and I'll tell you the best I can." He gestured with the rifle for Ramsey to walk in front. He and Abby followed a few paces behind.

"There was fighting all around Atlanta and Decatur," he began. "The Reb's were doing what they could, but no one but a fool was wondering how it would turn out. There weren't many of us. Mr. Alfred and Miss Susan let us live here. They had no desire to own us. He'd shut down his school two years before, and then he took sick. We were all just trying to make it through. We hid some supplies, and we had a garden. Seems like whichever side came by just took what they wanted, but we had enough they didn't find. Miss Susan, she was going over to Covington to help in the hospital. Mr. Alfred worried something awful about her. They argued, but she went anyway. The day when the Yankee soldiers came, we were out of cornmeal. Miss Susan rode off to the Coldwater place to see if they had any. I was out in the woods where our road turns off. I watched her ride back on her stallion, Prince. Folks said he wasn't a proper horse for a woman to ride, but she loved him and she could handle him all right."

They reached the wagon and horses. Gideon walked to his horse, untied him, and led him back to where Abby stood. Her left eye swelled. Soon it would be shut.

"I was out along the road that led up to Charlton. All by myself, just thinking about things. It wasn't long after I watched Miss Susan ride by, there came a wagon and some Reb troopers. All of a sudden, shooting started and the Rebs were killed. The Yankees came out of the woods and loaded the bodies on horses and the wagon. Then they rode off toward Charlton. I ran back as fast as I could to warn the people at the house, but it was no good. By the time I got there, the Yankees had everyone rounded up." His voice broke. "I couldn't do a thing. They shot Mr. Alfred and old Moses first. The big ugly one tried to force himself on Miss Susan, but she fought him. The others laughed and mocked her, grabbed and tore her clothes. Then the man inside there"—he nodded at the basement —"said something and the big man pulled a gun and just shot her. Shot her down like a dog."

Gideon paused to collect his composure, patting the flank of his horse.

"They made the black folk dig a hole in the field near the house and threw the dead Rebs in. When that was finished, most of the Yankees rode off, but two of them stayed behind with the wagon. They made our folk carry boxes into the basement and bury them there. When they got finished, they were shot down too. The Yankees just shot 'em down dead. Then they set the house afire. I was up on the crest of the hill and I saw. Couldn't stop it. Couldn't do a thing. But I saw it, yes I did."

The sky above was a thousand hues of gray. Lightning flashed. More thunder.

"You saved my life," Abby said. "You would have saved Susan's if there had been any way, any chance at all."

"I swore that I'd make them pay for what they did. You see, I found out what they buried, and I knew they'd come back for it. When they did, I'd be waiting. It took longer than I thought, but I knew they'd come. Weren't no doubt. I just waited."

Gideon drew close to Abby. "Some say it's up to God to punish evil, but I was done with God. I was done the day they killed Miss Susan and the black folk. I did what I had to."

Gideon mounted his horse and looked at Ramsey. "I'm sorry it took me so long to get off my shot. There was no way I could get in there till you folks started that ruckus. I came as quick as I could."

"We're grateful to you," Ramsey said.

"I've got to go now. There's too many questions I can't answer, and I sure don't want to see that sheriff. They would hang me quick as they found a rope. I'll leave you the horses, but don't come after me. Give me some time. You owe me that much. There's been enough killing."

Gideon searched Ramsey's face for a moment, then turned away. He spurred his horse and forded Snapfinger Creek. Drops of rain spattered in the dust. Abby pulled her coat up over her head for protection. Ramsey went back to the cellar and returned with his coat, the derringer, and Giles's gun. He climbed into the driver's seat where Abby waited.

"What are you going to do?" she asked. Ramsey snapped the reins, and they set off through the storm.

"Take you to Decatur."

"And Gideon? What of Gideon?" she asked.

"Yes, what of Gideon?"

"He wanted time. You can't betray him," she said. Abby used the wet sleeve of her coat as a compress for her eye.

"Gideon was right about the sheriff," Ramsey said. "A black man who kills a white man doesn't stand a chance. Gideon needs time to get as far away as he can." Ramsey turned to Abby, "But it isn't that simple, and he knows it. We have a choice to make. Either we send the sheriff after him as quickly as possible, or we never tell a soul he was here. That's it. Those are the options. Whichever we choose, we stick with forever."

Ramsey reined in the horses. "I think you know what we have to do."

She pulled the sodden coat from her head and turned her face skyward, letting the torrent wash down on her. The rain pelted her bruised face. She pulled her wet hair back and flipped it behind her shoulders.

When she spoke, her one eye shone with defiance. "There are times when the truth is only what we say it is."

"Did your father write that?"

"He wrote it over and over all his life."

"I suppose I can come up with a story that fits the facts and just insist on it. You can say Giles knocked you unconscious and you don't remember a thing. No one will argue with that face of yours."

Ramsey set the team in motion.

"What about the gold?" Abby asked.

"Gideon had it out of there long ago. He knew what was buried because he dug it up."

"Surely we must tell Mr. Sanbourne and Mr. Perdido. They deserve to know."

"We can't tell *anyone*, Abby, not ever. If the truth about these killings gets out, God only knows what will happen. A freedman has killed four white men—that's the South's nightmare come true. Will anyone stop to think why he did it? There are already rumors about an imminent black uprising. Otis Timmons was beaten because he argued for the rights of the freedmen. Not all of white Atlanta is afraid, but fear is rampant. We'll have to stick to our story and keep our own counsel. Rabun is a good man. We don't need to drag him into our secrets."

"And Mr. Sanbourne?"

"Gideon was riding a horse that belongs to Sanbourne. I saw it in the stable this morning when I left. We don't know where Heflin stands in all this, but perhaps he knows more than he lets on."

"I can't believe it."

"Maybe not, but belief is one thing and trust is another."

Abby raised her hand and pointed across the cotton field. "Look!"

A lone rider galloped toward them through the rain.

The trees basked in the long rays of the late afternoon sun. The recent dry spell promised to continue, ending a wet spring.

Papa Squirrel returned both well fed and newly clothed. He wouldn't, or couldn't, say where he came by this good fortune. His ravings about Angels of Vengeance were easily dismissed.

Allan Ramsey watched children playing between the houses across the street. When they ran off, he picked up his pen and tried to balance it on his finger. It fell onto the pile of mail—read but unanswered—that lay on his desk. None of the torn envelopes contained money. His finances were as precarious as ever. Perhaps he would take his chances in a poker game.

The door into the house opened, and Elijah's head popped in. "Soldier see ya, Cap'n Ramsey."

Johnny Bass entered the room. "Hello, Ramsey. They told me at the newspaper you had a room over here." Captain Jonathan Bass was in a clean uniform, groomed, and shaven. He took off his hat and sat down in one of the chairs across from Ramsey.

"I wanted to thank you."

"For what?"

"I've been transferred—posted to the Sixth Cavalry."

"That's great, Johnny, but what's it got to do with me?"

Bass laughed. "Don't try to fool an old trooper. General Grant signed my transfer. Stevenson and that Prussian bastard got hot as hell. I've come to say thanks."

"Maybe I suggested it, but other hands did the lifting."

"Well thank them too. I've got to go. I just wanted to see you before the train left. Stevenson doesn't want me in Atlanta one second longer than necessary."

"Good luck, Johnny."

Bass saluted and closed the door.

Well, thought Ramsey, that seals the bargain with McGrath—may it not be a deal with the devil.

The Isle of Capri wasn't crowded. Three soldiers sat at a table and called for more whiskey. Mr. Winks produced a bottle and brought it to them. At a table near the door, Fred Warren and his friends earnestly played a low-stakes poker game. Having finished with the weather, Chatsworth White and Joshua Brantley were talking about politics. Whitey was wearing a brand-new linen suit. It gave him an unwarranted look of prosperity.

Ramsey looked down at the chessboard and nursed a whiskey. The smoky recesses of the Isle of Capri were infinitely preferable to the solitude of his room. Rabun joined him. "Does it matter so much which piece you move?" he asked.

Someone walked up behind Ramsey. A shadow fell across the board.

"Mr. Allan Ramsey, local hero," said Ed Sprague. "Ain't seen you around. Not avoiding me or nothin', are ya? Man gets kinda lonely when his friends stay away." He threw his hat on the bar. "How 'bout some whiskey, Rabun, and not the swill you give them soldiers."

Rabun poured Sprague a glass. The soldiers looked uncertainly at their bottle.

"An early start for you isn't it, Ed?" said Ramsey.

"Well, like I said, I'm lonely and I got a lot on my mind."

Sprague sipped his drink and looked at the chessboard. "Never understood that game. Maybe I just ain't smart enough."

Rabun castled.

"Hell," Sprague continued, "I don't understand much of anything these days. I don't even understand what happened to you and the Maynard woman. Huh? Everyone sees it plain as day, but here I am, an' damn if I can't figure nothin' at all."

"Maybe there's nothing that needs figuring out."

"People tell me that." Sprague rolled his glass in his stubby fingers and took another sip. "Yup, it all turned out just fine. The Giles fella killed off his own gang, and then you come along an' rid the world of his crooked ass. Tied everything up with a neat little bow. The city's all smiles, from the mayor right down to the town drunk. Even the Army's happy. Am I right or am I right?"

Ramsey turned to look at Sprague. The deputy moved his hound-dog face close to Ramsey's and said, "All nice an' tidy, ain't nobody askin' questions. You told 'em just what they want to hear. Yup. They all happy."

"Except you."

"Except me. I ain't a cow so I don't like bullshit."

"What do you like?"

"A straight story. An' I ain't hearin' one."

Ramsey turned back to the game and moved his queen bishop.

"I took me a trip out to Charlton," Sprague went on. "That's something neither Powell or Anderson did. Powell just sent some men down there to collect your friends Giles and Turney. Whit didn't do a goddamn thing. Whitaker and the mayor talked with him for about an hour, an' it just turned Whit's ass to lead. Suppose when ya hear what ya want to hear, there just ain't no reason to go ask for more."

"If you say so."

"I do. I also say there was lots of footprints in the dirt out there. At least four people was walking around and none of 'em was Turney."

"It rained. There weren't any footprints."

"But I didn't look outside. I brought a lantern and looked down where you was diggin'. God only knows how many folks has trampled around in there since word got out about the gold, but I was there first. Not countin' the two sets of footprints that brought out the body, they was four more." He raised his hand and spread his fingers. "The Maynard woman, you, Giles, and—who? He weren't there long—wasn't many prints—but he was there."

Rabun, his hand suspended over the chessboard, stared at Ramsey.

"It was dark. I think you got confused down there, Ed."

"Yeah, just like Wilson got confused. But I suppose you're right. Ol' broke-down tracker like me. Had to happen sometime. But how 'bout this? You wanna tell me how you shot a rifle bullet outta that little toy pistol of yours. Takes a lotta different bullets, does it?"

Rabun took Ramsey's knight.

"'Course, maybe I'm crazy," Sprague continued, "but then so's Doc Bannister over in Decatur. He seen it too. He was the one that dug the rifle bullet outta Giles. Maybe my mind's goin' along with my eyes, but that bullet looked a lot like the one we got outta the wall on Decatur Road."

Ramsey kept his back to the deputy. "Ed, it's best to let this alone."

"Worried about your skin? Don't be. The city was hungry with questions, and you served up a platter full of answers. They fat and happy now. They ain't gonna bother you."

After a long silence, Ramsey spoke. "What if I tell you that you just have to trust me?"

Sprague knocked back the last of his whiskey, grabbed his hat, and strode out of the saloon without answering.

"This secret," Rabun said quietly, "is it worth the loss of a friend?"

"I hope the price isn't that high." Ramsey looked at the chessboard. "I resign."

"Ah, *mon ami*, we play poorly because we drink poorly."

Rabun left and returned with an ancient bottle of brandy and new glasses. He poured and they savored the bottle's contents.

"Do not concern yourself. I will not ask you questions," Rabun said. "Each man has his own truth. I have no need to share yours."

"It seems I am to be moving soon," Abby said. "Mrs. Hoehling says I've become notorious."

Her swollen eye was open. The bruise, now sporting various shades of yellow and gray, still dominated her face. Ramsey was struck by the carelessness with which she'd done her hair.

His luncheon invitation had suggested The Planters Hotel. She replied that her appearance made a public meal impossible. They were in Mrs. Carraway's house, dining after the other boarders had finished.

"Will you return to Boston?" he asked.

"There's nothing for me there. John's family never approved of our marriage and have dropped me entirely. Our circle shuns me since his death. I'm planning to remain in Atlanta. I've sent for my photographic equipment and will try opening a studio again. I don't know whether Atlanta is ready for the venture, but I can hardly do any worse here than I did in New York. Mr. Perdido and I are to be partners. We have bought property near his tavern. We intend to build. I will live upstairs and operate my studio below. I assumed he'd told you."

"No, he didn't," said Ramsey. "It appears that each man has his own truth."

"Denton Coldwater paid me what he kept in escrow for Susan and Alfred. He settled very promptly and without question."

"Like a man who wants the past to stay in the past?"

"One wonders. Allan, do you think the Coldwaters knew? Do you think they knew all along that Susan was gone? I"— she fought back her tears—"I wondered why they wrote to me. Do you remember their reaction when we went to see them? Do you think they knew about Susan and Alfred all along?"

"No, I don't. It served their interests if the world was aware of the fate of Susan and Alfred. If the deaths were known, the Coldwaters would have been better positioned to try to buy the land. But who can tell about such men?"

"They walk with the devil, yet they pay no price at all. You didn't tell the sheriff or the marshal anything you know about them. They profited from the losses of others, and you let them get away with it."

"What was I to say? Giles is dead. As for Munford's scheme, he didn't benefit and he would just deny everything. Justice is never absolute. We have to take what we get and hope it's enough."

"Well, they'll never have that land."

They ate for a time in silence before Abby continued. "Allan, the day at Charlton goes through my mind over and over like a nightmare. Does it ever get better?"

"The worst memories never leave, but they fade a bit with time."

"I expected to die. I thought Giles would kill us after I fired the gun."

"I did too. But that derringer was our last card. Whatever happened, I knew you would play it."

"So you waited."

"And so I waited."

Tears ran down her face. "I could endure my own death. Susan's is beyond me."

Abby wiped her eyes. "I never stop thinking of her. I thought I would find her. I really did. It's so hard knowing she's gone."

"But you're staying in Atlanta."

"I hope it's for the best. I never meant to come here. I barely knew Atlanta existed."

"Perhaps you saw it in a dream?"

For the first time since they'd left for Heflin Sanbourne's house, he saw her smile.

"Dreams have their truth, Allan."

"Well, let's look to the future." Ramsey raised his glass.

"To better days," he said.

"To better days."

EPILOGUE

Ramsey heard the footsteps on the stairs outside. After a quick knock, Mr. Henry entered, carrying a long thin package wrapped in old rags.

"I wondered how long it would take you to come by," Ramsey said.

Mr. Henry sat down and held the package in his lap. "Yes, sir, I'm here. Sorry to hear 'bout all your troubles. I stayed away so's not to intrude."

"Very thoughtful. Have you seen much of Gideon lately?"

Mr. Henry's face remained impassive. "No, Mr. Allan, I haven't. Him and Cassie, they went an' got married."

"Mr. Sanbourne's Cassie?"

"Jeremiah's Cassie. Yes, sir. 'Course they were courtin' for some time, so we weren't surprised."

"Well, since Gideon isn't around to speak for himself, perhaps you'd tell me a few things."

"Ain't nothin' a man like me can tell a man like you, Mr. Allan. I'm just an ol' black man tryin' to get by."

"You knew all along, didn't you? You knew Gideon killed Tully, O'Bannion, and Hackett, because you were with him from the beginning. Sprague and I were always just one step behind, but we never had a chance, did we? You were Gideon's eyes and ears, telling him everything we were doing so he always got there first. You even let Turney and Hackett get away that day at the newspaper."

The old black man said nothing.

"You knew, but you let me run blind. Thanks to you, Mrs. Maynard and I almost got killed."

The old man raised his head. For the first time Ramsey saw age and weariness in his eyes. Mr. Henry didn't raise his voice, but when he spoke, his words came at Ramsey like grapeshot. "It wasn't about you, Mr. Allan. It was never about you, an' it never mattered what you an' the deputy did. It didn't matter what you and Miss Maynard did, neither. We let you run 'round like fools 'cause it just didn't matter."

"They killed her sister!"

"And that's what you care about, ain't it. Mr. Alfred and Miss Susan was good people and that's sure. But a man like you wants white folks' justice for white folks' murders. Ain't that what you're sayin', Mr. Allan? Well, maybe you missed somethin', Mr. Allan. You're a clever man, but maybe you missed somethin'. Remember them colored folk layin' dead that day when Mr. Alfred and Miss Susan died? You remember them? Those Yankees made 'em work and then shot 'em dead. You remember? Well one of them was my son, an' every damn one of 'em belonged to someone. They weren't just darkies to us, Mr. Allan." In his anger the old man's breath came in short pants. "For us, it didn't have nothin' to do with you. We done what we done for us. You think any white man 'round here gonna lift a finger over what happened to them folks? You think that, you're a fool."

Mr. Henry stopped and composed himself. "Mr. Allan, you was on the outside lookin' in all along. We did for ourselves. Them white men killed my people, and we killed them. Every damn one of 'em is dead." Mr. Henry shifted the package in his lap. "You go call Sprague and let him hang me if you want. Don't make no difference now. I'm an old man. Got one foot in the grave. Besides, it's over. Can't bring back a dead white man just 'cause a black man killed him."

Mr. Henry's voice grew soft. "You lied to protect Gideon. We didn't expect it. I'm grateful to you. Gideon's all I got left. The reaper caught everyone in the family but me an' him. He's gone away, and at least he'll be safe. He took that gold and he left. Gone with some folks to start a new life. I'd like to see his and Cassie's babies if I live long enough.

"I suppose you know most of what we done. You're a clever man, Mr. Allan, and that's true. I guess you know it wasn't just Gideon and me. Other folks helped us. They knew what they was gettin' into, but they done it anyway. Be a shame if any of them came to harm. If anyone gonna hang, just let it be me."

"It's over, Mr. Henry. It's over for everyone."

Mr. Henry nodded. "Well, Mr. Allan, I got to go now. There's a business to run an' Gideon ain't 'round to help."

Ramsey stood and moved between the old man and the door. "Gideon had my rifle. At Charlton, he had my carbine, the one I lost when I was ambushed."

Mr. Henry said nothing.

"Gideon got that rifle from you, didn't he? And you got it the day I was shot down. You didn't just find me that day, did you?"

Ramsey looked hard into the old man's eyes.

"Maybe it was me that got you outta there. Can't say what folks helped me though. Who knows—any black man you see on the street might have been with me that day."

Mr. Henry set his package on the chair. "Somethin' else you should know, Mr. Allan. You don't have to worry 'bout them that shot you. God's done judged 'em long since. I knows that for a fact, but I can't say too much 'bout that, neither."

The old man eased past Ramsey to the door and swung it open. "Just be thankful for what you got, Mr. Allan."

He pointed across the room.

"That rifle of yours is sittin' on the chair. Gideon says you can have it back. He says he done with it now."

Author's Note

An Uncertain Peace is set *after* the Civil War because the struggle for peace is more significant in the arc of history than the war's battles, gore, and glory. In 1866, post-war American society, both North and South, was attempting to create a new and better nation. Sadly, many of the hopes for the future became the victim of confused goals and the divisive strains of the past. Racist aggression and legal repression replaced slavery. Questions of political power and economic fairness proved impossible to resolve. That our ancestors failed is no surprise; American society is still dealing with these issues.

The Civil War led to corruption in the North and left the South insolvent and angry. Slavery had ended, but the sharecropping system, controlled by a privileged oligarchy, resulted in generations of poverty for many Southerners. It would be a hundred years before the South began to catch up economically. Yet, despite their difficulties, people struggled toward healing, and in day-to-day life, the country muddled along as best it could.

Atlanta in 1866 was closer to a frontier town than a city. It was a place where one usually walked and people knew each other. The junction of four railroad lines—the Western & Atlantic, the Georgia Railroad, the Atlanta & West Point, and the Macon & Western—was important for the war; after, these connections fueled rapid growth. Atlanta's population in 1850 was 2,500; by 1860, the city had grown to 9,500, and by 1870, it could boast 22,000.

Incorporated in 1845, Atlanta developed a civic culture distinct from that of older Southern cities. When the Civil War ended in 1865, so recent were its beginnings that Atlanta had little past to cling to. The city looked directly to the future with boundless confidence and endless boosterism. People came from many places seeking their fortunes. Due to its commercial, rather than agricultural, origins, Atlanta had a relatively small Black population, approximately 20 percent. It had a surprising number of people of foreign birth for a Southern city, as well as a dynamic Jewish community. The rest of Georgia viewed Atlanta as a brash and suspect place, despite the city's prosperity—or perhaps *because* of it. This view remains today.

My interest in this period of Atlanta's past began while working for *The Atlanta Journal-Constitution*. At that time, the newspaper's main office was at 55 Marietta Street, not far from the 0-mile marker, which was at the center of early Atlanta. Of course, all the buildings of 1866 and most of the nineteenth century were long gone—Atlantans are careless of their past—but the streets remained, and I could walk where Ramsey walked and, at times, reconstruct his world through my imagination.

But imagination alone is not enough to create a historical novel. From the numerous sources I consulted in my research, two stand out: James Michael Russell's *Atlanta 1847–1890: City Building in the Old South and the New* is noteworthy for its research and clarity. *Atlanta and Environs: A Chronicle of Its People and Events Vol. I* by Franklin Garrett is arranged chronologically, which at times makes following a pattern of long-term changes challenging, but it gives the reader a sense of unfolding events as a local might have experienced them.

Garrett's racial attitudes are at times dated—he wrote the book in 1954—but his facts are accurate, well chosen, and useful.

Acknowledgments

The author offers his sincere thanks for the dedicated efforts of his editors at Wandering in the Words Press: Jennifer Chesak and Michael Mann. Jennifer's skillful guidance and attention to detail through multiple drafts, and Michael's knowledge of the period and his willingness to challenge the text were essential to the final result.